❧ THE ❧
INNOCENTS

❧ THE ❧
INNOCENTS

——— *a novel* ———

Caroline Seebohm

ALGONQUIN BOOKS OF CHAPEL HILL 2007

Published by

ALGONQUIN BOOKS OF CHAPEL HILL

Post Office Box 2225

Chapel Hill, North Carolina 27515-2225

a division of

WORKMAN PUBLISHING

225 Varick Street

New York, New York 10014

LIBRARY OF CONGRESS CATALOGING-IN-PUBLICATION DATA

Seebohm, Caroline.

   The innocents : a novel / by Caroline Seebohm. — 1st ed.

     p. cm.

   ISBN-13: 978-1-56512-500-1

   ISBN-10: 1-56512-500-2

   1. Twins — Fiction.   2. World War, 1914 – 1918 — Fiction.   3. New York
(N.Y.) — History — 1898 – 1951 — Fiction.   4. France — History —
1914 – 1940 — Fiction.   I. Title.

PS3619.E35156 2007

813'.54 — dc22   2006027518

10 9 8 7 6 5 4 3 2 1

First Edition

⊰❦⊱

In memory of my great-uncle
Captain Julian Royds Gribble, VC,
1897–1918

⊱❦⊰

AUTHOR'S NOTE

Events in this book are based on fact, and certain historical figures appear under their real names. The story and characters,
however, are fictional.

ACKNOWLEDGMENTS

I AM DEEPLY GRATEFUL to the Bogliasco Foundation for
granting me a fellowship at the Liguria Study Center in Italy,
where, in ideal surroundings, I wrote much of this book.

I should also like to thank Tom Wright for offering me time
and space to work in his house in Vieques, Puerto Rico;
Joan Mellen for giving a close reading to an early draft; and
Kemp Battle, whose genielike appearances with books, pictures,
objects, and other items from his collection of World War I
memorabilia gave me direction and inspiration when I most
needed it.

❧ THE ❧
INNOCENTS

Prologue

When we received our travel documents to return home, naturally we were ecstatic. But as we scrambled to find transportation out of France, in some quarters the celebrations were strangely muted.

I had met the Crosby twins occasionally on leave in Paris. What they did was tragic, of course. But frankly, I think several of us felt we might have done the same thing.

—Private diary of Maud Lessing, war correspondent,
February 1919

~ NEW YORK ~

Chapter 1

WHAT FUN IT WAS! The New York society columns were full of it for days afterward. Even in a time when such extravaganzas were commonplace, the event somehow outdazzled the most jaded of partygoers. On January 6, 1911, Mrs. Hermann Oelrichs, one of New York's most prominent hostesses, gave a fancy-dress party at Sherry's. Of course the venue was Sherry's; nobody would think of giving such an important party anywhere other than at Stanford White's gorgeous Forty-fourth Street establishment opposite Delmonico's. But even the staff at Sherry's found themselves conceding that they had not witnessed such a glamorous evening in years.

Mrs. Condé Nast, wife of the magazine owner, came as La Tosca in a gown of white satin embroidered in gold. The interior decorator Elsie De Wolfe, whose claims to beauty were tenuous at best, had transformed herself into a frilly Dresden shepherdess. New York society's doyenne, Mrs. William Jay, was dressed as Brunnhilde (she was not asked to sing), while the hostess, Tessie Oelrichs, a personage of ample proportions, was covered from head to foot in a pearl-encrusted gold and blue robe, with a dangling gold headdress that reached down from her ears to her gleaming bosom — the very essence of Amneris. (Characters from grand opera were all the rage that year.)

George Crosby, who, like most of the guests, hated opera, decided to go as Louis XVI. His wife, Lavinia, was a rather pinched-looking Marie Antoinette. (Her wig aggravated her migraine.) They were some of the younger set at the party, although George did not really notice. His impression of the evening was largely shaped by the presence of his twin sisters, Dorothea and Iris, whom, after much cajoling, he had persuaded to attend.

At this time, Dorothea and Iris were nineteen years old, and like all identical twins, their distinctive appearance was difficult to forget. Their skin was pale and transparent looking, as though rarely exposed to the sun. They both had huge dark eyes that seemed unusually solemn in creatures so young. They wore their thick raven black hair parted in the center and tied back in a chignon, accentuating the oval contours of their faces. Their foreheads were high, above finely sculpted cheekbones, with noses perhaps a little too sharp for such a fragile framework. Their mouths were full and sensual, another paradoxical gesture from the designer of these unorthodox beauties. The subtle conflicts in their features created an impression of mystery, setting them apart from the innocent prettiness of many of their contemporaries.

At first, the twins had refused to attend the party, declaring all such extravagant social events a waste of time. But their brother, beginning to get anxious about their marital prospects, had made an extra effort to get them to change their minds. Standing in for their parents, who were both dead, George felt very deeply the responsibility of introducing his younger sisters into society. Their social shyness had become, in his view, a serious obstacle to their future. If they appeared at Tessie Oelrichs's party, he felt sure that their charm and grace would be noticed and that before too long they, like all the other debutantes, would be announcing happy matrimonial news.

Shortly after receiving the gilded invitation, he ordered a large gin from the butler and padded reluctantly down the corridor of the apartment to his sisters' suite, as always stopping to admire the oil paintings of Crosby family horses that lined the walls of the long gallery. Most of them were painted by the highly regarded English horse painter Ben Marshall, and George would always smile as he remembered the artist's famous remark that a man would pay him more for doing a portrait of his horse than of his wife. This brief moment of good cheer instantly vanished as he knocked on his sisters' door and waited gloomily for them to invite him in.

The twins' sitting room had the classic look of the late Victorian period—red damask walls, fringed lampshades, Persian carpets, and pictures inherited from their father, who had collected a serious set of old master drawings before his untimely death. Bookshelves lined the walls. A small gold goblet from classical Greece and a pair of seventeenth-century glass vases from Venice gleamed in the soft light. All these objects were kept in pristine condition by the twins' personal maid, Anna, whose duties for her reclusive mistresses were otherwise not arduous, requiring only the laundering and ironing of their simple shirtwaists and riding clothes and the bringing of tea and cakes during the long afternoons when the twins were working at their writing.

The overall effect was inappropriate for two young women, George thought as he stepped gingerly over the threshold. It was a room that might belong to someone who had lived long and cautiously, with an eye to the prevailing standards of conventional taste. There was no youthful touch to liven up the furnishings. It was an old person's room.

Dorothea liked to sit in an armchair upholstered in dark green velvet, with a small mahogany table beside it covered in manuscript pages, on which she was always working. Iris preferred a wicker chair with quilted cushions, close to the fire, where she warmed her feet. For George, the sight he most dreaded when he ventured into their sanctum was that of the twins bent over the large table in the center of the room, whispering together, Dorothea eagerly guiding her sister's pen as Iris struggled over the streams of romantic verse that George found utterly incomprehensible. They were thus positioned when he made his latest foray into what he had begun to call—privately, to Lavinia—the doghouse. ("I'm always in it when I go there.") Anna was collecting their teacups and placing them on a porcelain tray when he entered.

"I've got another invitation for you," he said with false heartiness, waving the stiffly engraved envelope.

The twins looked up from their writing and sighed.

"Darling brother, you know we don't really like parties," Dorothea told him.

"Well, we like them well enough, but we find them boring after a while," Iris added helpfully. "People seem so uninterested in talking about anything except the next ball or trip to Newport. Perhaps you'd like some tea?" She looked at Anna, who held out the tray expectantly.

"You read too much poetry," George said, waving Anna away. The young girl curtsied and left the room. "That awful school you went to has a lot to answer for."

The twins laughed, and Iris went over to him and kissed his cheek.

"Perhaps we'll publish some poetry and surprise you," she said. George groaned and took a large drink of gin.

"What am I going to do with you?" he demanded with a note of irritation.

"*Do* with us?" Iris repeated. "Are we such a trouble to you?"

"Of course not. I wish you were *more* trouble."

"Don't worry about us," Dorothea said. "We are really very happy here."

George got up, moved to the door, and cast his eyes back into the room, wistfully remembering the playful boudoirs he had visited during his bachelor years.

"We dine as usual at eight," he told them. "I think Lavinia has ordered salmon tonight. And a very good white Burgundy from Father's cellar." He looked down at the invitation once more. "I wish you'd come," he pleaded. "Won't you do it for me? People are always asking about you both. I never know what to say."

After he had gone, Iris returned to her chair. "We *are* a worry to him," she observed.

"He wants us married," Dorothea said.

"Do you think we will ever marry?"

"I can't bear the thought."

"Well, you've never been in love."

"In love? How could we fall in love with the bores and fools George keeps introducing us to?"

"I know." Iris looked dreamily out the window. "But the poets talk about it so."

"Well, I don't want anyone intruding into our lives here." Dorothea indicated her handwritten pages on the table. "We have much work to do if we are to produce anything worth publishing."

"Perhaps we're getting like the madwoman in the attic," Iris said.

"You and I are enough for each other, Iris. We always have been. That's all that matters. There's no room for anyone else." Dorothea got up and put her arm around Iris's shoulder.

"You're right, darling." Iris smiled and stroked Dorothea's slim fingers.

Dorothea looked carefully at her sister. "You really want to go to this . . . extravaganza, don't you?"

"Of course not," Iris replied quickly.

Dorothea turned away and sat down again, picking up her pen. "I should be able to correct some of these verses before dinner." She bent her head and started to write. Iris watched her for a while, then raised her eyes to the window, where the rays of setting sun struck the panes like gilded darts.

"It's a beautiful evening," she murmured. "I've never seen such a golden light." She sighed deeply.

Dorothea put her pen down. "All right, Iris," she said. "We'll do it—to please George." Iris ran to her sister and embraced her. "Thank you, dear Dorothea," she said eagerly. "You always know everything I feel."

"Haven't I always?"

They laughed and went to the window together, watching the sun slowly fade into darkness.

So it was that the twins agreed to go to Mrs. Oelrichs's ball. With the help of Anna's nimble fingers (she was an excellent seamstress), they designed for themselves identical costumes made up in the diamond-shaped patterns of the commedia dell'arte. Dorothea had seen pictures of this form of theater in an illustrated book on sixteenth-century European stagecraft and was charmed by the disguises worn by some of the performers. It was the masks that particularly appealed to her.

"Wearing masks makes one unrecognizable," she told her sister. "We can hide behind them. Isn't that the best solution to the ordeal George is putting us through?" Iris was delighted by the idea. After much preparation, they finally left for the party dressed in multicolored pantaloons, black satin shoes, and capes. Like princes in a fairy tale, they wore their hair tied with black ribbon in a braid down their backs. Clutching their jeweled masks, the twins felt confident that they would be able to carry off the evening without difficulty.

The entrance of Dorothea and Iris Crosby into Tessie Oelrichs's ballroom caused a sensation. Having naively supposed that by disappearing behind their masks they would therefore be rendered invisible, the sisters quickly discovered that the opposite, of course, occurred. All eyes were on this intriguing pair, so provocatively dressed in identical Harlequin costumes. Who were these masked creatures? Were they male or female? A married couple or strangers? Where had they come from? Even the chandeliers seemed to tremble with excitement. Curiosity reached such a pitch that George felt it incumbent upon him to reveal their identities. The twins, mortified at the attention, fled.

Poor George! This was not the kind of social entrée he had intended for his sisters. What were they thinking of, wearing those strange clothes? Poor Lavinia! Humiliated once more at the eccentric behavior of her sisters-in-law, she tore up her wig and threw it into the fireplace, where it burned to ashes. Poor Dorothea and Iris! In equal measure, they found their expectations of delightful anonymity cruelly betrayed. The lesson they took away from the experience was that social engagements such as this were too painful to pursue.

On the following day, George groaned as he read the newspaper report of the Crosby twins' dramatic arrival and departure from Tessie Oelrichs's ball. The prospect of having two spinster sisters on his conscience for the rest of his life was becoming alarmingly close to reality.

Chapter 2

A PHOTOGRAPH OF THE TWINS exists, taken with a group of debutantes at a garden party during the year of Mrs. Oelrichs's ball. Most of the girls wear large hats, high-necked blouses with fashionable bows at the throat, and flowing skirts. Their faces reflect optimism and confidence, a cheerful mirror of the times. The twins wear identical dark dresses, with no ornamentation or decorative flounces. Their heads are bare; their hands hang stiffly at their sides. The overriding impression of their appearance is of austerity and plainness. The most striking aspect of the photograph, however, is that the twins are not sitting together. Their expressions reflect this aberration. Compared to the self-conscious poses and smiles of their companions, they are guarded. Dorothea in particular looks resentful, almost angry. Her mouth turns down, while Iris's forms a tense line, as though suppressing the urge to cry out.

When George was shown the photograph, he was astonished that the photographer had managed to separate them. It must have taken a threat of violence, he said to himself. It did not help the picture, of course, to have his sisters look so disagreeable. Why did it matter so much, he wondered — their inseparableness? Had he not given them everything a young woman might require in order to make a good marriage? Clothes, horses, domestic skills, and excellent dowries for them both? Was that not enough? Why did they always have to be together? They lived in a realm that even his wonderful wife, who was so good with people, could not penetrate.

In fact, Lavinia had mostly given up on the twins, thinking them irritatingly unworldly and selfish in their failure to make the slightest effort to catch a good husband, as she had so successfully done. But George felt that he, as their brother, should attempt an understanding. Without a mother or a father, who else could assume the role?

The twins' father, Chanler Crosby, had been a senior member of the New York Stock Exchange and founder of the distinguished brokerage house that bore his name. His wife was a Thayer, from Boston. In spite of these optimistic credentials, tragedy struck the marriage early. On December 3, 1892, Laura Crosby died giving birth to the twins. She was over forty years old and not strong. The pregnancy had been unexpected and perhaps unwanted. George was already twelve years old when his sisters were born. It was a sad Christmas that year.

Then shortly before the twins' thirteenth birthday, their father died after a fall from a horse while hunting near their country house in Far Hills, New Jersey. All the Crosbys were excellent riders, and the accident was a cruel shock. It appeared that the horse shied after the unexpected appearance of an untethered bull and threw its rider onto a rock that marked the entrance to the stables. Mr. Crosby survived for a day before succumbing to a fatal head wound. George, angered by the accident, wanted to destroy the horse that had killed his father, but Iris interceded. Although she rarely questioned her older brother's judgment, she knew the horse well and would not see it put down. In an unusual division between the twins, Dorothea sided with her brother.

The scene that ensued was unprecedented. The grieving siblings stood in the driveway near the stables. Two horses put their heads out of their stalls, hoping for a piece of carrot.

"The horse is bad, Iris," Dorothea told her sister. "He's unreliable. He'll do it again. We can't keep him."

"He was scared by something," Iris protested. "He's never done it before. He's a wonderful horse."

"Wonderful horse!" Dorothea scoffed. "He threw our father. He killed him."

"It wasn't his fault!"

The twins glared at each other. Each was trembling, cheeks flushed, hands clenched. The dispute between them had suddenly become enormous, a collision of fragile identities formed with the care of an artist. It was as though a piece of Ming porcelain had suddenly cracked in two. Alarmed at the damage, Dorothea walked away. Iris burst into tears. One of the horses tossed its head and snorted anxiously.

"I can't bear it," she sobbed. "Do what you have to do."

For several days after the grim sentence was carried out, Iris did not speak to her sister. George watched them anxiously, knowing the exceptional nature of the rift. Dorothea was pale and withdrawn, suffering equally the loneliness of their separation. Finally she persuaded Iris to walk with her to the stream at the bottom of the garden, far away from the stables. "I can't bear it, either," she said, taking Iris's hand. They fell into each other's arms. "I'm sorry," Iris whispered. "It's worse than anything, being away from you."

"I know," Dorothea said. "We'll mend quickly now." They sat down and picked some daisies from the lawn and made a chain, something they had often done as little girls. When it was long enough, they divided it in half and placed the two necklaces of white flowers around each other's necks, like garlands. "There," Dorothea said. "We're whole again. Let's tell George."

George worked in the Crosby brokerage house. After his father's death, he and Lavinia moved into the family apartment on Park Avenue and brought his twin siblings to live with them. It was a rich life in the material sense. There was a cook, a butler, a housekeeper, and several maids who worked for the Crosbys full time. The twins employed Anna as well, who was devoted to her mistresses. Her dark eyes and sad expression made George and Lavinia sometimes feel that she was another twin, a shadowy third player haunting the apartment.

The place was stylishly decorated in the fashion of the times, with French antique furniture, Italian silk curtains and upholstery, colored-glass lamps by Tiffany, and paintings by various artists of beloved family dogs, as well as portraits by the current society favorites, Boldini and Sargent. As young girls, Dorothea and Iris showed no interest in these matters and divided their time between the apartment and the country house they had inherited in Far Hills.

The twins' passion was riding, and much of their lavish annual income was spent on acquiring the finest horses and carriages, which they drove daily in Central Park. People later remembered them from their days driving a four-in-hand through the park, sitting upright and looking straight ahead, holding the reins firmly, sometimes caressing their horses' necks or murmuring to each other in soft voices. They were always beautifully dressed in English riding habits and hats, with suede gloves and gleaming brown leather boots. They rarely greeted people, as though fearful of an intrusion into their private world.

But it was the fact that they were twins that set them apart from most other young people promenading in the park in those early years. Identical twins were an uncommon phenomenon, so that observers sometimes had to look several times to make sure they were not hallucinating. The duality of their physical presence was unnerving.

Their delicately chiseled, unsmiling faces, seen in double exposure, provoked a feeling of unease, almost as though they were exhibits at a freak show. The very idea of twins seemed to some people unnatural, a biological mistake, a check in the smooth progress of human reproduction. (Gemini's signature, for those who gave credence to astrology, included the traits of instability, intellectuality, and brittleness.) Passersby on the street sometimes actually stepped out of their way to avoid them, as though still adhering to the primitive notion that twins were the handiwork of evil spirits, or a mother's punishment for sinful behavior (particularly if she died in childbirth).

Dorothea and Iris, already thrown together more than most twins because of their family losses, were aware of the effect they had on people and clung together in self-protection. They would look at themselves in the mirror, intently analyzing each other's features, conceding the identical nature of their appearance. Sometimes these examinations gave them a pleasing sensation of confidence, suggesting that each one's individual character was duplicated in the other, thus lending form and resonance to their personalities. More frequently, the suspicion that they were indeed anomalies caused by nature's perverse trick made them reluctant to leave the apartment.

Buffeted by these conflicting emotions, they learned to cultivate their interdependence with their own abbreviated style of communication, developing a kind of extrasensory mutuality of support. When one laughed, so did the other. When Iris was sick, Dorothea followed suit. They finished each other's sentences like a long-married couple. Their self-sufficiency was almost insulting to those who knew them. It was as though they had created an invisible barrier between themselves and the world. Holding hands, they seemed protected against the everyday afflictions to which most mortals are prey. Many people found this social quarantine discomfiting.

George worried about them more and more as they grew older.

The twins made few demands, and if sometimes they seemed a little melancholy, he attributed it to the general feeling of emptiness that accompanies the premature loss of one's parents. But their reclusiveness was not encouraging for the long term. George loved his younger sisters and admired them immensely. But maternal warmth had been denied them, and this lack of intimacy as children, he feared, might handicap them in arriving at the destination that all young women of their class hoped to fetch up at—a splendid marriage.

George sometimes wondered if their education had not exacerbated the problem. Following plans laid out by their late father, in the fall of 1905 Dorothea and Iris registered as students at Saint Mary's School in New York. Saint Mary's, founded in 1884, was created on the provocative assumption that girls were the intellectual equals of boys. Most private New York girls' schools of the period offered the normal institutional experience that would turn their students into good wives. Saint Mary's was dedicated to producing candidates for higher education. This enlightened approach infected every aspect of school life, from the students' scholastic endeavors to their musical and athletic activities. Of course, not all Saint Mary's girls went on to college; indeed most of them did not, preferring to become volunteers with the Junior League or the Red Cross or simply to bide their time until they married. But the teachers were of the highest caliber, and if all Saint Mary's pupils did not enter the academy, it was not because of any failing on the part of their pedagogic advisers.

The twins flourished at Saint Mary's. The school offered them a secure society of females who could provide some of the warmth and affection they lacked at home. The fact that they were twins made little impression on their schoolmates, most of whom came from educated backgrounds and were sophisticated about such matters, although the twins' insistent aloofness evoked an air of spirituality about them that sometimes found its outlet in melodrama. "Their mother died because her stomach split apart," the girls whispered to one another. "The twins nearly drowned in the blood." "They were born with only one umbilical cord," said a girl who had embarked on the study of anatomy. "That is why they are identical." "The horse that killed their father belonged to them, and he was trying to school it for them. That is why they only talk to horses." These rumors added to the aura of tragedy surrounding the twins and made their fellow students a little wary of them.

There was one teacher above all who dominated the twins' time at Saint Mary's. Her name was Adeline Wetherall, and she taught English literature, with an occasional class, for those of particular talent, in French poetry. Miss Wetherall was a tall, thin woman with wiry fair hair cropped like a cap, thin lips, and a slight limp that was frequently speculated upon by her students. She had fallen off a horse, some said. (Horses dominated the imagination of many of these young girls.) Others believed that she had been born with the defect. Still others preferred the dramatic story that, as a young woman, she had jumped out of a window because of a disappointed romance. Whatever the truth, Miss Wetherall was an electrifying teacher, reading the English lyric poets with a fervor that seemed to confirm the possibility of earlier tragedy in her life. She inspired the girls with passages from Byron and Tennyson ("St. Agnes' Eve" was a particular favorite), urging them to develop their vocabularies in order to produce great works of poetry or prose.

She gave a famous introductory speech each year to the incoming class. "You and I have a very special task together," she would say, "the task of education. It seems appropriate today that I explain what I mean by education." She would then quote part of a poem by Emily Dickinson about an oriole singing in a tree.

"The tree is there. The song is there. The bird is there, but the tune comes from within, from the person herself," she would say to the puzzled faces looking up at her. " 'The "Tune is in the Tree—" ' . . . "No, Sir! In Thee!" ' " The students looked blank. Ignoring them, the schoolmistress continued. "A Frenchman once said that a landscape was really only in the mind of the person who looked at it. In other words, young ladies of Saint Mary's, we teachers can only do so much. We can only implant in you the vision of wisdom. It is up to you to hear the unheard music and follow it where it leads."

Such exhortations made Miss Wetherall both alarming and stimulating to her students, most of whom, while finding her remarks incomprehensible, strove to gain her commendation. Like many dedicated teachers, she was always eager to discover exceptional talent. She would ask students to read something they had written, and then take their efforts apart in flowery language. She would summon them individually to her office, asking them to choose a favorite passage in a book and explain why they had chosen it. Such tests would indicate to her what potential was latent in each girl's budding intellect, and over the school year she would single out the one or two in whom she saw the most promise.

The first indication that Dorothea and Iris Crosby would pass the test was their insistence that they go up before Miss Wetherall together. For their classmates, this was not a surprising request. The twins did everything together—everyone knew that. They pushed their desks together, their lockers were side by side, their books had both their names inscribed in them. They wore the same clothes, they shared their food and drink, they stayed together in recess. They were inseparable.

Miss Wetherall at first demurred, insisting on separate interviews. But something in the twins' faces made her change her mind, and she finally agreed to their unusual condition. Dorothea and Iris entered Miss Wetherall's book-lined room with their usual self-possession. Their eyes fixed upon a marble bust of Wordsworth on her desk and then, fleetingly, on each other. "Well," Miss Wetherall said, looking at them. "Which of you will read first?"

Dorothea read Keats's "On First Looking into Chapman's Homer." Iris followed with the same poet's "Ode on Melancholy," both choices carefully selected to appeal to their teacher's taste. As each read, the other watched intently, moving her lips in time with the words. This synchrony gave the uncanny impression that both were declaiming at the same time. Miss Wetherall was enchanted. Their soft, impassioned voices, their tenderness toward each other, and their delicate manners combined to give an impression of considerable intelligence and sympathy. "My dears, you read beautifully," she told them. "You seem to know the works so well and, in some part of you, to understand them. I believe you may have the beginning of wisdom."

Dorothea and Iris looked at each other, and a faint blush suffused their pale cheeks. "Thank you, Miss Wetherall," Dorothea said. Iris bowed her head.

"You may go now, girls," the teacher said in more distant tones. "And please refrain from discussing what went on in this room." Miss Wetherall was always sparing with her praise. It did not do to become intimate with one's pupils, although in this case she had looked up the Crosbys' financial assets and found them to her liking. "We shall work well together if you listen and are willing to receive the mysteries of language," she told them. "Life is only tolerable when the imagination roams free." With a regal wave of her bony, black, bombazine-clad arm, she dismissed them.

By the time they reached the twelfth grade, Dorothea and Iris had both shown their exceptional abilities in literature and music and had been placed on the second teams in the school's sporting programs. They were not elected to any senior class position, since, as their fellow students pointed out, one would have to vote for both of them, and that did not seem fair to everyone else. On their vacations, the twins attended plays and concerts in New York and occasionally had small tea parties in the Park Avenue apartment, but school friendships seemed mostly an intrusion into their fond togetherness.

Miss Wetherall was an exception. The teacher had formed a powerful attachment to the twins. Her attention to them flattered and excited them. Her soulful recitations and romantic flourishes enveloped them in an embrace that inflamed their senses. Nobody had ever talked to them in this fashion. She would lyrically describe foreign places where she had traveled—France, Italy, Germany. She would paint word pictures of castles, gardens, and lakes that had led her to a deeper understanding of beauty and love. She would visit the Crosby apartment with books and read to them, inviting them to respond, suggesting they write their own poems and essays.

Dorothea in particular discovered in writing a new passion. By her senior year, she had realized that putting words on paper satisfied her far more than personal interactions (apart from those with her sister, of course). Disappearing into the magic of language, her mind teeming with poetic images, she experienced a liberation from the real world by entry into a literary one. Miss Wetherall noticed her dedication and singled her out in lessons, lauding her work in front of the others. She also encouraged her in private sessions to write the poetry that seemed to come so naturally to her. "We are just mortals," Miss Wetherall would say to her, "but we share the vision of justice, beauty, love, and truth. If you can see beyond the eye and hear beyond the ear, you are becoming an educated person."

Iris admired her sister's devotion to writing. Dorothea urged her to pick up her pen as she had done. "I do not have your talent," Iris demurred.

"Nonsense," Dorothea said briskly. "We are the same. You must work at it. Miss Wetherall will help you."

Although Iris found her sister's immersion in literature difficult to emulate—words came less fluently, she was not always convinced by Miss Wetherall's abstract nouns—at the end of the year, it was no surprise to anyone that Dorothea and Iris had won the school's literature prize jointly, the first time it had ever been so awarded. They went up to receive the prize together. It had been necessary for the administration to purchase for them two separate copies of the customary luxurious gilded and leather-bound *Complete Works of Shakespeare,* an unexpected drain on the school's graduation budget.

It was after this triumph that George began to be seriously concerned about his sisters. While most of their friends plunged into the world waiting for them on Fifth and Park avenues—the teas, the evenings at the theaters, the soirees, the picnics, the football games at Yale and Harvard—Dorothea and Iris seemed content to while away their time at home, writing, or riding in Central Park.

Miss Wetherall had urged the twins to apply to college, believing that their talents would be well served at Vassar or Wellesley, institutions that Miss Wetherall herself, owing to family constraints one did not mention, regretfully had not attended. She wrote to George, suggesting he encourage them, hinting that Dorothea's poetic gifts, in particular, deserved a more public forum than the school magazine. "We can surely allow Emily Dickinson a little competition!" she exclaimed. Being unfamiliar with modern American poets, George did not understand Miss Wetherall's reference and neglected to show his sisters her letter. In private he thought that the all-female institutions of higher learning proposed by Miss Wetherall would be a deadly fate for them. Vassar and Wellesley would only encourage the hermit qualities and bookishness already apparent in the twins, characteristics he regarded as brilliantly effective in deterring possible candidates for their hands in marriage.

Lavinia thought her husband somewhat obsessive about the subject, but then she fancied all the Crosbys were a little intense. George had told her how his mother, when she was over thirty-five, had tried desperately to become a concert pianist, taking endless lessons from various European virtuosos and practicing ten hours a day without respite, making life hell for him and his father. Could such propensities be inherited? Lavinia was grateful George had gone to Princeton, where any tendencies to unconventional behavior were directed into more acceptable social paths such as drinking and playing football. Now, she was pleased to see, he had settled down nicely into his position running the family firm. If his sisters would stick to riding their horses in the park and going foxhunting, where they looked reasonably handsome, she felt confident they might one day have at least some chance of achieving domestic contentment. Besides, she hadn't told George, but she had already decided that the twins' bedrooms would make a very nice nursery.

Chapter 3

DOROTHEA AND IRIS DECIDED to prepare for the college entrance examinations even without their brother's support. They hoped they might find in the libraries and corridors of higher learning some easing of the distant longings that sometimes disturbed them so, longings that found no respite at the debutante balls and countless Red Cross and Junior League benefits to which they were invited, however worthy they seemed. When George reluctantly confessed to them that Miss Wetherall was in favor of their decision, they pressed ahead enthusiastically.

Although few of their contemporaries would consider leaving the amusements of New York for a women's college in some remote country town, the twins were not daunted by the prospect. Their only anxiety was attaining the standards required by the entrance examinations. They were encouraged by Helen Keller's book *The Story of My Life,* which had been published in 1902 to wide acclaim. If a blind girl was able to master the demands of algebra, geometry, and physics as well as Greek, Latin, French, German, and English well enough to enter Radcliffe, surely the Crosby twins, with their excellent elementary education, could succeed equally well.

The decision made, they entered into the process with characteristic intensity. Their rooms were made over into study centers, with piles of documents and test papers everywhere, augmented by regular arrivals in the mail of scholarly books. They also had a weekly visit from a tutor who had been recommended by Miss Wetherall to bring them up to the level required by the college admissions office.

"Do you think it matters that we are not writing poetry anymore?" Iris asked one Sunday morning. They had just returned from church, where prayers had been offered for the missionaries in China.

"I think it is more important for us to train our minds in a more disciplined fashion," Dorothea said briskly, laying down her hat and picking up one of the arithmetic books they were working on. "Although I must say that addition and subtraction do not take the place of Wordsworth."

"Train our minds for what?" asked Iris, picking up a sheaf of papers and looking at them with an expression of discouragement.

"Surely you remember what Helen Keller wrote," Dorothea said. "Let me read it again to you." She went to a bookshelf and, picking out their copy of Keller's autobiography, turned to a marked page. "'Knowledge is happiness, because to have knowledge—broad, deep knowledge—is to know true ends from false, and lofty things from low.'"

"Perhaps we should be going to China instead." Iris was at her favorite place, looking out the window. It was a chilly day in late March, and the trees were still bare. A wintry sun leaked its pale light onto the street below.

"Perhaps you think we should be blind, too," Dorothea volunteered.

Iris turned to her sister and laughed. "All right, I know I'm silly."

"China can wait. I think it's time for luncheon." Dorothea looked at her watch. "Shouldn't Anna be calling us?"

She snapped Helen Keller's book shut and was putting it back in the bookcase when Anna suddenly opened the door and, with a high-pitched cry, sank to the floor.

"Isn't it lunchtime, Anna?" Dorothea asked, then turned and saw her crumpled on the ground. "Why, what's the matter?" She ran over to her and tried to lift her up. Anna began to weep hysterically.

"Anna, dear, what is it?" Dorothea asked again. "What's that on your apron?" Smudged black marks covered the front of Anna's starched white uniform. Anna stared down at them and tried frantically to brush them off. A smell of burning rose from her hands as she wiped them helplessly on her sleeve.

"Anna, tell us—please, you must tell us, or we can't help you!" Iris put her arms around the girl and turned her face toward her own. "Tell us, what has happened?"

Anna lifted her head up, tears streaming down her face.

"My cousin, Maria, my family, friends, everyone . . . dead!"

She broke off and began speaking in a torrent of foreign words. Dorothea leaned down and took her by the shoulders.

"Anna, you must calm down and tell us what has happened." Anna tried again to speak, but only guttural foreign sounds emerged. Dorothea and Iris looked at each other in alarm and then stared at the piteous figure sobbing on the floor.

"Anna, stop—speak English. What happened? Who is dead?" Dorothea's firm voice penetrated the troubled air. Gradually the girl calmed herself and in halting sentences told the terrible story.

The day before, on Saturday, March 25, a fire had broken out in the Triangle Shirtwaist Factory of Harris and Blanck, at Washington Place and Greene Street. Three stories of the ten-floor building had burned. The bodies of the young factory workers who had tried to escape were heaped in piles on the ground. Girls in the hundreds lay in grotesque rows, filling the sidewalk and the street, their charred remains unrecognizable.

"Maria, my cousin, I look for her," Anna said in a strangled whisper. "Maria, so pretty, but I see nothing—just legs, arms, black like soot in your fireplace . . . girls in rows like this"—she brought her hand up and cut the air in a slicing motion. "I could not tell who was it there . . . faces all turned inside out . . ." She squeezed her cheeks in a grimace. "My family . . ." She moaned like a small animal. "Sonya, Olga . . ."

The twins listened in increasing horror as Anna's story unfolded. "I search, I search, people cry, 'Mama,' I dare not look, touch. How touch such—such things? I see a headscarf, half-black, but red, yes, I can see, like Maria's . . . but who's is it really? So many headscarfs . . . Sonya, going to be married, I look for her ring. Everyone Russian like me . . . We cry out in our language, but no one hears . . . All night, no sleep, no sleep, no go home, just looking at ashes . . ." She looked down at her hands with their blackened fingernails and rubbed them frantically on her apron.

"Anna, oh, poor darling Anna, we must go and get help for you." Iris hugged the shaking girl and kissed her wet cheeks. A smell like singed fabric filled the room. Anna looked around, her eyes mad with grief. She grabbed Iris by the hand and stammered in Russian, then in English. "See, whole families come here to find new life, and now find only dead, all people dead . . ."

The newspapers called it one of the worst catastrophes ever to befall New York. It appeared the fire had broken out nearly five hours after closing time. The one little fire escape was almost at once filled with smoke. "Some of the workers escaped by running down the stairs," a reporter wrote, "but in a moment or two this avenue was cut off by flame. The girls rushed to the windows and looked down at Greene Street, 100 feet below them. Then one poor little creature jumped. Then they all began to drop. The crowd yelled, 'Don't jump,' but it was jump or be burned."

The twins read and reread the grim details, then agreed that they should report to the Red Cross Emergency Committee, representatives of whom had arrived on the scene almost immediately. Nothing could be done for the dead, but the organization hastily set up a relief fund for the families of lost children, opening a special headquarters in the Metropolitan Building on Madison Avenue to cope with the problems caused by the disaster.

Most of the victims were between the ages of sixteen and twenty-three, recent immigrants to the United States, working overtime to send money back home to their families. The stories of these young women piled up like their heartbreaking corpses, their brief little lives transformed into tragic biographies of hope and desperation. Dorothea and Iris were put to work at once, sifting through the information so that letters might be sent, cash put aside for coffins, and medical assistance made available for the parents and children left behind. They worked in a tiny office in the Red Cross headquarters, devastated by the litany of pathos before them.

C.D. 18 years old, dead, earned $7 a week; in this country eight months only, union member, lived with aunt, sent about 20 rubles a month to mother in Russia.

M.F. 17 years old, dead, union member, lived with uncle, very needy dependents in Poland—small sums sent when possible.

L. and M.G., twins, 17 years old, dead, union members, earned $8 a week, sickly mother here, formerly clothing cutter; father, stepbrothers in Białystok, Poland, sent money monthly.

"Twins, Iris." Dorothea read this last entry aloud. "They were all seamstresses, machine operators. Imagine them working so hard, so late. Why were they working on a Saturday afternoon?"

"How their fingers must have ached from so much work." Iris looked at her own smooth hands and tucked them out of sight under her desk.

"Anna was lucky," Dorothea went on. "She had found a better place to work. She sewed and ironed for us instead of being imprisoned in a sweatshop. Many of her family must be listed here. I wonder if she sent money home."

"Białystok," murmured Iris, reading another entry, pronouncing the word slowly. "Such a peculiar name. I wonder what it's like. So far for them to come. Such hardship."

"Such hope," Dorothea said. "And then such hopelessness." She turned back to the task.

Every day for a week they went to the Red Cross center and continued their bleak assignment, increasingly exhausted by the relentless efficiency of the bureaucracy of death.

S.R. 19 years old, union member, dead, in this country 5 months, lived with and supported only surviving family member, from Russia.

This last pitiful obituary, a terse few lines just like all the others, closed the twins' file. Iris put the document down on the desk, made a notation, and then stood up, staring at the dog-eared jumble of papers they had worked through for seven long days. She turned to Dorothea and said in a voice that was choked with shame, "*We never even knew Anna was Russian.*"

The Red Cross and the Ladies' Waist and Dressmakers' Union were later congratulated for their speedy response and effective collaboration in dealing with the tragedy. Distinguished New Yorkers, particularly those with suffragist leanings, like Anne Morgan, daughter of the financier J. P. Morgan, and her friend Elsie De Wolfe, the decorator, came to help and raise funds for the victims' families. On one occasion, seeing the Crosby twins' white faces as they bent over the seemingly endless descriptions of tragedy, Miss De Wolfe invited them to take tea with her at the Colony Club. The twins declined, but they were grateful.

"We saw her before, you know," Dorothea said to her sister later.

"Think of it, only two months ago we were at Mrs. Oelrichs's fancy-dress ball. How ridiculous it all seems now."

"She came dressed as a Dresden shepherdess," Iris remembered. "But there's nothing fragile about her. She's tough. One can tell."

"She became like that through struggle and hard work," Dorothea said. "I know her early life wasn't easy."

They were sitting in their room as usual. It was freezing cold. Since the catastrophe, they had not been able to bring themselves to light the fire. George was beside himself and urged them daily to change their minds, but they continued to wrap themselves in their sable coats and shiver.

"Is that what it takes?" Iris asked.

"Obviously," Dorothea retorted. "At least it's one way."

Iris put her feet up to the empty grate, as though looking for warmth. "Is entering the university another?"

Dorothea darted a look at her sister. "We must believe so," she said.

Iris picked up a page of arithmetic from the floor by her chair, looked at it blindly, then crumpled it up and threw it into the grate.

"Don't do that, darling," Dorothea chastised her. "It's all we've got."

Iris stared at the piece of paper nestling in the fireplace. "I can smell it," she said. "I'll always smell it. It'll never leave me."

After several months, they began riding again in Central Park. At home, Dorothea wrote feverishly, page after page of descriptions of children dying in outlandishly named foreign lands where she had never been. She read Keats, Byron, Shelley, Wordsworth, drowning herself in their honeyed language. Iris spent more and more time with her horses, riding long hours in the park or in the fields of Far Hills, exhausting herself so that she might sleep at least a few hours at night. They ordered flowers to be sent all over the city to clinics and shelters, and brought armfuls of daffodils, lilies, and lilacs into their own suite, as though the sweet scent might eradicate the smell of charred flesh in their nostrils.

They refused all invitations. After a while, they ceased to study for their examinations. They threw out all the books and papers they had once so attentively studied, and canceled the tutor's visits. They hardly left their room, except to call on some of the families who had survived the fire and were struggling to survive in the tenements of lower New York. George was alarmed at the effect the disaster had had on the delicate constitutions of his sisters. They would come back from these visits ravaged and feverish, and George feared that this new preoccupation, like the earlier preoccupation with higher education, would not only damage their chances for a normal future but threaten their mental health.

He had asked Anna to leave, realizing that her presence would only continue to remind the twins of the tragedy. He gave her money and offered to pay her passage home to Russia. "Home?" Anna repeated. "I have no home." After making inquiries, George found her a position with a friend from the bank whose wife had just had a baby and needed extra help. The twins made no objection. In their shame, how could they?

Friends told him that his sisters should take time away from New York, to get over the memory of the Triangle disaster. He knew this was good advice, but he saw no way to act on it. His prayers were answered in the form of Adeline Wetherall, who favored trips to Europe during her summer vacations—when her health and her bank account permitted—and had several times invited the twins to accompany her. At George's suggestion, she decided she could manage to arrange a tour with them through France. Doubtless his offer to foot the bill for the trip aided her in her decision.

"You are doing the right thing, Mr. Crosby," she said when they met to discuss the journey in the Park Avenue apartment. "Excuse me, is that a Bouguereau?" She looked at a painting on the wall with a little cry of excitement.

"Yes, yes," George said testily. He was anxious to complete the interview before his sisters discovered his plan and refused it.

"Get them to forget," he begged the teacher. "That is the only cure. Forgetting."

"Rest assured," said Miss Wetherall, reluctantly staying her hand from the rich Aubusson tapestry hanging near the fireplace. "I'll bring them back restored and refreshed. France is the cure—with a little guidance from me."

George eyed the spindly-looking schoolmistress. "It's the memory of this terrible catastrophe that haunts them," he explained carefully. "They've never seen anything like it. Their lives have been so protected. Can you really erase such things from people's minds?"

Miss Wetherall was confident. "The power of the present will replace the past," she asserted. "I direct you to the words of the poet: 'Better by far you should forget and smile / Than that you should remember and be sad.'"

George made a few unidentifiable noises. "I'm sure you're right. Perhaps France will help them forget. I can't think of any other solution. Thank you, Miss Wetherall."

He shook her hand and added, "Take all the time you need."

"I shall," she agreed. "Until my school needs me, that is. I am so grateful to you, Mr. Crosby, for this opportunity to be with your wonderful sisters."

"They are wonderful, aren't they?" George said, brightening. "That at least is certain. I only want them to be happy. And now I wish you *bon voyage*." He paused. "I'm afraid my French is rather spotty."

He handed her a large envelope, which she placed carefully in a voluminous black velour bag.

"*Merci mille fois,*" she responded. Her French accent was impeccable. George bowed in recognition of her superiority. She smiled kindly. "I'll bring them safely back to you, I promise."

She took his hand and pressed it to her bony bosom. "And now, like you, I say *bon voyage.*"

When he told his sisters the good news, he thought he saw a flicker of interest in Dorothea's drawn face.

"Thank you, dear brother," Dorothea said. "I suspected you had a plan. We shall make preparations immediately."

"But must we leave here?" Iris wailed. "Dorothea, you didn't warn me. I don't want to go anywhere." She cast around for an objection. "I'm just breaking in a new mare . . ." Her voice trailed off.

"We shall go, Iris," Dorothea said firmly. "George is right. We can't stay here now. Think how we have wanted to go abroad all these years. Think of France."

"France," Iris said listlessly. "Yes. We can't stay here now."

"*Très bien,*" George said. " 'Better by far you forget and smile.' "

Dorothea looked at him. "George, are you feeling all right?"

"It's Rossetti," Iris exclaimed. "Goodness me, dear brother!" Laughing, she bowed to him. Dorothea, amused, did the same.

"Never mind," George said sheepishly. "I got it from Miss Wetherall."

"We always told you she was a wonder." The twins stood each side of him and embraced him. "We'll go on your grand tour, George, dearest," Iris said. "It has worked magic for many. Who knows, it may work for us."

Later, George told Lavinia that he thought Adeline Wetherall needed a few days out hunting. "She should see a dead fox or two," he remarked. "That would put some color in her cheeks. But she's all we've got to help our girls, so I must go along with her, poetry and all. God bless her, let's hope she succeeds." Lavinia, pleased that the twins would be going away for an unspecified period of time, enthusiastically agreed.

Chapter 4

ON JUNE 8, 1912, the twins and Miss Wetherall sailed from New York on the SS *Caronia*. The plan was to visit Paris, Chartres, and Rheims, the choice of venues reflecting Miss Wetherall's passion for French religious architecture and the life of the spirit. For many Americans, France was indeed the Holy Grail. It represented to them everything America lacked—history, sophistication, wine, art, style, sensuality, irony, leisure, *douceur de vivre*. In the first decade of the new century, "The French do everything better" was the accepted mantra of *Vogue, House and Garden,* and the other taste-making publications of the day.

Miss Wetherall, of course, heartily endorsed this view. Constantly at her side was a book written by one of her favorite writers, Edith Wharton, who fueled the Francophile flame in many an American breast. The "hoarded richness of France" was how Mrs. Wharton described it in *A Motor-Flight Through France*—a book that Miss Wetherall read aloud with biblical reverence to the twins as they journeyed by boat and train to Paris. The English teacher also recited to them passages of French romantic poetry in the throbbing tones that they had come to know so well at home and in the classroom. *"Ô France, quoique tu sommeilles / Nous t'appelons, nous, les proscrits!"* (She admired Victor Hugo's passionate nationalism.) *"Elle était belle, si la Nuit / Qui dort dans la sombre chapelle / Où Michel-Ange a fait son lit, / Immobile peut être belle."* (De Musset's heated musings on love and death particularly appealed.)

In Paris they stayed at the Hôtel de Crillon, on the place de la Concorde. It had been open as a hotel for only three years, and Miss Wetherall was relieved to see that the new owners had kept the quality of the original palace intact. "Such fine moldings, such elegant paneling, such decoration!" She waved a thin arm at the ornate ceiling of the Salon des Aigles, with its eight gilded eagles at each corner guarding the blue and white panels depicting Fortitude, Truth, Wisdom, and Abundance, four of Miss Wetherall's favorite virtues. "This hotel is a favorite of dear Mrs. Wharton's, you know," she added.

Adeline Wetherall's supposed intimacy with the famous novelist gave the twins a moment of doubt as they pondered over their teacher's heretofore faultless character. Spirituality while romping with the poets was one matter; suspect claims to friendship with exalted personages, quite another. It was on the foreign soil of France that the first flickers of suspicion about Miss Wetherall entered the twins' minds. It was possible, they agreed, that outside an enclosed context, such as Saint Mary's School, people might well reveal characteristics that had never been asked of them or recognized within the sanctuary.

"Are we behaving differently, too?" Iris asked her sister as they trudged after Miss Wetherall through the Crillon's Salon Marie-Antoinette, a smaller room hung with Gobelin tapestries and illuminated by ceiling-high French windows. "There are obvious similarities, you know."

"You mean," Dorothea said, "that we are being taken out of ourselves? Being different?" Her question lingered in the fine dust of the gilded salon.

"Isn't this what this trip is supposed to be about?" Iris persisted. "Somehow changing us?"

"Changing us?"

"For George, anyway."

"For George, of course," Dorothea said briskly. "For us, we don't really know yet." She paused. "I don't imagine some magic wand transports us into a new dimension, do you?"

They stepped out onto the balustraded balcony of the hotel and gazed down in awe at the vast expanse of the place de la Concorde, imagining Napoleon's imperial army marching down the Champs-Élysées to the cheers of the crowd.

"Well, that's magic enough," Iris exclaimed.

Dorothea shrugged as they turned back into the salon. "If you like Napoleon," she observed.

Picking up a car—a later model of the Panhard favored by Mrs. Wharton—Miss Wetherall dashingly took the wheel and they set off, amid the usual discomforts of automobile travel (no windshields, no heat, modest springs, and a great deal of noise). The champagne country, with its soft green hills ribbed with vines, and charming little villages where they could taste the bubbling wine fresh from the vineyard, was of particular delight. They visited Château-Thierry, birthplace of the fabulist Jean de La Fontaine. They stopped in Épernay and visited the caves of the famous champagne makers Moët et Chandon and Pol Roger and enjoyed the elegant formal gardens of the Trianon Palace, built in the early nineteenth century by Jean-Rémy Moët, as Miss Wetherall explained, to please Napoleon. They sat at dinner and recited La Fontaine, drinking wine freshly bottled from the local château. "This is the real champagne," Miss Wetherall would say to the girls, holding up the pale golden liquid that fizzed gently in its long-stemmed glass. "The rest is a poor imitation. This is the elixir of the gods." And a rosy glow would tint the tip of her nose.

The twins were intrigued by the revelation of the two sides of

Miss Wetherall—the austere, dedicated teacher who lived modestly in New York, and the energetic traveler who transformed herself, once in France, into an enthusiastic schoolgirl.

"Which one do you like better?" Iris whispered to her sister as they hurried after Miss Wetherall through yet another Romanesque church in an obscure village.

"They are two sides of the same person," Dorothea said. "That's what they say about us, you know. The dark twin and the light twin."

"Don't be absurd," Iris protested. "They do not say that about us, because they can't make such a distinction."

"I'm not so sure," Dorothea said. "You are much more tolerant than I am."

"And you are much braver than I am."

Dorothea turned and looked at her sister. "That is not true, and you know it," she said.

Iris stared back at her. "We haven't been tested."

Hundreds of young girls, their arms and legs charred and broken, their necks torqued like a felled deer's, called out in reproachful silence. Iris hid her face in her hands.

"I know what you are seeing," Dorothea said gently. "Wasn't that a test?"

"It was nothing," Iris replied, shaking her head as though to clear it. "We were observers, that's all. Outsiders. We didn't even know Anna was Russian. She was invisible to us."

"But it affected us. Terribly. Isn't that enough?"

Iris shook her head. "I don't think so. If we didn't experience it, how can we say that we lived it?"

"People live in different ways, Iris."

"But how can we know which is our way?"

"We're going to Rheims," Dorothea said. "This is Adeline's way."

She quoted La Fontaine's epigraph: "'No town is dearer to me than Rheims, / The Honor and Glory of our France.' What a recommendation! Don't waste it, Iris."

Iris nodded and smiled at her sister. "You're right, of course. We must immerse ourselves. Perhaps this is also our way, after all."

The party spent several days in Rheims. The hôtel de ville, the marketplace, the archbishop's palace, the twelfth-century church of Saint-Jacques—all confirmed for them the validity of La Fontaine's apostrophe to the city.

But the thirteenth-century cathedral of Rheims was the highlight of their visit. The three Americans tirelessly walked around it, their heads turned like sunflowers to the dazzling facade of the building. How they exclaimed over the flying buttresses, masterpieces of delicacy; the elegant statuary; the dramatically ornamented doors and gables; and the finely wrought towers, higher than those of Notre-Dame in Paris. Equally awe-inspiring was the interior, with its massive nave, towered over by the graceful vaulted ceilings typical of the High Gothic architecture of the period. Most overwhelming to the twins was the sumptuous stained glass, particularly when the late afternoon sun struck the rich, pulsating colors of the rose windows at the west end of the nave, flooding the magnificent interior with a jewel-like glow.

As they basked in its glory, Miss Wetherall read again Edith Wharton's appreciative prose: "'It enters into the imagination, less startlingly but perhaps more completely, than any other of the great Gothic monuments of France.'" Miss Wetherall paused after this sentence. She felt her "dear" friend Mrs. Wharton did not go far enough. Her complaint was the famous author's notably secular approach to what was a religious encounter. "We are experiencing nothing less than a spiritual epiphany," she said firmly. While the twins felt Edith Wharton had expressed herself most admirably, they also conceded that Dorothea's quest for magic had been wonderfully achieved.

Returning to Paris by way of Chartres, the party agreed that Rheims won the contest for magnificence. Similar in appearance and in ornateness, the two cathedrals could not be faulted in any way, and at first neither twin was prepared to vote for one over the other. Dorothea ventured that the rose windows in Rheims were perhaps even more astonishing than those in Chartres. Miss Wetherall, faithful to La Fontaine, cast the deciding vote by reminding her listeners that Joan of Arc, having rescued Rheims from the English, presented the keys of the city to the French king at the high altar in 1429. "Rheims Cathedral is not only a sublime example of religious expression," she declared, "but it is also part of the fabric of the history of France."

THE YOUNG AMERICAN TOURISTS returned home full of stories about their trip. Miss Wetherall had distracted them brilliantly. But was it the "cure" that George had hoped for? Were the dark memories haunting the twins being expunged by the brilliant light of the art and architecture of France? A careful observer might have noticed how Dorothea flinched at a charming ruffled shirtwaist on display in a shop on Madison Avenue, or how Iris sometimes sat at dinner as though in a dream, her fingers tapping on the table and her lips moving silently as though repeating to herself a list of names. George was not convinced.

But the hedonistic world of New York began once more to claim their attention. The present was demanding, aggressive, painted in brilliant colors. When the twins found time to look back, the past years seemed to be gathering dust, like the souvenirs of a vacation tucked away in an attic. They discussed making another attempt at taking the university entrance examinations, but their concentration faltered and the idea was soon dropped.

There was a new restlessness in the air. The twins stayed with George and Lavinia in Newport for the summer months, attending picnics and boat excursions. They were painted by Boldini in ornate eighteenth-century gowns for a Junior League benefit. As a special gift to George for his birthday, they posed for the fashionable photographer Arnold Genthe in Japanese kimonos, their black hair piled high with combs like chopsticks, holding fans that partially concealed their artificially whitened faces. (George was not sure what to make of these alien apparitions. Their Kabuki poses would surely be unlikely to arouse any of the romantic feelings that he prayed might still be cajoled from a young bachelor's breast.)

Through the long summers of 1913 and 1914, there were receptions and dances, with gold and silver decorations, gardenia-strewn floors, champagne pouring from fountains, turtledoves set free under tents on the lawn, girls in long floaty dresses twirling parasols while boys ogled them, yearning for a kiss later under the stars. Along with all the others, Dorothea and Iris danced the turkey trot and sang along with Irving Berlin's "Everybody's Doin' It Now." Like everyone else, they found themselves swept along in the energy of America's carefree young century. There was a sense that time was getting short, that decisions should be made, that futures should be secured.

George, who watched his sisters hopefully during these sparkling occasions, noticed that at times they seemed to be sleepwalking through them. They stood on the sidelines, as though waiting for something. He observed how their escorts, at first so enthusiastic, gradually began to drift away, realizing that there was no way of extracting satisfaction from the twins' relentless doubleness. The young men grew impatient with the "Which one are you?" jokes, tired of trying to separate them or tease out their differences. On occasion, a particularly persistent admirer might somehow manage to persuade one of the sisters to agree to a glass of champagne or a dance, only to watch the reticent Iris or the remote Dorothea grow paler and paler as the evening wore on, until, finally released, she could rush back to her twin and become attached again. It was as though they required an infusion of each other's blood to keep them alive.

Discouraged, George continued to pay for Miss Wetherall to take his sisters to Europe each summer. At least during these trips they seemed more engaged and came back looking healthier. Part of the reason for their changed appearance was that, thanks to George's continuing largesse, Adeline, without a bleat of regret, had abandoned the spiritual themes of her earlier tours in favor of Baden-Baden, Trouville, and Biarritz, fashionable watering holes of the American rich, where she enjoyed most agreeable accommodations for herself and her charges. "Salvation may be found in unexpected places," she would declare, settling into a comfortable deck chair overlooking the ocean, with a glass of Bordeaux and a dish of pralines close at hand. The twins, unversed in such temptations, found themselves easily accepting the liberating powers of French humanism. What else was there to do?

On June 28, 1914, while the twins and Miss Wetherall were sampling the pleasures of fine late spring weather in Biarritz, the Austrian archduke Franz Ferdinand was assassinated on a visit to Sarajevo by a Serbian revolutionary. With this single act of violence, the simmering tension in the Balkans broke open, and the consequences, challenging the frail treaties between Europe's major powers, tipped the balance so catastrophically that within only a few weeks, all-out war had been declared across the Continent and beyond.

At the time, a seemingly isolated murder in a distant and unfamiliar eastern European city cast hardly a ripple on the other side of the Atlantic, where the summer was slowly giving up its heat to the beaches and resorts of Newport and Bar Harbor. Blithely unaware of any unpleasantness blowing through their beloved Europe, Adeline, Dorothea, and Iris returned home. The teacher as usual urged her charges to return to their desks. No time should be wasted, she explained, in writing up their experiences of yet another inspiring period of exposure to French culture. "This is our duty as educated observers. Poetry expects it of us!"

On October 12 of that year, George persuaded his sisters to attend the Harvard-Princeton football game. It was being played in Princeton, a less arduous journey from New York than Cambridge, and George, who had always enjoyed the reputation of doggedness, floated the idea that the twins might connect to some of his single friends who would drive up for the game. It was a perfect fall weekend, with parties from New York, Philadelphia, and Boston arriving in their autos packed with hampers of caviar, foie gras, smoked salmon, and cases of beer and champagne, while the leaves of the red and yellow maple trees lining the stadium tumbled down like flakes of gold onto the festive scene.

George's friends had told him of the famous class of '15 athlete who had transformed Harvard's ice hockey and football record into something even the hard-boiled New York sportswriters were amazed by. His name was Harry Forrester, and George promised his sisters that they would see something very special in the stadium that day. Knowing nothing about football, the twins watched obediently as the young legend appeared on the field. He was immediately noticeable, without a helmet, his thick, wavy fair hair like a Greek god's; his presence on the field turned it into an Olympic arena. The ball found him time after time, and as he effortlessly raced up and down, twisting and turning in the autumn light, he seemed to leave behind tracers of lightning. He seemed both untouchable and untouched, and as the game progressed, his speed and agility made the old men's cheers hoarse with emotion. Harvard won, but the only thing anyone remembered afterward about that day was Harry's performance on the field.

After the game, George took the twins to the Ivy Club, a handsomely paneled private meeting place for Princeton students, where George's friends were congregating. Despite Princeton's loss, George was in a happy and gregarious mood and dragged the twins into the throng with enthusiasm. All the talk was of the wonderful athlete they had seen and whether anyone would ever be so great again.

Suddenly the room went oddly quiet. The players rarely joined the celebrations after a game, but to everyone's surprise, Harry Forrester had entered the room. Off the field, he seemed smaller and more vulnerable. The slight flush in his cheek and the beads of sweat on his forehead, turning some strands of hair dark, betrayed the physical demands the game had made upon him. George boldly went up to him.

"Congratulations," he said. "You played magnificently."

"Thanks." Harry seemed uncomfortable with the praise and looked away. Beside him stood an older man, tall and very thin, with black hair slicked back and shining as though treated with boot polish. He had long, thin lines running from his nose to his mouth, giving a gaunt appearance, and his blue eyes were shaded by heavy lids.

"Everett Grayfield," the man said, introducing himself to George. "I think I was a few classes ahead of you."

"Of course," George said. "George Crosby. These are my sisters, Dorothea and Iris." Everett gave them a cursory glance, then put his hand on Harry's shoulder.

"Come, my dear," he said to him. "We are expected in New York. A good dinner awaits you after your brilliance this afternoon."

Harry looked at Everett and smiled awkwardly. "Whatever you say," he responded. "I'd better go and grab my things."

Harry walked off quickly through the crowd, receiving the back-slaps and cheers from admiring students with his hands up to his face, as though protecting himself from blows. Everett watched him go and then turned to say good-bye. "Good to see you, George," he said smoothly. "We must have lunch sometime. I believe we belong to the same club. Excuse me."

"Absolutely," George replied. Everett disappeared after Harry, waving to a few acquaintances as he left the room.

Dorothea and Iris looked after them curiously. "What a paradox," Iris said. "So sure of himself on the field and so adrift everywhere else."

"I expect he's shy," George said. "People make such a fuss."

"I feel sorry for him," Iris murmured. "I read something I think Barrymore said once, that the only time he felt he really lived was when he was onstage."

"But you can't live your whole life on the football field," Dorothea pointed out.

"I suppose not. And the other? Is he the alternative?"

"The jackal and the prey," Dorothea suggested.

"Don't be absurd," George protested. "Everett has been very generous to students over the years. Lots of Harvard alumni are in his debt. I'm sure he's just being kind. I heard that Harry hasn't got any family."

"That's not surprising," Iris said. "There's something sad about him."

George burst out laughing. "You're talking about the most famous man at Harvard," he scoffed. "People hero-worship him. Look at those cheering crowds. I don't know why he should be sad about anything. Anyway, we must go home. Lavinia will be wondering what happened to us."

That was the first and last time the twins would attend a game. By the end of the 1914 college football season, war between Germany, France, Britain, Italy, and Russia had already been declared, trenches were being dug deep into the soil of Belgium and northern France, and mortars had taken the lives of thousands of young men in the pursuit of their country's glory. All those students and players who had celebrated Harvard's victory in Princeton that fall would soon be involved in a very different kind of game, with victory defined in very different terms.

At first, Americans were slow to register what was really happening abroad. Minor inconveniences at home had not slowed their relentless pursuit of wealth and pleasure. But by the middle of 1915, the country realized that the war would not end as soon as expected. Reports from the front painted a grim picture of the theater of war in France. Society leaders were galvanized into action. Various organizations were formed—the Sewing Girls of Paris Fund, the American Women's War Relief Fund in London, the Children of Flanders Rescue Committee, and so on. Foreign visitors warned Americans that Paris was plunged in darkness at night and that the streets were too gloomy to navigate. Friends were particularly concerned for well-known expatriates such as Elsie De Wolfe, who had a house in Versailles, and Gertrude Stein, who was a resident of the French capital. What would happen to them if the Germans reached Paris?

As they rang in 1916 with no signs of the war's abatement, the twins anxiously sifted through the increasingly distressing news from Europe. But it was when Edith Wharton began publishing dispatches from the front in *Scribner's Magazine* that they knew they would have to act. They were shocked by the novelist's expressions

of despair at how her adopted country was being systematically destroyed—the ashen emptiness of the villages, the soldiers back from
the trenches, "battered, shattered, frost-bitten, deafened and half-
paralyzed . . ." Dorothea and Iris read and reread to each other her
descriptions of the terrible look in the soldiers' eyes as they accepted
cigarettes or food while their wounds were being tended to, and of
the indomitable sisters of mercy who nursed these men in pitiable
conditions, only to return them to the horrors they had for a precious moment escaped.

What was Iris doing, riding in the park? Why was Dorothea still
in her room, trying to write a poem? The sisters relived their annual
visits to France, a France now under siege, and they understood that
they were finally being shown the way to participate in a world they
had shunned all their lives. This time they would not be outsiders.
This time they would not be found wanting.

While Adeline Wetherall bemoaned the fact that their European
trips were for the moment impossible (their favorite liner, the *Caronia,* had already been refitted as a warship), the twins knew they
must get to France by other means, and as soon as possible. Miss
Wetherall did not understand their perverse desire. Going to France
at this point was both irrational and lacking in spirituality. What
good could they do, such talented and refined souls, in that messy
conflict? She urged them instead to return to their poetry while the
unpleasantness in Europe lasted.

George was equally horrified when he heard of his sisters' absurd
scheme. He was aware that they had stepped up their involvement
with the Red Cross, but many of his friends' wives were equally
taken up with volunteering on behalf of the poor, benighted French,
so this was perfectly normal and understandable. He also discovered that his sisters were taking advanced French lessons, but he refused to believe that this was anything other than a sign of solidarity

with their beloved France and further proof of their devotion to French literature. France had saved them earlier, yes, he conceded that. But actually going over to France now was of course out of the question.

His wish to stay out of the fray was shared by many of his fellow countrymen. As the war dragged on, many Americans watched with mixed feelings the deliberations of President Wilson and his government over the call to join the struggle. In May 1917, the United States declared war on Germany. It was finally official. The next day, Dorothea and Iris announced that they would go to France as soon as they could arrange passage. George tried in vain to dissuade them. The twins were galvanized, on fire with energy, shopping, packing, making arrangements, putting their financial and legal affairs in order. They were never still, calling to each other, checking lists, writing notes, contacting other volunteers who were making plans for France. Dorothea threw away in disgust a much-reworked volume of poetry she had been working on. Iris, with only a momentary twinge of regret, said good-bye to her favorite horse and gave him to the local stable.

George could not believe what he was witnessing. He had never seen them so animated. Their faces had an inner glow, their dark eyes flashed, their voices rang with confidence. Even when applying for college against his wishes, they had not looked so vibrant. To him, they looked beautiful, as beautiful as they should have looked during all those years when New York was poised to receive them. Any man would desire them now.

"We are needed," Iris told him. "It's as simple as that. We have seen enough from a distance. Now we must join in. We are like actors. We've been given parts in a play and we are eager to perform them."

"At last," Dorothea agreed. "George, believe us. We have been waiting all our lives for this moment. It's a gift. The gift of visibility."

"Authenticity," Iris added. George looked bewildered.

"The only question now is whether we can do it. Whether we can pull it off." Iris looked at her sister with a blazing smile and started to do a little dance, grabbing her brother's reluctant hand. "Can we pull it off? Can we, Dorothea and Iris, pull it off, George? *Est-ce que c'est possible?*" she sang.

"Ah, yes, Iris. Yes. That is the only question now." Dorothea clapped her hands in approval, and Iris danced faster, feverishly twirling around her brother. George pulled his hand away and stared at her in alarm. His sisters had clearly lost their minds.

Like George, Miss Wetherall was helpless against the whirlwind. She gave each of them a large bound volume titled *The Hundred Greatest English Poems* and an equally large companion volume titled *French Poems to Remember,* meanwhile urging them to reflect on their decision. "I cannot understand why you want to do this," she lamented, a note of querulousness in her voice. "What am I to do without you?" The twins laughed gaily, and Dorothea pointed her to a line of Keats: " 'Ever let the Fancy roam, / Pleasure never is at home.' Remember what you said to us about freeing the imagination?"

"I didn't mean it like that," Miss Wetherall retorted crossly. "What about the celebrations for your twenty-fifth birthday? You forget we were organizing a trip to Maine this summer. I have so many new books to read with you. And you will miss my retirement ceremonies at Saint Mary's. I was depending on you to be there to help me through this difficult time."

"But what about opening wide 'the mind's cage-door'?" Iris quoted airily. "We'll 'dart forth, and cloudward soar.' Thank you, dear Adeline. We'll do all those things another time. And don't be concerned about your retirement; we are making sure you'll be taken care of. For us now, the door is opening elsewhere."

The twins embraced their longtime companion. "I'll write, I promise," Dorothea consoled her. "You mean so much to us. Your spirit will always be with us in our beloved France, the country that you have made us love beyond all others. '*Ô République de nos pères, / Grand Panthéon plein de lumières . . .*'"

Tears flowed. Adeline Wetherall was not comforted.

The twins did not include in their luggage the volumes of *The Hundred Greatest English Poems* or *French Poems to Remember*.

There were a few months to wait while the country mobilized and the volunteer services were organized for departure overseas. On Thursday, November 1, 1917, the twins embarked for France.

Chapter 5

EVERETT GRAYFIELD STOOD at the window of the library of his Fifth Avenue apartment, smoking a cigarette and looking out at Central Park. He was dressed in a dark green velvet dressing gown, with matching monogrammed slippers. His movements were graceful as he raised and lowered his hand, the cigarette pressed into service between the narrow, curled lips.

The winter air had penetrated the tightly closed windows of the room, so it was both stuffy and cold at the same time. The park looked dry, brown and pinched, already an old woman, Everett thought. The youthful vision of the great landscape designer Olmsted had faded sooner than anyone could have imagined. "All visions fade," he said aloud as the smoke from his cigarette wreathed his long, varnished fingers before escaping them and drifting aimlessly into the thick air of the room. He lifted up his little finger and examined it; an appointment with the manicurist was in order. He brought the cigarette again to his lips.

There was a knock at the door, and the butler entered, carrying a silver tray.

"A letter just came for you, sir," he said in an English accent.

Everett crossed the room. He made little sound on the richly patterned Persian carpets that covered the parquet floor of the library. The floor-to-ceiling books also muffled any noise. He moved easily between the eighteenth-century French gilded chairs and small tables, covered in silver, ivory, and porcelain knickknacks, that were placed at various angles around the room. Over the Adam-style fireplace hung a portrait of a boy with black curly hair and red lips, wearing a Little Lord Fauntleroy suit. Everett was ten when Boldini had painted the portrait, at the insistence of the boy's mother. The artist's flattering renditions could be seen in many of the drawing rooms of New York's ruling grandes dames. Mrs. Grayfield had planned for him to paint her portrait also, when Everett's was finished, but events intruded in the form of an attractive French violinist with whom Mrs. Grayfield bolted to Europe. Everett glanced at the picture with his usual twinge of nostalgia as he took the letter from the tray.

"Thank you, Willis," he said. "Please bring me a large bourbon in the conservatory, and do not disturb me until dinner."

"Very good, sir." The butler left the room.

Everett turned the letter over carefully. It was crumpled and dirty, and he handled it with some distaste. Letters, however, were all he had, and this one was not to be treated lightly.

He walked into the long marble hallway, with its glass sconces and mirrors, toward the conservatory. On the way he passed a heavy paneled mahogany door. It was closed. Hesitating, looking up and down the hall as though not wishing to be seen, he opened it. It revealed what seemed to be a child's room. There was a narrow bed with a large, brightly patterned coverlet on it, a big mahogany armoire, and a tufted rug. Its most distinguishing feature, however, was what was on the walls. Every space was covered with memorabilia of college athletic events—photographs of football games and hockey games, newspaper headlines about games, team photographs, individual photographs, photographs of stadiums and hockey rinks.

Shelves beneath these displays held framed pucks, footballs, sporting trophies, and plaques.

The wall behind the bed was even more specific: it was hung with pictures of a young man. He was portrayed in various team uniforms, kneeling in front of a ball, wearing a hockey jersey, alone on the football field. In some he wore a helmet; in others his head was bare. It was Harry Forrester. In all the photographs, he looked at the camera with the same distant expression, unsmiling, boyish, disengaged, except for his somber, disdainful eyes.

Everett went up to one of the photographs and stroked the glass with his fingers. Then he slowly left the room, closing the door quietly behind him. He walked on into the conservatory, a long, light room with glass windows from floor to ceiling and a central island of tropical plants. In a corner near a wicker chaise upholstered in green damask, Willis had placed his master's drink on a small round table. Here Everett sat down and opened the letter.

It was dated November 3, 1917, from Paris:

My dear Everett,

I have just arrived in Paris after completing my training at Issoudun. I couldn't write before, as the work at Issoudun was really tough and there was no place or opportunity to put pen to paper.

I love flying. There's nothing like it. It takes me back to the days when I played hockey at Harvard, the diving and banking, the quick-fire reflexes and correcting direction all the time, only now it's not a fellow on skates but a fellow in a flying machine.

Mind you, I could say something about the flying machines. The Nieuports are pretty heavy and difficult to maneuver, and they break down continually. The French are now experimenting with Spads, which are much lighter and easier to handle, but we aren't going to get a chance to fly them anytime soon, as they insist on passing on the Nieuports to us new boys. How about using your influence in Washington, Everett, to get them to make planes for us? We are sure going to need them.

The boys here are a fine bunch of people. My French is still a bit weak but I am getting better by the day. There are quite a few fellows around that I knew at school, so there are comrades here. I have been spending a lot of time with Maurice Aronsohn—you may remember him from Harvard. He was at Issoudun with me and is now in Paris, waiting like me for our marching orders. He's a good man—likes writing, unlike me!

Looking back on my three years since graduating, I believe a lot of my problems came from hating the work I was doing at the bank. I never could get the hang of it, and the only reason I could keep going was that you took me in and made things OK. That and playing pickup hockey for Saint Nick's. So I just want to thank you, Everett, for saving my life during this time. Your generosity has been extraordinary, and I know my mother feels the same way, only she is always too far gone to say so.

Now, of course, everything is different. I wish I had gotten over here earlier, like some of the fellows. Last week I met Raoul Lufbery, who joined the Lafayette Escadrille way back last year. Think of it—while I was wasting time behind a desk! If I'd started earlier, I might have had a better shot at getting a reasonable number of victories. As it is, some fellows like Lufbery have already notched up an impressive score. Anyway, soon it'll be my turn. I can't wait to get up there and shoot down some Boches. I'm an airman now, and when it's just me and the sky and the enemy, I think I can do well—with luck.

I hope to hear any day now where they are sending me, so I'll write again when I know. The waiting is the only hard part. Meanwhile, don't worry about me. I'm really in great shape and enjoying myself. I'll make you proud of me, I promise.

All the best,
Harry

Everett read the letter twice before placing it back carefully in the fragile, stained envelope and slipping it into his pocket. His face was impassive, but the lines around his eyes seemed deeper than before, and when he got up from his chair, he moved stiffly. He drank from the glass and then moved back through the hall to Harry's bedroom. He opened a drawer near the bed and drew out a small package of letters, tied with a green velvet ribbon. He placed the one he had just read on top and replaced the package. Looking around the room, he gave a faint sigh, then closed the door and returned to the conservatory.

"Willis?" he called.

The butler appeared at once. "Yes, sir?"

"Do you remember the party I gave for Harry for his twenty-fourth birthday?"

"The one at Delmonico's, sir?"

"Yes, the dinner with the French theme."

"Of course I do, sir." Willis remembered it clearly, as did many people in New York. It was one of the most famous parties ever thrown at Delmonico's. The restaurant was closed to the public and was decorated for the evening like a Parisian street, with cafés, bars, musicians, and flower sellers. The guests were all male, twenty-four of them (the same number as Harry's age), dressed in white tie or costumes of Napoleon's court. Those with suitable proportions chose the latter—such flattering britches! Harry wore conventional attire, but his body seemed constrained in his stiff collar and heavy jacket. He should, Everett thought with a smile, have been naked. Those who were known for their wine cellars were requested to bring a favorite Bordeaux for the evening. The others, younger and less wealthy, brought only their good looks and charm. The party lasted all night and the gossip columns wrote about it for days.

"Was a young man called Maurice Aronsohn there? Harry's Jewish friend?"

"I don't think so, Mr. Grayfield. He was unable to attend, as he was working at the time."

"I'm trying to remember what he looks like."

"Rather serious, if I recall, sir. Wears glasses. If I may be so bold, Mr. Grayfield, to me he looked something like the conductor Mr. Mahler. The Viennese gentleman. I found the similarity quite remarkable."

Everett looked at his butler in surprise.

"Well, sir," Willis explained, "my wife likes the classical music, and we sometimes manage to get to the Sunday concerts at the New York Philharmonic. Mr. Mahler was the conductor there until his sad demise."

"Dark, I suppose. Semitic looking."

Willis was not sure how to respond to this. "Mr. Aronsohn has dark hair, sir, yes."

"Yes, he would." Harry always seemed to like the dark ones. Everett put a hand to his hair and stroked it absently. "Like Mahler, you say? I believe I recall some reviews of his performances. Of course I am not a lover of the Philharmonic. It is still a provincial orchestra." He waved his hand. "That will be all, Willis. Bring me some writing paper."

Willis withdrew and returned with pen, paper, and a blotter.

"Thank you. I shall dine at eight o'clock."

The butler bowed and left, and Everett Grayfield picked up his pen. This war, he thought. Why? It is just over twenty years since we engaged in another war, also fought on foreign soil. What did we gain? Spanish land. And a taste for world power. Who will gain what from this European war? The winners, more world power; the losers, humiliation. Harry, like his contemporaries arriving every day now in France, is just a child, seeking thrills, fame, victories—an insignificant cog in the great wheel of national aggression. Harry is fighting for France, for French freedom—and yet he can barely even speak a word of French.

Everett sighed, shook his head, and in the silence of the conservatory began to write.

~ FRANCE ~

Chapter 6

THE BAR AT THE HÔTEL DE CRILLON is crowded with Americans. Many of them are drinking excessively, excited by being in France, by the proximity of war, by the strangeness of being so far from home. Most Parisians are delighted to see these fresh-faced visitors who are suddenly populating their deserted streets and bars, evidently embracing the freedom of a foreign city. *"How are you gonna keep them down on the farm, after they've seen Paree?"* The American presence provides an infusion of energy for the weary capital, as the bureaucrats of war fill hotels, offices, and apartments with the young men and women who have arrived to help the Allied cause.

Dorothea and Iris are at the bar with two young women. All four wear Red Cross uniforms. The twins look anxious, pink spots in their cheeks and eyes bright as they greet their companions, trying to be heard over the noise of American voices and laughter.

"What a piece of luck," Iris cries. "Meeting two Saint Mary's girls here at the Crillon!"

"You'll get used to bumping into people," says the taller of the two women. "Everyone's in Paris."

She is Isabel Lexington, a baby-faced beauty with big blue eyes and bobbed hair that falls in ruffles around her face like a bonnet. She smokes a cigarette slowly, circling her lips around it as though kissing it. Her friend is Grace Pope, small and thin, with the rapid movements of a bird. She also smokes, in light, hurried puffs as though wanting to use up the cigarette as soon as possible. Isabel looks around impatiently as they talk together. There is the possibility, she tells them, that their friends Harry and Maurice will join them before setting off to their postings.

"I can't stand the waiting," Dorothea says. "We really want to get started. We've been here two weeks already. What's the point of being here if we just stand around all day spending money in bars?"

"I expect you'll hear this week," Isabel assures the twins. "God knows you're needed."

"We took such an inadequate nursing course in New York," Iris says with a sigh. "I'm certain we won't know what to do."

"You needn't worry about that," Grace tells her. "First of all, you'll get a head nurse who will be much worse than any of the old battle-axes at Saint Mary's. They just scream orders at you until you're dizzy. Not know what to do? You'll get to know what to do before you can even find your way to the bathroom. 'Here! Nurse! Over here! What do you think you're dillydallying for?' You don't want to know too much, actually," she adds cheerfully. "The less you know, the better."

She puffs violently on her cigarette.

"What do you mean?" Dorothea asks.

"Well, it gets pretty disgusting. All that blood." She makes a face. "Until I got here, I thought too much blood was the droplet that appeared when I cut my finger. You get to faint a lot, you know." Dorothea and Iris exchange nervous glances.

"Don't listen to Grace," Isabel says. "She's just homesick, that's all."

"I'm not," Grace says indignantly. "You couldn't pay me to go home. Back to Connecticut and all those boring sewing parties? I'm having a whale of a time, and you will, too."

"Oh, look," Isabel interrupts her, waving. "There are Harry and Maurice. Hurrah!"

Two young men push through the crowd to the four girls. Harry's handsome face is instantly recognizable. His hair is as fair as Dorothea and Iris remember it on the football field at Princeton. Harry Forrester—the name alone conjures up that bright autumn afternoon and the thrilling sight of a young athlete in his prime. It seems quite natural to see him here in Paris, dressed in an airman's uniform.

Isabel does the introductions.

"Harry Forrester, Maurice Aronsohn, Dorothea and Iris Crosby. Grace, of course, you know."

"We thought we wouldn't make it," Harry says. "We finally got our orders, thank God. I have to leave tonight, and Maurice tomorrow at dawn, so we can't stay long."

Harry gives them a gleaming smile. Iris and Dorothea remember the contained energy he radiated after the football game. That golden quality is still there. He smooths back his unruly hair and shakes his shoulders like a dog after swimming. "At last, dear friends," he declaims, as though addressing an audience, "the call has come. I'm prepared. Harry Forrester is on the team, ready to have a go and get the damn Boche." He clenches his fist as though manipulating a joystick and lets out a wild whoop.

"Down, buster," Maurice says teasingly, patting Harry on the arm. "All in good time."

Maurice is much darker in coloring than his friend, and smaller boned. His rimless glasses, long dark hair, and serious expression give him the appearance of a scholar. He is not wearing a uniform but the kind of light open-collared shirt and blue jacket Frenchmen wear. He looks more like a poet than a pilot.

"So what are we drinking?" Harry asks. "Beer for us, wine for the girls, OK?" Harry orders for everyone.

"I think we saw you play football once at Princeton," Iris ventures.

"Everyone says that," Isabel says, putting her arm around him. "Harry's the most famous athlete in the world, aren't you, darling? People come up to him all the time."

Harry smiles awkwardly and shakes her arm off his shoulder.

"We came with our brother, George, to one of your games," Iris continues. "It was back in 1913, I think. At Princeton."

"Nineteen fourteen," Harry corrects her. "That was some game."

"It seems a long time ago," Iris says dreamily. "I remember it was quite cool, and autumn leaves were falling everywhere."

"That's all you remember?" Harry asks with a sly grin. Iris stares at him in mock surprise.

"Can you remember anything else, Dorothea?" she asks, shaking her head. "I really don't think so."

"You mean Harry didn't make an impression?" Maurice asks her in shocked tones. "You didn't see him kick a field goal? Intercept the ball? Return a punt? I can't believe it!"

"Wait a minute." Iris holds up her hand. "You didn't wear a helmet," she declares, as though suddenly remembering. "And I think Harvard won." Maurice laughs and gives her an approving nod.

"Of course Harvard won!" Isabel exclaims. "Harvard always won with Harry!"

"Not always," Harry corrects her. "But that was a lucky game for us. Princeton played great defense."

"Harry never forgets a game," Isabel explains. Harry shakes his head dismissively. "He was just as good on skates, you know," she continues, kissing him on the cheek. "Played hockey for Harvard, too."

"Really?" Dorothea murmurs politely.

"Wait till you see him in the air," Maurice says. "He thinks the sky's a skating rink."

"How do you know?" Harry demands. "You've never been up with me."

Maurice looks at him and rolls his eyes. "I know, buddy," he says, laughing. "Trust me. I've been in an automobile with you and that was enough. With wings, I'm sure it's worse." Harry shrugs, his expression a mixture of annoyance and pleasure.

"Well, since this is the last night of your leave, let's go dancing," Isabel says. "How about it, Harry?"

"I don't know," he demurs. "Dancing seems—I don't know . . . We always had to go to bed early before a game."

"Don't be silly," Isabel protests. "You're out of college, remember? You can make your own decisions. And I want to dance." She tosses her head back.

"Besides," Harry adds stubbornly, "I'm no good at dancing. Never was. Always stepped on the girl's foot. You wouldn't want that, would you, Isabel?"

Isabel glares at him. "Oh, you're such a slug sometimes. Well, if you won't, I'll find someone else. Look, there's Mac and Pete over there." She flounces off. Harry shrugs and drinks his beer.

"Don't mind her," Grace says. "She just doesn't want to waste any time. She feels the war may somehow get in the way of her plans."

"Plans?" Iris asks.

"To get married, of course. With all the boys we know being called up to fight, there may not be such good pickings in the future. The odds are getting worse every day."

"Lordy! I hadn't thought of that," Dorothea says in a tone of alarm. "Iris, how is it that we hadn't thought of that?" Iris shakes her head rolling her eyes in mock horror.

Harry quickly drains his beer. "Girls always think of that," he retorts, turning away and merging with the crowd.

"What did we say?" Grace asks.

"He's probably gone to find Isabel," Maurice says. "He really adores her, you know."

Grace snorts. "You'd never know it."

"Give him a break, Grace. He's not some awful parlor snake, thank God."

"You're very old friends, aren't you?" Iris observes.

"Since college. But I shall be seeing him less from now on."

"Aren't you in the same squadron?"

"No," Maurice answers. "Harry is stationed in Toul and I am near Saint-Mihiel. I'm much lighter than he is, and the lighter machines are based in Saint-Mihiel. I've met some fine people there, but I'll really miss being with Harry."

"Is he really such a good aviator?" Dorothea asks.

"Good aviator?" Maurice laughs. "He has such natural abilities it's like a sixth sense."

"What a marvelous gift," Iris says thoughtfully. "But he obviously doesn't like people mentioning it. I remember noticing his discomfort at being praised when we first saw him that time in Princeton."

"He'd rather do it than talk about it, if that's what you mean. I'll tell you something about Harry." He takes a drink and lights a cigarette. "We were at a house-party weekend during spring break," he begins. "It was our senior year. The house had a garden with a lake at the bottom. One night I couldn't sleep and went out walking, and found myself down by the water. We'd had a cold spell, and the lake was frozen. I got there after midnight, and it was pitch dark. I could hardly see a step in front of me. But then the moon appeared, and in the pale light I saw a figure gliding across the ice. He had a hockey stick, and he pushed a puck in front of him, invisible on the black ice, identifiable only by the thwack of the stick as it connected with it. I knew it could only be him—Harry. He was skating across the lake in a kind of trance—a state of grace. He never saw me, and I watched him for what seemed like an hour. For the first time, I understood what poetry in motion meant."

Maurice stops. "Then I realized how cold I was and got the hell back to the house."

"How extraordinary," Iris says.

"Why?" he asks.

"Taking your hockey stick to a house-party weekend."

"Exactly." He looks at her and grins. On her skin she feels his warm brown gaze behind his glasses.

"Well, that's the real Harry for me—always will be. Skating to the moon."

"You're worried about him, aren't you?"

"This war has changed everything for him. Ever since I've known him, all he's ever wanted to do is skate or play football. He came off three lousy, miserable years behind a desk in New York to come here to fly. And now, damn it, he's flying. And he's a new man. You can see—it's all he lives for. If he lives, that is. That's the irony, of course." He gives a short laugh. "'If he lives.' Now there's a line."

"So you are a writer," Iris says. "You're fortunate."

"Fortunate?"

"Because you have something real to write about."

"Real? As opposed to what?"

"As opposed to the fatuous sentiments we scribble in the safety of our nice warm apartment back home."

Maurice looks at her with sudden interest.

"We?"

"Dorothea and I. She's really a poet. But we both try to write. I hate to think how silly that sounds."

"It's not silly." He pauses. "Do you do everything together?"

Iris looks over at Dorothea, who is deep in conversation with Grace. "I believe so," she murmurs.

"How confusing." Maurice holds up his hands and slides them, like two screens, across his eyes. "Twin visions of beauty are almost too much to bear."

Iris flushes and laughs. "Try writing about that," she suggests.

"I think I shall." He pauses. "Iris." As he says her name, their eyes meet and lock, like magnets. Then equally suddenly, they pull away. "I must go to my sister," Iris blurts out. Maurice takes a cigarette from his pocket and lights it. He offers her one. She puts her hand out to him, then withdraws it. "I must go to my sister," she repeats. She backs away from him carefully, as though wishing not to startle a wild animal, then turns and hurries to join Dorothea, who is busily hunting through her purse. "Dorothea?"

"I'm tired," Dorothea announces. "I'm looking for our passes. I think we should go back."

"Of course." Iris has a guilty expression as she studies her sister's impassive face. "Is everything all right?" Dorothea continues to rummage through her purse, humming. Iris looks back furtively at Maurice, but he has turned away and is talking to Grace.

"Why so serious?" Isabel rejoins them, her eyes sparkling, her cheeks pink. She has Harry by the hand.

"We found each other," she says, snuggling up to him. "I'll always find you, Harry. Never fear."

Grace laughs. "Is that a threat? Look out, Harry. She'll always find you."

Harry holds up his hands. "And I thought it was the Boche who was after me." They all laugh. Harry takes out a cigarette from his breast pocket. Iris watches him intently, remembering precisely the same movements from Maurice a few seconds ago. "Anyone?" Harry asks, offering the pack.

"We don't smoke," Dorothea informs him.

"You will," Grace says darkly, taking one. The twins look puzzled. "Oh yes, you will," she continues, drawing the smoke deep into her lungs. "You'll understand soon enough."

Dorothea regards the clouds of smoke with distaste.

"Surely not," she remarks. Iris starts to say something, then stops herself.

"How little you know," Maurice bursts out. Dorothea looks startled at his vehemence. "Sorry. It's just that you are going to see things out there . . ." He looks at Iris's innocent face. "Never mind."

"We should go and check our status," Dorothea says, interrupting him. "We are still hoping to be sent somewhere tomorrow. We need to start work. I am really tired of all the waiting."

"I don't blame you," Harry agrees. "Waiting is the worst. I go crazy with the waiting."

"What a disagreeable thing to say," Isabel says, pouting. "When you're waiting, you can be with me. What's so terrible about that? I think you like your war planes better than me."

Harry gives her a pat on the back. "Isabel, we'll meet in a month when I am back, and then we'll do all the things you want to do."

"Oh, Harry." Isabel throws him a flirtatious smile. "You are such a darling, and I shall miss you dreadfully."

"Come on, Maurice," Harry says. "We must get over to the Union. There may be mail."

"What's the Union?" Iris asks, staying their departure.

"The American University Union in Europe," Maurice explains. "A group of universities got together and set it up as a kind of center for alumni to use as a base—drop things off, spend the odd night, meet people, report casualties, get information from home. It's on the rue de Richelieu—they rented the Royal Palace Hotel. It's very useful. And you can get dinner there for five and a half francs."

"One of its major benefactors is Everett Grayfield," Harry adds.

"Well," Maurice observes, "I'm not sure that's such a great credential."

"I don't know what you mean." Harry turns on him, annoyed. "You know that stuff gets on my nerves."

"Sorry, Harry," Maurice says. "But you know how I feel about him."

The twins exchange a glance. They remember the older man who hovered over Harry after the football game.

"The jackal," Dorothea whispers to her sister with a grin.

"Anyway," Maurice goes on quickly, "you can also rent a tennis racket there, which is just the thing when you're on leave with nothing to do."

"Oooh," exclaims Isabel, "I adore playing tennis. Daddy and I used to play all the time back home. We have a lovely grass court. Let's get up a game, Harry."

Harry looks weary. The golden lights have gone. "Sure," he says, "I'll play, but it's not my sport. I didn't grow up with my own tennis court."

The two men make their good-byes. Maurice, his expression enigmatic behind his glasses, holds Iris's hand slightly longer than necessary before leaving. Iris follows him with her eyes, conscious of his slender figure alongside the strong, athletic build of his friend.

"Maurice is such a sweetie, isn't he?" Isabel coos, noticing Iris's gaze. "But he's awfully intense. I'm really more for sporting types, aren't you, Dorothea? They're much more fun."

Dorothea looks at Isabel and raises her eyebrows. "I'm not sure we can answer that," she replies. "We haven't had much experience, I'm afraid."

"Well, now you're over here, that should change," Grace assures them. "The place is just teeming with handsome fellows looking for a good time. Makes the old US of A look terribly stuffy. It's really wild here. As long as Isabel doesn't get to them all first."

Isabel giggles. "Oh, my heart's set on Harry," she declares with a toss of her head. "I'll leave the others to you."

"Thank you," Grace says sardonically. "How generous of you."

The four girls shake hands and wish one another luck on their mobilization, agreeing to meet again whenever they find themselves back in Paris.

"These leaves in Paris will save you," Grace says. "Don't ever turn one down. I'm actually being serious for a moment."

"We won't forget."

The twins make their way through the overheated and smoky atmosphere of the bar, past clusters of uniformed men and women, most of whom are now drunk, passing precious time, waiting for orders that will send them to unknown destinations. A few tipsy soldiers wave at the twins, staring in confusion at their likeness. They whistle, making mock bows, jokily crossing their eyes to indicate double vision. One of them grabs Dorothea and kisses her wetly on the lips. She pushes away from him and stumbles toward the door, wiping her mouth. "Wrong one," commiserates his companion, pointing at Iris and cackling loudly. Escaping their laughter, Iris rushes after her sister and covers her with her cloak.

As the twins struggle out of the Crillon into the cold November air, someone starts singing the "La Marseillaise." The mood changes at once. People at the bar suddenly go quiet, drawn back into the reality of who and where they are. The reedy voice of the singer ebbs and then dies. There is a pause, like an inhaled breath, then the noise inside resumes, even more frenziedly than before, as though to drown out this moment of vulnerability, of fear.

The unexpected interlude has also affected the twins. Even though ragged and tunelessly rendered, for a moment the song has made the ugly night beautiful.

"We haven't heard any music for so long," Iris says.

"Do you remember Mrs. Wharton's description of a chant she heard in a village church?" Dorothea asks. "What was it? '*Sauvez, sauvez la France, / Ne l'abandonnez pas.*'"

The twins walk with firm steps into the place de la Concorde. After the riotous din at the Crillon bar, it seems eerily still. They can see their breath. The pedestals of the statues standing at the corners of the huge plaza are piled high with sandbags, like funeral pyres. How could they once have imagined Napoleon's triumphant armies in this sad arena? *Save, save France. Don't abandon her.* They pull their cloaks around them more tightly and make their way toward the Champs-Élysées. It is beginning to rain.

Chapter 7

My dear Everett,

Well, I am finally at the airfield, not far from Nancy. It is a grim place, almost as bad as Issoudun, horribly muddy and wet. We are still flying Nieuports, but they have promised us some improvements early next year. I have flown some successful missions, although nothing like Rickenbacker and Lufbery, whose records are stunning. It's such sport up there, waiting for the Hun to appear—usually from behind, out of the sun, cunning devils. We get to know their tricks, and it's not so difficult to get the upper hand. Frankly, it's exhilarating. I only wish I had joined up earlier and been of use before this.

I was in Paris briefly last week and picked up your most recent gift package from the Union. That is the best address, by the way, to send things. Your contribution to getting the place up and running is hugely valued by all the fellows arriving from the States. We use the place all the time. I see lots of friends there—it's just like being back in Cambridge!

Your package, as usual, was overwhelming. You are too generous. The cigarettes and delicious Swiss chocolates are most welcome, but the gold engraved cigarette case was quite unexpected, and the mother-of-pearl cuff links are too elegant for words. (To tell you the truth, I have no idea when I will ever wear them!) I must ask you to stop sending me such beautiful things; they are quite out of place here and I am afraid they will be stolen. I feel so ungrateful writing this, but you have no idea of the kind of life we are living. The conditions are pretty hellish, and I feel very burdened by being in possession of such expensive objects.

In your last letter you said you wanted to come to Paris. I strongly urge you not to do so. The city is in a state of siege, with all the best restaurants closed or without proper supplies, and the hotels full of military personnel from England and the U.S. You would not find it to your liking at all. I think you are much better off in New York, where you can be with your friends and be safe. I miss you, of course. I look at the photos you sent me and feel homesick for a while, but then I hear the engines tuning up on the airfield and I know I'm in the right place.

Right now, we are waiting for the weather to clear—it always seems to rain in northern France—so we can go up again. The squadron gets a little restive at the inaction, as do I. We seem to do so much waiting around here. But I tell myself all will be fun and games soon enough. The difficulty is to stay ready. I try to follow the same kind of exercise program we had with the football team. It keeps me going.

I saw Isabel and Grace a few times in Paris with Maurice. The last time I saw them, they were with the Crosby twins. I think you know their brother; wasn't he a class or two below you? I recall your showing me his beautiful house in Far Hills when we were out there once. The twins seem nice, rather quiet. Apparently we met after the Princeton game in 1914. You'd think I'd remember, seeing double like that. Quite a game, wasn't it? We only just pulled it out at the end. That's probably why I didn't remember. I always found it difficult to be sociable after a big game—as you well know! Maurice seems to like one of the twins particularly well, but I don't see how he tells them apart. Isabel is lively and likes sports, which of course puts her up there in my book. They say she's a prom trotter, and she's certainly rich, but she seems to have taken a serious liking to me, which is a little embarrassing. You'd probably think her fast—although most of the girls I've met over here seem fast, at least compared to the ones back home. I suppose it's something to do with the war and everyone living on their nerves. And away from their parents!

Not much other news, so I'll sign off. I can never thank you enough for all you have done for me, Everett. I feel I don't deserve it. If I were a better writer, I would be able to express it all better. It was such a dark time for me, the last few years. Only now, when I take a plane up, do I get to that place I used to find when I played hockey and football. This is really it for me, and I am grateful that the opportunity came before it was too late. I feel truly alive again.

All the best,
Harry

Chapter 8

IT IS ONE OF THE coldest winters in memory. Even the Seine has frozen over. Here on a flat plain near the small village of Plotières, the wind is particularly fierce. It shears through the canvas flaps of the hospital tent like scissors through paper, blowing away bandages and surgical instruments, knocking down water canteens, tearing off the nurses' kerchiefs. Pieces of bloody dressing fly through the air, landing on patients' faces. Dirty washrags wrap around the legs of the rusting iron beds. Buckets of vomit topple over onto the muddy floor. The stove flickers and goes out, allowing a vicious wave of cold to rage through the tent.

But the worst aspect of these winter storms sweeping France from Nancy to Amiens is the noise. When Dorothea and Iris first arrived here, they found the constant din of the shelling at the front to be almost intolerable. Now, three weeks later, the shelling is like a muffled obbligato, almost reassuring in its consistency. The noise of the tent's flapping and howling in the wind is far more distressing. If the tent falls, the hospital falls, and if the hospital falls, only the dead will remain.

"We weren't prepared," Iris calls over the wind to her sister as they struggle to contain the chaos in the tent.

"It's certainly not Park Avenue," Dorothea responds, her hair tumbling over her face as the wind tears at her chignon. Iris pulls out her tortoiseshell hair clips, letting the dark hair loose.

"It's better this way," she shouts. "We can tie it back with our kerchiefs." Dorothea nods and follows suit.

"What would George say?" she cries, trying to tie the kerchief against the tugging of the wind.

"What would Lavinia say?" Iris asks, laughing, as she pushes her hair inside the kerchief. "There, that's better."

But Dorothea does not hear her. She has turned away to attend to a soldier, who is shivering in little gusts as he tries to wrest his blanket from the greedy wind.

"*Voilà, mon pauvre,*" she murmurs, wrapping him up as best she can. "*Il fait chaud maintenant.* You'll be warmer now."

Because the twins speak good French, the Red Cross has assigned them to a French hospital. It is a complex of hurriedly constructed tents and *baraques,* or huts, the latter slightly stronger than the tents in order to house the more seriously wounded. A special hut at the far end of the complex, conveniently located near the morgue, is set aside for the *grands blessés*—the dying. The twins, being novices, have not yet been invited to serve in these exceptional quarters. The soldiers on their watch are supposedly on the way to recovery. Indeed, the directrice has specifically instructed her nurses to patch the patients up as quickly as possible so that they may get back to the trenches. "I think she has a quota," Dorothea observed to her sister after their first week. "The more men she returns to the front, the bigger her medal. Ten per day gets you a silver star; twenty gets you a gold plaque."

The directrice is a frightening woman. Grace's warnings in Paris were accurate. Big, brassy, red-faced, the tireless French matron shouts at the nurses and patients alike, insisting on a regime of discipline that would do justice to a military prison. "Up, up," she yells to a boy whose eyes and body are almost entirely covered in bandages. "No lying about here, *mon vieux*, we must get you on your feet." She props up the young soldier into a sitting position. Blood immediately starts oozing from his chest. "Who did this dressing?" she exclaims in fury. The boy lies down again, gasping for breath.

"Nurse, at once, over here!" the directrice calls out. Both twins jump at her summons and run to get clean bandages. "Did you learn nothing in America?" the directrice excoriates them, unwrapping the dressing, which is already soaked through. She wraps the wound with clean gauze in efficient, tight circles and slaps the soldier on the shoulder. "Tomorrow you'll be out of here," she tells him briskly. She is probably right. Her willpower is irresistible; she seems almost to hypnotize her victims into recovery. The soldiers are weakened by trench warfare, but here in the tent they are equally victims of the directrice's relentless force. The twins hate her and admire her in equal measure.

It does not take long for Dorothea and Iris to learn the drill. The directrice wrote and tacked up their schedule immediately after their arrival, and any deviation from it earns her fury. Make beds. Wash linen. Scrub lockers. Disinfect medicine cabinets. Fix patients' identifying labels from dressing station and medical charts to beds. Pack swabs and gauze. Roll bandages. Change and wash dressings. Fold blankets. Prep for night.

At first they move around the ward in a daze, inhaling the sweetish, rotten smell of festering wounds and congealing blood, hearing the constant moaning of the soldiers, unable to tear their eyes away from the oozing craters that cover the men's stricken bodies. But in a surprisingly short time, the conditions become normal. They learn what to do, where to go, how to insert themselves into the routine that has been set out for them.

They smoke.

The directrice keeps a firm eye on her inexperienced team. "You must eat regularly," she tells Dorothea and Iris in her blunt way. "What is the point of a girl working for me who is not at full strength?" For most of the wounded, "eat" is a euphemism. The nurses spend much of their time trying to get even a drop of liquid down the soldiers' ruptured throats. Even if the liquid can be persuaded to trickle down into the digestive tract, it often triggers violent interior spasms, and many patients choke, throwing up a mixture of clotted blood and vomit. These men have been living in conditions that make their bodies indifferent to food, numb to appetite. Like prisoners, they live on blood, rum, and cigarettes, a diet that keeps them alive long enough to hurl themselves one more time over the top into No Man's Land.

For the twins, despite the directrice's orders, food has become an equally meaningless word. They drink a lot of cocoa, which is both warming and energizing. Any extra food they are given—old bread, dried meat, and biscuits—they smuggle to the horses and dogs who live on the farm outside the hospital. Most days, they have no time to think of anything but the next instruction on their schedule. They are on call constantly, rushed from task to task, always fighting to keep up with the insatiable demands the makeshift hospital and its suffering inmates make upon them. The mindless activity, of course, is part of the process that allows them to endure the terrible work. Both the directrice and her trainees know that. The routine becomes their satisfaction, the accomplishment of daily tasks their fulfillment.

Iris stands over a soldier who has four bullet wounds in his stomach. They are round and black, and as she stares at them she is suddenly back in the kitchen of her brother's apartment, a child again, alone with a freshly baked chocolate cake the cook has left on the table. She surreptitiously sticks her finger into the soft, warm flesh of the cake and lets the sponge cling to it. Pulling it out, she sticks it in her mouth and licks it, slowly savoring it. She does it again, and then again.

It is not the remembered taste of the food that is so dangerous. It is the reentry into that other world, a place that she has now turned her back on, that sets up the possibility for weakness, for failure. Half-fainting at the memory of that long-ago kitchen, in that faraway apartment, Iris gazes at the fingertip wounds in front of her, which are now beginning to suppurate with the usual corrupt mixture of pus and blood. Her stomach heaves and she feels a rush of bitter liquid fill her mouth. Grabbing the soldier's basin, she bends over it and lets the bile erupt jerkily into the filthy mixture it already contains.

"Nurse! Nurse!" The directrice is calling her. Iris puts the basin away and starts dressing the boy's wounds. Furious at herself, she works on the moist holes, cleaning them, covering them with iodine, wrapping them in gauze. The soldier complains faintly. She does not hear. How could she have slipped so badly? How could that image of the past have crept into her mind without her noticing? Usually she senses the warning signal that her memory has temporarily awakened, and she closes everything down. It's the only way. Keep focused at all times. Make beds. Wash linen. Scrub lockers. Disinfect medicine cabinets. Prep for night.

"Iris?" She hears her sister's voice and looks up, tight lipped, still under the spell of memory. "Iris. I'll be right there. Let me help." Dorothea joins her sister in dressing the wounds of the next patient. His abdomen has been ripped away, showing what looks like a string of skinless sausages, with blood bubbling around them in a red stew.

"Your eyes look remarkably big today," Dorothea goes on in a strong voice. "I fear it is because you have lost weight with this magnificent diet we are fed. Still, it makes you look very fine."

Iris stops working for a minute and looks across the bed at her sister. Her expression lightens, and she licks her dry lips.

"Very fine?" she repeats vaguely. She puts her hand to her eyes. "They look big?" She is quiet for a moment, tentatively touching her eyelids. "Well done, Dorothea," she says finally, looking at her sister's stern face — the reflection of her own. "You've pulled me out of it. You've brought me back." She briskly shakes her head.

Dorothea hands her a cigarette and lights it. "It's just a question of the imagination, you know. Too much is dangerous for us here."

"Keep it on a firm leash, like the dogs at home. I know," Iris says. "Thank you, darling." They exchange a small smile and return to work.

Later in the afternoon, the wind picks up and the tent sways and teeters dangerously. The flaps swing open constantly, hurling in dust and rain, drenching the beds and the floor. Iris and Dorothea move down the ward, mopping up, reassuring patients, trying to fix shaky tent poles.

"It's a pity we never went camping," Iris says, tying a rope more firmly. "We'd be better able to do this."

"I don't think camping was Miss Wetherall's idea of a summer vacation," Dorothea replies, removing a metal dish filled with a dark yellow fluid from under a bed.

"Miss Wetherall." Iris repeats the name slowly, stepping back and looking at the row of injured men huddled on their cots. Dorothea turns her head away from the dish as she flushes it into a sink.

"I can just see her here, can't you?" Dorothea adopts Adeline Wetherall's pedagogic position, head cocked, fingertips together. " 'Thou still unravished bride of quietness . . .' "

Iris rolls her eyes. "You're so good for me," she tells her sister. "What would I do without you?"

"How about this," Dorothea goes on, enjoying herself. " 'O sweet and far from cliff and scar — ' "

" ' —The horns of Elfland faintly blowing!' " Iris finishes the line, waving her arms and laughing.

They suddenly see the directrice down the ward, looking disapprovingly at them. The sudden reminder of their fierce tormentor sobers them.

"We learned a lot from Miss Wetherall," Dorothea whispers, turning back to the sink. "She counted, once."

"Once," Iris says. "A long time ago."

The directrice starts moving toward them. Dorothea watches her as she approaches with firm, angry strides, her eyes blazing.

"How different, these two women in our lives," she mutters. "Who counts now? Quick, Iris, back to work."

"I must find more bandages," Iris says, hurrying away from the directrice's onslaught of reproof.

A soldier puts out an arm and stops her. He lies on his back, a lock of hair over his forehead. His eyes stare up, cornflower blue, with dark lashes. For the moment, it is not possible to see where he is wounded. Iris puts her hand on his tunic, which is as stiff as cardboard, encrusted in dried mud. All the buttons are ripped off. She brings scissors and starts to cut the tunic open on the sides, where the fabric is less resistant. She raises it like the lid of a box, and immediately a huge gush of blood spouts out, staining her apron red. The blood pours across the boy's body in a stream. It has black bits in it. Shrapnel. The stiffness of the tunic is now explained. It comes not from mud but from dried blood. The soldier's tender body has been enclosed in a carapace of blood.

Iris sways slightly, her face ashen.

"Hold on," Dorothea says fiercely from the other side of the bed. "Iris, hold on."

The boy puts a hand to his chest and feels the sticky liquid. "Lor',

I'm ever so sorry," he says in a weak voice. "Wot a mess. And on your lovely clean apron, too."

"You're English," Dorothea says, starting to mop up the blood. "How did you get to a French hospital?"

"I dunno," the boy says. "I think they thought I was dead and left me, the sods. Some Frogs picked me up and brought me 'ere."

"Well, you'll be fine," Dorothea says.

"It's a bit o' luck you speak English," he says. "I thought I heard you spouting something. I can't speak a word of French except . . ." He stops, looking at the twins. "Never mind," he says with a saucy grin.

Iris bends over him, covering his chest with iodine, and then helps Dorothea pass a bandage beneath his torso.

"You've had a bad injury," she says, "but I think you were lucky."

The English soldier looks up and sees the twins above him, their faces as pale as marble. He looks from one to the other and back again.

"Lucky?" he asks. "Blimey, I must be a goner. I'm seeing double." He closes his eyes.

Later, returned to the front, the Tommy will tell his comrades of the double vision he experienced in the French hospital. Soon others will live to tell the same story. The French soldiers received at Hôpital Chirurgical Mobile no. 3 begin to look forward to seeing for themselves the twin American nurses who seem to have such magical healing powers.

"You mean there are really two of them? Two for the price of one, eh?"

When they first arrived, Dorothea and Iris put different-colored markers on their armbands so they could be told apart, but the soldiers could not remember if Iris was red and Dorothea blue or the other way around. Anyway, what did it matter? The twins perform their duties anonymously, pale, floating figures entering and disappearing from their patients' consciousness, just like the other nurses in the ward. As long as they do their job properly, who cares what anybody's name or number is? The hospital is a place for transients. Nobody is going to stay here long enough to remember. The twins abandon their identifying tags.

The record-cold winter of 1917–18 shows no signs of relenting. It is often so frigid that the twins go to bed in their clothes and wake up with their stockings stiff with frost. They sleep fitfully. They listen to the roaring wind, to the remorseless explosions of shells that always seem closer at night, and to the wrenching cries their soldiers utter through the darkness. Disembodied voices call out, *"Vite! Vite! C'est nous!" "Je ne tiens plus!" "Où est mon camarade?" "S'il vous plaît, coupez la fil de fer barbelé! Vite!" "Non, c'est pas possible!" "Mourir, Jésus . . ."* Cries of random desperation—please, quick, help, I can't die—dredged up from a too-short past, a past without a vocabulary of pain.

Dorothea and Iris lie shivering on their cots, shielding their ears from the hideous lullabies. "What is *fil de fer barbelé*?" Iris whispers. "They say it all the time."

"Barbed wire," Dorothea answers. "It has to be cut so they can go over the top." She pauses. "And sometimes it isn't. Sometimes the wire doesn't get cut."

The twins huddle down under their thin blankets, seeing the impaled bodies of young men who have been betrayed in the futile effort of gaining—what? Three feet of ground, perhaps. Three feet of human mud.

"Mademoiselle, mademoiselle, où êtes-vous?"

Iris jumps up and rushes into the tent, past the narrow beds rocking with their sweat-drenched cargo. "I'm here," she calls. She finds the boy who cries out. She knows his voice. He is going to die.

"*Je suis ici,*" she says. "Shhhhhh." The boy's head and eyes are covered, so she cannot stroke his brow. One of his hands has been shot off, and the stump is badly infected. As his arm twitches in recognition of its loss, it releases a putrid smell from the wet bandages, enveloping Iris in suffocating waves of a hot, sweet stench that rises up and fills her nostrils. She longs for a cigarette or a sachet of lavender, which the nurses sometimes use to cover their noses and mouths. Instead she takes rapid, shallow breaths and looks for the boy's other hand, which has long, graceful fingers like those of a pianist. Her own hands are no longer smooth, but coarsened from the cold water, rough towels, and acid disinfectants that they are constantly assaulted by, and her carefully arched nails are now short, with jagged edges. But of course he wouldn't know the difference. She caresses his fingers, one by one, over and over.

"*Dis-moi quelque chose,*" he whispers. "*Quelque chose, Maman.*"

Iris stares into the darkness of the tent. What can she tell him? What would his mother tell him? Her French deserts her. She looks down at the soldier.

" 'It is a far, far better thing that I do, than I have ever done,' " she suddenly finds herself reciting. " 'It is a far, far better rest that I go to than I have ever known.' " Then she whispers, "I'm sorry. *Je m'excuse.*"

But the boy does not respond. He has already gone.

Chapter 9

THE ROYAL PALACE HOTEL is one of the great Paris hotels that sprang up at the beginning of the new century. Designed by Charles Lemaire, it first opened in 1908, a year before the Crillon. It sits on the corner of the rue de Richelieu, facing the place du Théâtre-Français, a tree-filled park with a fountain in the center. Its six floors, with wrought iron balustrades protecting the high French windows, rise above an elegant gun store called Fauré le Page. Over the ornately carved front entrance is a sign reading AMERICAN UNIVERSITY UNION.

Dorothea and Iris stop to admire the gleaming metal and wood of the firearms displayed in the store windows. "We don't see any like that in Plotières," Iris observes.

"These are for sport," Dorothea explains. "For game."

"Isn't the enemy game?" Iris asks. Dorothea laughs.

"They are for Harry, certainly."

They walk through the arched doorway into the lobby. A few Americans in uniform are sitting on sofas and chairs, reading mail or newspapers. Dorothea reads aloud the sign over the information desk: "The general object of the Union shall be to meet the needs of American university and college men and their friends who are in Europe for military or other service in the cause of the Allies."

"Isn't that nice," Iris says. "And to think the jackal is behind it."

"Perhaps he's a good man after all."

"Maurice didn't seem to think so."

"Well, in that case . . ." Dorothea shoots a penetrating look at her sister. Iris blushes.

"Can I help you?" a man at the information desk asks, taking a pipe out of his mouth. "You're looking for Maurice?"

"And Harry Forrester," Iris says quickly.

"I think they're in the library," the young man says. "I'll show you the way."

They follow him through the lobby into a small room with leather chairs and shelves lined with a modest selection of books. The books, however, are not the typical leather-bound volumes that normally adorn a library, but shabby, thin, stained, dog-eared objects that look as though they might have been picked up off the street.

They see Maurice at once. He is standing by the window, one of the decrepit books in his hand. He is smoking a cigarette, and the smoke spirals up around him, partly concealing his face.

"Maurice," Iris says. He turns quickly, the smoke parting like a curtain to reveal the slim, dark figure by now familiar to them.

"Iris," he exclaims, beaming. "And Dorothea. I'm so glad you could come. I only have a few hours, but when I heard you were in Paris, I thought it worth a try."

"Where's Harry?" asks Dorothea.

"He couldn't be here. I think he's trying to get to the center where Isabel works. He hasn't much leave, either, so every minute counts." He raises his eyebrows suggestively, and they laugh.

Dorothea begins to move toward the ragged collection on the shelves with a dubious look.

"The books?" Maurice waves at them with a wry expression. "They don't look like much, I agree. But what's the cliché—never judge a book by its cover?"

"So what are they?" Dorothea asks.

"They belong to men at the front. Mostly English, I guess. Probably either brought from home or sent to them by friends or family. They say it's useful to have something to read in the trenches when nothing's going on. A lot of it is poetry, oddly." He holds one up and looks at its damaged spine. "This, for example. By Rupert Brooke. Ultimately they somehow find their way here to the library, either donated by the books' owners who have returned home or—" He breaks off with a grimace.

"We understand," Iris says hurriedly.

"Rupert Brooke?" Dorothea asks. "I don't know his work."

"He was English," Maurice explains. "Hadn't written much. He died almost at the beginning."

Iris picks a small softbound book from a shelf. "Julian Grenfell?"

"Another Englishman. Died at Ypres a month after Brooke." Maurice takes the book and opens it. The pages are loose, and he has to shuffle them back in order to read them:

> The fighting man shall from the sun
> Take warmth, and life from the glowing earth . . .

He pauses.

"Go on," Iris urges him.

"I don't really want to," Maurice says. But he continues:

> Speed with the light-foot winds to run,
> And with the trees to newer birth;
> And find, when fighting shall be done,
> Great rest, and fullness after dearth.

He gives a sigh and puts the tattered volume back.

"That's wonderful," Iris says.

"No, it's not wonderful," Maurice says sharply. Iris looks startled.

"I'm sorry," he says. "It's complicated. I'll explain some other time. We aren't supposed to be talking war talk. This is our leave, after all." He leads them out of the library. "There are other rooms here, you know, more cheerful rooms, where they have receptions for the ambassador and sell theater tickets and deliver mail and parcels. Last week a parcel came filled with two hundred toothbrushes and two hundred tubes of toothpaste. Donated by an anonymous American benefactor."

"Not the jackal again?" Dorothea inquires. Maurice looks puzzled.

"Never mind," Iris says hurriedly. "I don't think he's interested in teeth." The twins suppress a laugh.

"Who are you talking about?" Maurice asks. "He sounds charming."

"You wouldn't be amused," Dorothea says. She grins conspiratorially at her sister, and they again try not to laugh.

Maurice looks at them both with irritation. "Well, I'm interested in teeth," he announces, covering the awkwardness. "We Americans have our reputation to live up to." He gives Iris a large artificial smile, baring his teeth. She smiles back.

Dorothea winces. "I'd rather think about the theater," she says. "Now, there's a delightful thought."

"Let's see. I think they were putting on *When We Dead Awaken* last week," Maurice says. "Or was it *War of the Worlds*?" The twins stare at him. He bares his teeth again.

"Yes, of course," Iris says with sudden amusement. "I expect they did *Dance of Death* as well."

He nods solemnly. "That was done several times," he tells her. "It was the most popular play this season."

Dorothea makes an impatient sound. "You're both being silly," she says. "*Dance of Death* was a painting."

"Sorry," Maurice says. "Being silly helps at times. You should try it more often. What you are doing is far harder than what we do, you know."

"What do you mean?" Iris asks.

"You are confronted every day with the worst consequences of the trenches. You see at first hand what the soldiers are going through. You smell and touch the blood and mud and wounds. It's right in front of you, day and night. We airmen have all heard of the horrifying conditions, of course, but we have never so much as stepped on duckboards, or seen the barbed wire, or experienced a shell attack a few yards from where we stand. We don't stay up nights guarding ten feet of pointless ground, in the freezing darkness, listening to the endless firing of the mortars, staring at the blasted tree stumps and stretches of muddy plain, knowing that in the morning we will have to climb out and run over it toward almost certain death. For us, the war is clean, oh yes, so clean you wouldn't believe it. Fighting in the air, the only thing we see is blue sky and white clouds. As romantic as hell."

He stops short. "I'm sorry. I got carried away. The war in the air is a glorious thing." There is an uncomfortable silence.

"Flying may be clean," Iris ventures, "but the end comes just as quickly—and finally. The odds are terrible. What is it? One in three don't come back?" She realizes what she has said and puts her hand over her mouth.

"Probably marginally better odds than that," he says, laughing. He gestures to Iris as though to take her hand down. "Please, don't be sorry. It honestly doesn't bother us. Anyway, I just wanted you to know I admire what you do immensely. Not many women like you could do it at all, let alone go on doing it day after day, indefinitely, never knowing when it will end."

"Like us?" Iris and Dorothea repeat the phrase in unison, looking at each other.

"You mean women who grew up on Park Avenue and went to the right schools and summered in Newport and never saw a drop of blood in their lives?" Dorothea asks demurely.

Maurice laughs. "Well, I suppose I did mean that."

"It's not really so hard," Iris explains. "We don't really have time to think about it."

"Anyway, we didn't have any choice," Dorothea says. "We knew what we wanted to do. We are lucky, really."

"For the first time, we feel we're doing something worthwhile," Iris agrees, her eyes bright. "That's a fine feeling. We are the lucky ones."

They fall silent. Dorothea offers her sister a cigarette and takes one herself. Maurice quickly brings out his lighter and lights them both.

"Not everyone would agree with you there," he persists. "You deserve the medals that get parceled out to the dead in such pointless quantities."

The sisters shrug. Maurice looks from one to the other. They are both studying their cigarettes, distant, secretive.

"All right," he says cheerfully. "I see you're not going to explain further. Let's forget it. You deserve a drink. I know I need one." He looks around the Union lobby, which is filling up with off-duty soldiers. "Let's go somewhere else. I'm sick of seeing so many old college friends here. You can't think of anything to say after a while except what you can't say, if you know what I mean. We'll walk through the Palais-Royal and find a café that's open. Would you like that?"

"We should go back to Red Cross headquarters," Dorothea says. "We have to make a report."

"Must you both go?" Maurice says, directing the appeal to Iris.

"Well . . ." Iris glances doubtfully at her sister.

"You can't both leave me," Maurice argues. "They only need one, surely. They won't know which one of you it is, anyway. Besides, I don't want to walk down the Palais-Royal on my own. It scares me." He looks from one to the other several times, as though choosing a painting. "I'll take this one," he says, pointing his finger at Iris.

Iris blushes and looks at her sister.

"By all means," Dorothea says easily. "I'll see you back at the hotel, Iris. Don't be late; we have to make an early start tomorrow." She kisses Iris on the cheek, nods at Maurice, and, with a slight smile, leaves the hotel. Iris frowns anxiously as she watches her sister leave.

"Should I not have done that?" Maurice asks. "Don't you ever do anything separately?"

"Of course we do," Iris says in an uncertain voice.

"Then let's not waste time. We'll stop off at a little bar I know and then walk for a while around this wonderful, wounded city."

He takes her to a small café on the place du Théâtre-Français that is miraculously open. He orders two *vins rouges*.

"Would you have preferred something more exotic?" he asks. "Absinthe perhaps. This is still Paris, after all."

"It's a nice color," she says. "But a rather odd taste."

"Popular with artists. Gives you hallucinations."

"Not sure I need any of those."

"Quite." He darts a look at her, but she seems relaxed. He watches as she drinks the wine, her skin so transparent that he can almost see the burgundy coloring her throat.

"I'd prefer bourbon," he volunteers. "But it's hard to get around here. My mother sent me some, but the bottle broke in transit. What a mess."

"Bourbon? I always think of Southern gentlemen when I hear that word."

"I am Southern—but not a gentleman," he adds. "I'm Jewish."

"Jewish?" Iris studies him. "What does that mean?"

"Oh, you know. An outsider. Looking for a homeland. The South certainly wasn't it."

"An outsider." Iris lingers over the word. "Is that why you don't sound like a Southerner?"

"Well, you have to remember I went north to school and abandoned my accent as soon as possible. But a Southerner is always a Southerner. Mah granddaddy fought in the war, and don't you forget it, honey," he drawls. "And you know what ah mean by the war, y'all?"

Iris laughs. "But you didn't go back?" she ventures.

"After Harvard, I spent some time in a bank in New York. But like Harry, I hated it and knew I wanted to go abroad. I had always loved France and so came here to try to write—like so many others. When the war came, I signed on with the French Foreign Legion, but they didn't see much use in me because of my poor eyesight. So I waited until I could get something with the air force, where for some reason my eyes were not an issue. I suppose they think even blind people can fly well enough to kill Germans."

"What did your parents think?"

"Funny you should ask. They were horrified. They were horrified at everything I did, from leaving the bank to wandering around Montmartre with a pen in my hand. They had been so proud of my getting into Harvard; they thought it was the start of a great future as a doctor or a lawyer." He smiles ruefully. "What about yours?" he asks.

"They are both dead."

"I'm sorry."

"Don't be. It's a great relief, in a way. Not to have to explain things. I have a brother, but he's much older and doesn't really care one way or the other. He'd like us to be married, of course. Instead of wasting time writing poetry."

"Have you published anything?"

"Not yet. Dorothea was preparing something for publication before the war started. She says it is by both of us, because everything we do, we do together. But she wrote most of the verses, not me. What about you?"

Maurice shakes his head. "Everything I have written seems pointless and irrelevant now."

"Is that why you didn't like the Englishman's poem?"

"I have been here a long time, remember. Since the war started. That's nearly four years. I spent some time with Alan Seeger before he died. He was a friend from Harvard and was wandering around Europe like me before the war broke out. Once he joined his French outfit, he began sending home stuff that was just outrageous—high-flown sentiments about the greatness of dying and so forth. He told me once that he was in a kind of ecstasy about the war, that he had always thirsted for this kind of experience and that now he was playing the biggest role of his life. How he loved being with the other soldiers, the comradeship of it all, how he pitied the civilians who would never see or experience the things that he was seeing or experiencing, how thrilled he was embracing his destiny, how proud of his 'Rendezvous with Death.' That was the name of a poem he wrote. Perhaps you have read it."

Iris shakes her head. "But I can understand how he feels," she murmured. "I think we feel on a bigger stage somehow, in a place we've never been before. This is something new for us, remember, and it's very exhilarating."

"Well, I simply cannot accept that fatalism, that grandiosity. This war is a pointless journey to pointless death for thousands of innocent young men who are being used as fodder by the generals to gain two inches of French or German soil. What's glorious about that? What is that to do with honor? What kind of destiny do they have in mind? That is why I can't read the English poets like Grenfell who died right at the beginning. They were dead before they knew the reality of what they were writing about. *Pro patria mori?* Let's talk about the rats picking over piles of rotting corpses." He lights a cigarette brusquely, snapping the lighter top so hard that it almost clips his finger.

Iris puts a hand on his arm. "Maurice, don't."

"I'm sorry," he says. "It just gets to me sometimes."

"I understand you well enough," she says quietly. "But I understand what Seeger said, too. About finding a role, about being involved, about experiencing something most people couldn't even imagine. There's something very . . . fulfilling about that. No longer being protected from the world, glassed in. We were outsiders, too, you know."

He looks at her. "My little Jewess," he says affectionately, smiling at her. She laughs. "You're right," he goes on. "We are in a new world. All of us here, doing what we are doing. We have shared secrets. We speak differently from how we spoke before. We think differently. We are acting in a play written in a language that nobody back home will ever understand."

"Every day, I feel more remote from the world I came from," Iris says in agreement, picking up his lines. "It is becoming an effort to remember the face of my brother." She moves her hand to her mouth again as though to deny such a shocking statement.

"That's exactly it. We can only imagine the present. We begin only to see and remember one another." This time, he takes her hand in his. "I am glad I met you. I should like it to be only you that I see—and remember."

Iris looks down at their joined hands. His is a warm color, as though tanned in the sun. There are a few fine brown hairs on his fingers. Hers is white, translucent, the skin worn down to the last layers. Every vein stands out, coursing through her hands like the tributaries of a river. Maurice touches the blue lines gently, tracing the fragile map that charts her life.

"When did Seeger die?" she asks.

"On July third, 1916. At Belloy-en-Santerre, near the Somme. A 'heroic martyr.' He must have been delighted. And the day before Independence Day, too. The perfect ending for a patriotic writer like him."

Iris's hand moves in his. He turns it over, cups her palm, and drinks a kiss from it.

"I think we must all go mad here," he says to her cheerfully. "But if we must go mad, let's go mad together."

She laughs and pulls her hand away. He looks at her, then takes her by the shoulders and kisses her again, this time on the lips. Under the kiss, he feels her body stiffen. Her long neck arches, and she begins to tremble. She pulls away again, and he lets her go.

"We couldn't be doing this back home," she says, blushing.

"Hoorah!" Maurice exclaims. "I knew the war was good for something." He starts to kiss her lips, her nose, her eyes. She draws away from him, fearing his passion, breaking the spell. They quickly find each other's hands again, however, as though wanting safe harbor after a perilous journey. Maurice pays the bill and they get up from the table, Iris's face reflecting the gold candlelight of the bar. He keeps hold of her hand as they walk slowly down the rue de Richelieu into the Palais-Royal. The great courtyard is plunged in darkness, the unwelcome darkness of wartime stringencies. Sinister shadows play among the colonnaded galleries like Halloween ghosts.

"This place was used as a hospital once," Maurice tells her. "I think it was 1832, when Paris was overrun by the plague. They closed all the public buildings, like the Comédie-Française and so on, to house the sick, and put the overflow, mostly the very poor, in any open spaces they could find. Think of these arcades with rows and rows of bodies on the ground, all dying . . ."

"You don't have to go on," Iris says sharply, pulling her hand away. Maurice stops short.

"I'm sorry, Iris. Stupid of me. My imagination runs away with me sometimes."

"You don't understand." She tells him in rapid bursts about the Triangle Shirtwaist fire. As she describes it, her voice shakes. Maurice listens, watching her face. When she stops, they are silent.

"My favorite cousin drowned when I was fifteen," he says finally. "I was on the beach, and I saw it all. I couldn't help him—I had broken my leg and couldn't swim. But I saw him drown. Two years later, I was at the ocean in Wilmington, North Carolina, on vacation with my parents. Suddenly, right at the edge of the water, I burst into tears. The memory was completely fresh, you see. I wondered then if I'd ever escape it."

Iris takes his hand again.

"I understand you better now," he goes on. "What you just told me explains in part how you came over here—had to come over here, really—and your remarks about feeling fortunate. All of us here are involved in something that seems to us more real—greater—than anything we've done before. In that sense, it's true, Seeger was right." He pauses. "I don't know what happens to us in the end, however. Because one day the war will end. And then what will we be left with?"

His question hangs suspended in the chilly air of the galleries. Iris keeps her hand clutched in his. He traces its shape with his thumb, caressing the mounds, the joints, as though rehearsing how it feels, the warm flesh of her slight hand enclosed in his. She responds to his tender examination, feeling with equal intensity his touch on her tingling veins. Thus, as the electricity passes from his palm to hers, they begin haltingly to create a memory of each other.

The city is empty. No men, old or young, stroll through the long arcades. A few solitary women, veiled in mourning, step aside to let Maurice and Iris pass by. The youth of the American couple is noticeable, but there is something more, a connection linking them through their entwined hands that acts like a password to those who can still feel the pulse of life. "I'll open a bottle of wine tonight," murmurs a withered old crone to herself as she turns to watch them walk down the shadowed colonnade. "Maybe two." And a small, toothless smile undoes her face, so that for a moment she looks twenty years old.

Chapter 10

My dear Brother,

I apologize for being slow to respond, but we have taken some time to settle in. Because we speak reasonable French, the Red Cross sent us to a French hospital. It has three sections, one for the wounded who are expected to go back to the front, one for the more seriously wounded, and the last for soldiers who are likely to die. Our knowledge is shamefully inadequate, but we have a splendid directrice who never fails to show us the correct procedures. We are grateful to be here and eager to do the best we can to help the poor "poilus" (that's the French word for the young men fighting in the trenches) who are assigned to us.

We were astonishingly lucky to meet up with Isabel and Grace so early in our time here. I think I mentioned them to you in my first hurried letter after our arrival in France. Their enthusiasm keeps our spirits up when things seem very grim, with news from the front becoming worse and worse daily. They both know so much more than we do about everything; we depend on them enormously. Harry and Maurice, whom I think I also mentioned to you, have also become friends. Harry and Isabel seem to be getting rather serious about each other, but any kind of personal connection is intensified in this wartime atmosphere, and it seems to me foolish to place too much importance on these abbreviated encounters. As I pointed out to Iris, we cannot be sure even if we will meet them again. There are no guidelines anymore.

Before we left Paris last November (how long ago it seems!), we wanted to visit a little café in the place des Vosges where we once spent such happy times with Miss Wetherall. It all seems impossibly distant now. The place was shuttered, of course. But it hardly matters. We shall never go there again. The word *Vosges* is a synonym for *horror*. Almost four years ago (so long has this war been going on), a battle took place on the summit of the Vosges Mountains, and thousands of Frenchmen perished there. The casualties could not even be counted. Soldiers we met in Paris who lived through that offensive could not speak of what they had seen. So many other places that once were innocent are now stained with blood and death—Mons, the Somme, Verdun . . . I passed the rue d'Arras and could see nothing but frightened men in the rat-infested mud of those hateful trenches. You may be interested to know that the soldiers who fought on the Arras battlefield called it the Sausage Machine.

No Man's Land is an equally vivid phrase. I wonder if it will have any other meaning ever again. We have now heard many strange new expressions coming from the front, and we read about them in the newspapers. It's almost a writer's war in some ways. I was hoping to write something myself, but I must confess my mind is weary and not much gets down on the page. The distractions are distressing, but nothing compared to what our poilus endure. Some of them hear whistles in their heads incessantly—can you imagine it? (Whistles are blown to send them, in as orderly a fashion as possible, over the top.) I doubt even the best writers in the world could make much poetry out of that.

Please forgive the brevity of this letter. We are kept busy almost every moment of the day and night, and when we finally get time off to try to snatch a little longed-for sleep, my hand trembles so that it can hardly hold the pen. We hope to get to Paris again soon. As one of our friends said, the leaves are absolutely essential.

I trust that you and Lavinia are flourishing. Iris and I are thrilled about your news. Imagine us being aunts! Please keep us posted as to the baby's progress. America seems very far away these days.

We both send loving wishes.

Your devoted sister,
Dorothea

Chapter 11

THE CONCERT HALL IS freezing. Most of the audience, who have paid over fifty francs to attend, are dressed in furs, hats, and gloves. Since it is a benefit (for the French Orphans of the War), the required accessories, such as diamonds and emeralds, are also on display. (In such circumstances, it is regarded as perfectly acceptable to wear a jeweled bracelet on the outside of one's glove.) Even in the coldest winter in Paris since 1895, the opportunity to dress up in one's finery cannot be resisted.

Harry, Isabel, Maurice, Iris, and Dorothea are seated in a row close to the stage. The twins and Isabel are huddled in cloaks and scarves; Harry and Maurice, in their leather flying jackets. Their noses are red with cold.

"We look like circus clowns," Iris says to her sister, looking down their row.

"We should have brought our sables from home," Dorothea comments. "Think how useful they would be."

"Thank goodness we didn't," Iris responds. "It's embarrassing enough having to send back all our ridiculous linen and lace underwear. What were we thinking of?"

Dorothea laughs. "You mean, we should have brought our tiaras instead."

Iris rubs her arms against the chill. "Well, you're right. Our fur coats would have been very welcome just now," she concedes. She glances at Maurice, sitting next to her, and hopes he hasn't heard her, but he is reading a book. Harry and Isabel are playing a game with a French coin. The audience waits, shivering, chattering, determined to have a good time.

Finally the featured soloist enters the stage. He is Gabriel Fauré, the distinguished French composer.

"Who?" Isabel asked when the twins had suggested they all go to hear him.

"It will be splendid," Dorothea assured her. "Maurice and Harry are coming."

"Well, if Harry's going, so will I. I don't want to leave him alone for too long. He'll forget who I am."

Fauré looks like a weary old pine tree. His long white mustache droops down as though weighted with snow. He is dressed in a huge overcoat lined with fur and wears a thick wool scarf. He walks over to the piano and sits down. His hands are encased in gloves without fingers. He rubs his hands together as though to rustle up a spark before applying them to the chilly keyboard. His fingers look pale. There is an anticipatory silence.

Fauré begins to play one of his most famous barcarolles. As soon as the music starts, Maurice stiffens. With his eyes fixed on the stage, his body subtly moves as the music unfolds. Iris feels the tension in her arm, which gently rests against his. The contact between them produces a little flame of warmth that seeps through her sleeve. As the barcarolle comes to an end, the music spirals through her like Maurice's jacket brushing hers, enfolding them both. He smiles at her ardently.

Fauré stops and stares at the keyboard. The applause is enthusiastic but muffled; leather- and wool-covered hands beat against one another like birds' wings. The composer stands up, bows stiffly, and disappears. He does not return.

"It's too cold for the old man," Maurice whispers. After a long pause while the people in the audience wonder whether to leave, an announcer comes out and tells them that a substitute will finish the concert. His name is Alfred Cortot. Maurice, Iris, and Dorothea exchange appreciative glances. The fledgling genius they have heard so much about! What a substitute! As they settle back contentedly to wait for the young virtuoso, they become aware that the two seats next to them are empty.

Harry and Isabel have left.

At the end of the concert, the three Americans make their way out of the theater, exhilarated by the music.

"Better Cortot than Fauré," Dorothea comments.

"But I'm glad I saw Fauré," Iris says. "He's so great. And sad. He looked like a general from the Civil War."

"No wonder he's sad, then," Maurice says with a laugh. "I expect he was on the wrong side."

Dorothea gives him an odd look.

"He's Southern," Iris explains.

"Don't worry," Maurice says. "I lost an uncle, but I found a cause."

"Better the cause than the uncle?" Dorothea inquires.

"You didn't know my uncle. Anyway, one always feels better fighting a war with a cause."

"Doesn't it depend on the cause?"

"Of course." He smiles wickedly at Iris. "Particularly when it's Iris." She blushes.

"So, Iris, how does it feel, being fought for?" Her sister's voice is sarcastic.

"Please, if there's going to be a fight, let's fight over something worthwhile, like a pastry," Iris says briskly. "It's Friday. The patisseries will be open."

"I'd like something stronger," Maurice says.

They find a café that will serve them an aperitif. The place is not full. Most people are jamming the confectioners' shops, which, because of rationing, do not sell sweets on Tuesdays and Wednesdays.

"Wouldn't you rather have marrons glacés?" Dorothea asks her sister.

"This is fine, thank you."

Maurice has ordered absinthes for them all. Dorothea tastes hers cautiously, with a look of faint disapproval. Iris downs hers fast and asks for another. Maurice is eager to oblige.

"So what happened to our favorite couple?" he inquires.

"I don't think Isabel is very musical," Dorothea observes. "She had never heard of Fauré."

"All the French she knows is *l'amour,*" Iris adds. Maurice laughs.

"Harry's French isn't much better. I think all he knows are the names of the great French aviators, like Captain Guynemer."

"Who?"

"He counted fifty-four victories before getting shot down last September. That's pretty incredible—even I can see that. Harry never stops talking about him. Apparently he always wore a black and red uniform that marked him out from everyone else."

"The French are so vain," Iris murmurs fondly.

"Not just the French," Dorothea retorts. "I think all aviators are vain."

"Present company excepted," Iris adds hastily. Maurice shrugs.

"She's right, of course."

"I can't think of a less vain person than you." As Iris turns her gaze on him, a pleased glow suffuses his face. "You are like a Georges de La Tour portrait," she announces impulsively. Her own cheeks are quite pink.

"And you are—actually by an artist whose name I forget," he says. "Darn it. But Ingres will do very well. More absinthe, everyone? You'll notice it's French painters we're talking about."

"Well, French music, painting, art—isn't that what we are fighting for?" Dorothea demands irritably, getting up from her chair.

"Of course, Dorothea," Iris says in a soothing voice.

"Music, painting, art?" Maurice says scornfully. "I don't think so, Miss Crosby. You're referring to the 'cause' again, I take it. If only it were that simple. No, it's just a hideous political chess game with thousands of young men as pawns. Art?" He drinks his absinthe with a disgusted expression.

"He's right, Dorothea," Iris says quietly. "Not much art in our tent, is there?"

Dorothea glares at her. "So you have lost your starry eyes as well, have you? How could you have become so cynical?"

"I'm not, really." Iris bites her lip, looking pleadingly at her sister. "I only feel that we should be realists now we know what it's really like here."

"But what do we know? Do we know anything?" There is a tense silence.

Maurice looks from one to the other and then at his watch. "I'm sorry I started this," he says. "Foolish of me—I apologize. Finish your drinks, girls. No more talk about art and the cause tonight." He drains his glass. "Let's just move on, being grateful for the music of Fauré's barcarolle."

"Yes, grateful," Iris repeats his word. "I wonder if we'll ever hear it again."

"Except in our heads," Maurice says to her. He taps her forehead gently. "That's the wonder of it. We can play it for each other there, you know, whenever we wish."

"No, not there," Dorothea says sharply. "There's no room. At least, according to Mr. Aronsohn." She puts her glass down, half-finished, and moves toward the door. Maurice holds Iris back. "You are my art and my cause," he whispers to her. "My dream, my barcarolle." He opens the palm of her hand and kisses it fervently.

"I'm sorry about the argument," she murmurs, trying to maintain her composure. "We're just a little tired."

Maurice looks up at her. "'This is a delicious evening,'" he declaims melodramatically, "'when the whole body is one sense, and imbibes delight through every pore.'" He stops, laughing at her embarrassed look. "You should read Thoreau sometime. It would do you good. In fact, it would do you both good."

"Dorothea hates him," she explains. "Don't you, dearest? Dorothea?"

But Dorothea has walked outside and does not hear her.

Maurice drops Iris's hand impatiently. "Oh, Dorothea! Dorothea!" He almost spits out the words. "Dorothea!"

"Wait, Maurice!" Iris cries. "Don't say her name like that. Please!"

Maurice picks up Dorothea's glass and drains it. Slamming it down on the table, he blows Iris a mocking kiss and starts to walk away. She stands and watches him, hoping he will turn back to look at her, then gives up and runs to join her twin. Dorothea does not take her arm. They walk through the darkened streets of the city toward their lodgings. The heads of the statues in the squares are covered by wooden boxes for protection against the long-range German bombs that are expected at any moment.

"Look, Dorothea, it looks as though they're wearing hats!" Iris exclaims in a cheerful voice.

"They won't be any use. A typically absurd gesture."

"Just the vain French?"

"Exactly."

"You used to love the French."

"I did. But you've told me not to."

Iris pulls her to a stop. "Dorothea."

"Well, to be precise, Maurice told me not to. He's a bad influence, that fellow. Ruining our dreams."

"Let's not talk about him." Iris looks Dorothea squarely in the eye, then firmly pulls her sister close to her and wraps her arms around her. Dorothea, melting, puts her head on Iris's breast. They snuggle together, like children trying to get warm.

Chapter 12

HARRY FORRESTER SITS on a small wooden stool in his hut, his head in his hands. Outside, faint rolls of thunder reverberate over the airfield, like a distant bombardment. If only it were, he thinks, sighing. Gusts of freezing wind rise and fall, causing the roof of the hut to shudder. Although it is early afternoon, the hut is dark, its one small window looking out onto rows of other identical huts, and behind them bleak, flat terrain without trees or shrubs, the once-fertile farmland stripped of its bounty in order to serve as a landing strip for the American air force. In the late afternoon, the lingering frost is heaped like ashes over the deadly landscape.

Harry clenches his fists and sighs again. He looks up and reaches out to take a letter from his narrow, neatly made bed. He does not open it. He turns it over, wincing at the large purple handwriting that exposes his name with a flourish. A faint scent of lavender wafts up from the pink envelope. He has received such letters before. Many times, in fact. When he was at Harvard, he used to receive them regularly, often from women he had never met. They didn't just write letters, either. Once, he stepped into an automobile sent by Everett Grayfield to take him into New York after a football game to find two young debutantes in the backseat, waiting for him. They giggled and invited him to join them, but he made the driver stop and ordered them to leave. They were bewildered by his lack of enthusiasm.

But letters are all right, he thinks to himself. I can deal with letters. They keep their distance. They don't ask you to look them in the eye. They don't corner you like a hunted rat or make you want to climb the walls in an attempt to get the hell away. They don't make demands of you that you have to respond to before you have time to think.

This letter is from his mother. She doesn't write to him often. She must be between husbands — or drinks. He was quite small when he realized his mother was not like other mothers. He remembers the scene so well, his mother coming into the living room at the house in Pittsburgh, looking a little lopsided. Her hair has fallen from its chignon and her lipstick is smudged. His father is also in the room, reading a book. He is gaunt, the skin stretched over his face like paper, his color fatally gray. He is slowly and angrily dying. "Oh, Edith," he says with distaste, "not again. It's really getting to be too much. When are you going to pull yourself together?"

She ignores him. "Darling boy," she drawls, opening her arms to her son. Harry runs to her as he always does, feeling the usual mixture of repulsion and delight. She draws him to her, and he smells the familiar smell of smoke, lavender, and juniper floating up from her silk dress. She runs her hands over his sturdy bare arms, and his flesh tingles as though brushed by nettles. "Darling boy," she says again, in a voice worn with cigarettes and liquor. She crushes his head against her chest, pressing it down so tightly on the huge emerald pin she wears that it will leave a mark on his tender cheek. "Darling boy," she says once more, burying her ravaged mouth in his fair hair. "Please don't grow up to be like your father."

Harry smiles at the memory. He is all right with his mother now. In fact, he has become quite easy with her, as long as he is not alone with her for long. Luckily she "travels," as she calls it, and is rarely in one place long enough for him to meet her. Occasionally she sends him an unsuitable gift, like a bottle of absinthe from Paris or a glass paperweight from Venice. They are probably meant for someone else. She often urges him to marry—some "nice" girl, she says vaguely.

Would she think Isabel a "nice" girl? he wonders. She is the kind of girl Harry is drawn to—strong and confident. Isabel is slender, boyish, her lithe body set off by her curly cropped hair, a style only just coming into fashion. He knows she is "fast." But he likes that in her. He liked her leaving that dreary piano recital in Paris with him last month. That restlessness is in him, too. He finds it exciting, to get away from things. Their discussion in the bar afterward about their families was first rate. He was not the only one, it seemed, to have a crazy mother. She's the first girl he's really been able to talk to about it.

And how about Isabel on the tennis court? He starts to imagine her in a white tennis dress, running toward the net, but the image blurs. Before he knows it, the girl in the white dress is replaced by a line of hockey players skating down the ice. He hears again the roars of the crowd calling out, "Go, Harry!" as he lets fly shot after shot at the opposing goal. Yet another great game—although each game was always Harry's greatest, and the world adored him for it.

Harry shakes his head at the memory and then tries to bring Isabel back again. But she cannot compete with this triumphal history. Who could? It cannot be understood unless you have experienced it. He gets up and goes to the small mirror fixed with a rusty nail on the wall by a small metal basin and water pitcher. He stares at his reflection, lifting his head to see the line of his jaw, smoothing down the flesh on his throat with his hand. Keeping his hand in the mirror's sights, he curls his fingers up and down as though it is part of an exercise. Still watching critically, he raises his hand up and pushes the fingers through his thick mop of hair. He feels the texture between his fingers and moves more closely to examine the hairline above his wide brow. He brings both hands up to his face and cups them under his chin, gazing at the mirror with an expression of deep absorption—the look of a portrait painter estimating the features of his subject.

"What in hell are you doing?" Ken Johnson, one of the pilots Harry trained with in Issoudun, has charged into the hut. Harry jumps.

"Nothing." He quickly moves away from the mirror.

"You don't have to worry," Ken says, critically passing his own square-featured face before the mirror. "You have enough girls to keep an army." He picks up the scented letter from Harry's bed and puts it to his nose.

"Mmm. I'd say this was Forever Love."

Harry groans. "If you only knew," he says, snatching the letter from his friend. He moves to the window and looks out at the chilly airfield. "Doesn't the waiting just kill you?"

"So to speak." Ken laughs. "You really don't think of anything else, do you?"

"What's wrong with that? I just want to get a few victories and catch up with the other fellows, that's all. You're just as keen as I am."

"Not so keen that I'd do something crazy like you did last week."

"Oh, leave off, will you?"

The reference is to a recent mission that almost brought the two friends to blows. Harry was heading a patrol of six. As squadron leader, he flew above the others to protect them and alert them to danger. He spotted four Fokkers coming toward them, and he swung into their vision, hoping that they would attack him and leave the others alone. They came in at about forty-five hundred feet, with Harry a few hundred feet below and the patrol a thousand feet beneath him. Suddenly a burst of shrapnel exploded close to a French observation balloon near the ground, obviously the target of an enemy pilot that Harry had not yet seen.

Harry peeled off and swooped down low, gunning his motor as fast as it could turn, in pursuit of the Boche. The balloon went up in flames and the German pilot started turning back to his own lines. Harry raced after him, exhilarated by the sight of the black crosses on the wings and tail of his prey. He began to catch up with him and found himself in a good position to fire. "It was a perfect angle," he told his friends later. "I could see the back of his head. He turned when he spotted me, and I saw his face. We could have waved to each other."

Harry fired at least a hundred rounds before banking upward to avoid a collision. But he failed to bring the German plane down. Angry and frustrated, he flew back up to join the patrol, now surrounded by the enemy, and in the ensuing dogfight he hit a Fokker. This time there was no doubt. He watched as the plane spiraled down in flames, and he followed it long enough to see the black smoke rising up from the woods where the plane crashed. Ken, watching below, gave him the thumbs-up signal and mouthed congratulations.

Harry returned to the base. Two of the pilots in the patrol reported damaged planes, one with shrapnel in the rudder, another with bullets in the wing. They commended one another on a successful outing, but Harry could not shake off his frustration about losing his first target. He could still see the German's arrogant, smiling face, taunting him. Suddenly he turned around and ran back to the airfield. Cutting short the plane's refueling, within minutes he was airborne again, rising quickly to four thousand feet and turning toward the enemy lines. This time the patrol of Fokkers saw him first, and they started speeding toward him. With the advantage of height and going solo, Harry was able to dive and twist his plane at angles that confused them. He maneuvered his Spad as though he were on the ice, hurtling through the air and charging recklessly into the line of defenders. As he came down close behind the Fokkers, he started firing, and this time he had the pleasure of seeing his bullets reach their target. One Fokker started spiraling down, another was hit in the front of the wing and started wobbling wildly, and the third turned back in retreat.

Almost out of fuel, Harry brought his plane back home, to the usual mixture of praise and disapproval from the squadron. Ken was pacing up and down outside the officers' mess.

"How many times do I have to remind you what Eddie says," he told his friend angrily. "The experienced pilot does not take unnecessary risks. His business is to shoot down enemy planes, not to get shot down."

"That's what I did," Harry said lightly. He felt elated, giddy almost. His eyes watered; his head tingled. Somewhere out there, he could hear the crowd roaring. "This is the life," he said exultantly. "Why else are we here?" He slapped Ken on the back. "Come on. I'll take you and the boys into town for dinner. We should celebrate our victories."

Still aroused by the afternoon's sport, Harry went to the squadron office and made a telephone call to Isabel in Paris. He suddenly felt eager to see her again. He told her he wanted to meet her as soon as he was granted his next leave. But, he couldn't help adding, he hoped he would get more flying in first. "You're crazy, Harry," she said.

"Isabel says I'm crazy," he tells Ken now.

"So it's Isabel, is it? The one we met at the Union?" Ken makes appreciative noises. "Lucky man."

"I don't know," Harry says doubtfully. "It's hard to get in the right mood. Anyway, she's expensive."

"All the best girls are expensive."

"Well, I'd rather gamble on the weather." He indicates the cloud-filled sky.

"That's why I came here now and interrupted your toilette," Ken says. "I think we're going to get some action tomorrow. Apparently the weather is clearing."

"Yeah!" The two men slap each other's hands. "A dollar we go up tomorrow," Harry says.

"Done," Ken agrees, adding in a jeering tone, "better get some beauty sleep." He makes a lunge for the pink envelope on the bed, and as he grabs it, Harry pounces on him, attempting to trip him up. Ken drops the letter, laughing loudly. Holding his heart in a romantic clutch, he runs from the room, still laughing.

Much later, after the lights on the airfield have been turned out, Harry sneaks out of his hut, carrying his skates. It has been below freezing for several nights now, and he knows a pond where the ice is locked in, waiting for him. It looks black and forbidding when he gets there. A few stars shine in the sky, like flashlights from a distant audience. Harry laces up his skates and glides onto the ice. For the next hour, he silently moves over the gleaming surface of the pond, pushing out into the cold air like a heron on a long landing. After a while he changes direction and picks up a large stick, which he guides after an unseen puck, skating faster, more aggressively, twisting, braking suddenly, swiveling, whacking the stick on the ice. The cold air whistles in his ears. He hears the familiar voices: "Go! Go!

Go, Harry!" A sudden night wind swells up from the ground and blows through his hair.

Coming to the edge of the pond, he positions his stick for one last run, crouched and ready, his body leaning into the blades of the skates, picking up speed and then racing headlong across the ice, rotating the invisible puck in a final pivot of ecstasy under the moonless French sky.

Chapter 13

Darling George,

Thank you so much for your most recent parcels. We particularly loved the cans of fruit. Fruit of any kind is impossible to find here. The cashews and peanuts are always welcome, as we can eat them throughout the day to keep up our strength. Do continue to send them if you can. And the shortcake — we have acquired a very sweet tooth! But I know you must be very busy with the baby on the way. We are both delighted with the news. Please make sure that Lavinia gets lots of rest!

I think Dorothea wrote to you telling you the latest from here. Nothing has changed except the numbers of the dead. We continue to work hard, doing our best for the poor poilus, who are all so brave and cheerful that they put us to shame. We are both scared to death (so to speak) of our directrice, but she is extremely efficient and runs the place brilliantly under very difficult circumstances. She has little refinement and has probably never read or heard of any of the books with which Adeline Wetherall so beautifully educated us, but her gifts are of a different order, and I am grateful that we have been given the good fortune of working under such a fine, dedicated, unselfish human being. Without her, we should not be nearly so effective in our work.

It is April, and we try not to think about spring. The weather here continues to be cold and unforgiving, and the ground is still bare and wasted by the war. (Will it ever be green again?) I occasionally dream about the fields of daffodils in Far Hills, but they seem very distant now. I have completely forgotten their scent—can you believe that? I am sure it is better this way.

Darling brother, I should like you to do something for me. In one of the bookshelves in our living room is a book I'd like you to send me. It is a Ticknor and Fields first edition of Henry David Thoreau's *Walden* that I bought as a birthday present for Dorothea. She never took to Thoreau, so it has languished. I have now found someone who I think would like it very much. I assure you that it will be easy to find; it has a lovely dark brown cover with gilded lettering and is on a shelf with other American writers to the left of the fireplace. When you find it, please wrap it up carefully and send it to me c/o the American University Union, where you send us the other packages that we so love. *Please send it separately from any food parcels.* This is so that it does not accidentally get damaged, and also because I should prefer that Dorothea not know about it. (It was, after all, her birthday present!) So please don't mention it in a letter to us.

Please do this for me as soon as you receive this. Time is so precious here.

Thank you, dearest George.

Your grateful sister,
Iris

Chapter 14

My dear Mother,

I have just returned from a brief leave in Paris and found the cigarettes and books at the Union. Thank you immensely for the package; all the contents are most welcome.

At an exhibition in Paris before the war, I was struck by a painting by a not very well-known artist, whose name I think was Chassériau. It was a portrait of two young women — his sisters. They were dressed in similar pink and gold dresses with red shawls, and their skin was like ivory. They had almost identical oval faces framed in black hair smoothed into chignons, accentuating their long, bare necks. They gazed out of the canvas enigmatically, but their bodies were close together, arms touching, as though protecting each other from a threatening world. It was a very striking painting, and the images of those fascinating women stayed with me.

Well, I recently met the models for that portrait. Not really, of course, but during a leave before Christmas, Harry Forrester introduced me to twins, Dorothea and Iris Crosby, who remind me uncannily of that picture. (If you don't recognize the artist, think of Ingres instead. His portraits of remote, aristocratic women are comparable in mood and style.) The twins are from New York, both working in a hospital near the front. They had no former experience as nurses, so you can imagine what they are going through. It seems almost sadistic to give them such hellish responsibilities. They seem to be astonishingly brave about it all and are far more deserving of medals, in my view, than the much-decorated generals who direct this war from comfortable desks in London and Paris.

Twins are fascinating, aren't they? Such a fluke of nature. Can they ever really lead separate lives? One reads about their almost telepathic empathy for each other when apart. But surely this is both a blessing and a curse? The Crosbys are identical in looks and movement and, as in the portrait, seem to hold each other in a constant embrace. But this mutual dependency is clearly discomfiting at times. One of them, Iris, seems to me to have a distinctive quality, more fragile, perhaps, more open. She affects me deeply.

If you think I do not seem to have my mind fixed on the Ultimate Sacrifice, let me reassure you. I was flying a cross-country reconnaissance mission recently and began to have motor trouble. I looked around to see where I might make a landing and saw a château surrounded by fields that looked a perfect place to drop down on. I made a fair landing and stepped out to find an elegant French count waiting on the lawn to greet me. He invited me into the château, which looked something like Vanderbilt's mansion in Asheville, and there I was given a first-rate meal with the best Bordeaux, cognacs, and cigars and then shown a bedroom that would have done the president proud. He sent out for a mechanic to fix the engine, and in the meantime I fished in his river and walked with his dogs and was generally treated like a favorite relative. I should also point out he had two young daughters who seemed quite interested in me! My French was not up to the task of getting them to marry me, however. When I got back to the base, I was congratulated for landing the plane and returning it without damage!

As for the real war (which gets more and more unreal every day),

I can't tell you much about our operations at the moment. The weather has been terrible and we have not been able to fly as much as we would like, particularly since the Germans are packing in some offensive or other that we could really sabotage if we got the chance. If only the war were being fought in Florida, we would be seeing action the whole time! Whenever I see Harry, he complains about it. He gets really frustrated at being grounded so much. (Of course, I am secretly very relieved!)

I miss you and Tommy and the dogs and the camellias and the grits.

Your cowardly son,
Maurice

Chapter 15

THE DIRECTRICE HAS TOLD her staff there has been a big push. The twins know what that means. It means an avalanche of wounded men suddenly swamping them, so many that there will not be enough beds, or even enough room on the floor beside the beds, to look after them all.

It is almost dark when the first patients appear. The tent is soon filled with bodies, almost unidentifiable as such, so covered in mud and dried blood, their flesh so flayed and burned, so strangely misshapen in the head, arms, and legs. A painting of sinners in hell would look like this, Iris thinks as she and the other nurses address each one in turn, reading the tags hastily scrawled by the doctors at the dressing station, trying for information of any kind in order to treat what seems untreatable.

"Bad," Dorothea says matter-of-factly.

"Will you be all right?" Iris asks.

"Of course," Dorothea snaps. "It's you I'm worried about."

"What do you mean?"

"There's no time to talk. I need help here." Iris quickly runs to hold the head of a soldier bleeding in Dorothea's arms.

"Are you angry with me?" Iris glances at her. "It's Maurice, isn't it?"

"Iris, please. Not now. They need help." Dorothea indicates a corner of the tent, where a pile of makeshift litters have fallen on top of one another, burying several of the wounded. Someone laughs, and others pick up the laughter. Iris, eager to obey her sister, runs to sort out the confusion.

Suddenly, in the middle of the chaos, the directrice summons Dorothea and Iris to her side. "I need you to take a cart with water to the road." Her voice is urgent. "I am told there are many men struggling to get here on foot, who are desperately in need of water. Take as much water as you can, give it to them to pass down the line, and come straight back." She turns away, and then, seeing their surprise, says, "I understand you are good with horses. The cart needs an experienced driver; there has been no success with the poor animal so far. It's probably in as bad shape as our poilus. Another cart went ahead, but we need more."

This is the first time the twins have left the hospital on relief work. They quickly remove their armbands, put on their cloaks, and run out to the yard, where a broken-down horse is standing, its head drooping almost to the ground, a rickety wooden farm cart attached to its rump.

"*C'est impossible*," an old man shouts angrily. He has one leg and leans on a bent stick for a crutch. He hits the horse on the head with the stick and pulls roughly on its bridle. "*Il ne bouge pas.*"

The twins rush up to the sluggish creature and start talking to it, stroking its nose and ears. Iris runs a hand over its matted, muddy coat and feels the sharp bones of its ribs. It is hardly recognizable as the same species of animal that they used to ride in Central Park. "This horse has not eaten for weeks," she says, her voice lowered in indignation. "How can it take us anywhere?"

"It must," Dorothea replies. "The men need water."

Iris talks gently to the horse again, feeds it a scrap of maggoty bread, then wheedles its head into an upright position. Dorothea checks the cart, which is stocked with rusty barrels of water and battered tin cups. "Let's go," she says. They pull the horse and cart past the yard into a mud-soaked lane. The twins climb onto the cart, Dorothea holding the reins, her hands held high just as she and her sister had been taught as children. She makes a face at her sister, wondering whether her skills will help her now. The slow clip-clopping of the horse's hooves soothes them as they sway in unison to the creaking of the cart.

"How I loved that chestnut mare—what was her name? . . ." Iris begins dreamily, but Dorothea cuts her short.

"Don't, Iris. Don't think about those things."

Iris sighs at the anger in her sister's voice, then reflects how she always seems angry now.

"We can't go back there," Dorothea insists. "It's another life. That's gone, remember? We aren't there anymore. Going off into reveries of the past doesn't help. All it does is make us soft, sentimental, useless. This is all that matters now. This is our life. The other world is over." Iris bites her lip and nods, falling silent.

Dorothea calls to the horse, urging it on in the calm, firm voice of experience. The horse moves slowly and wearily to a command to which it once would have eagerly responded. The cart makes a grinding noise as its wheels bump over the rutted path. The horse drags it bravely along, head down, breathing heavily, stumbling, sometimes almost falling with the effort.

The twins shiver in the cold, but they sense the warm heart of the horse, and as they loosen the reins in response, their fingers accidentally touch. Suddenly they clutch each other's hands, the physical connection drawing them together. Looking at Iris's distressed face, Dorothea feels her anger fall away, and she follows her sister's lead, allowing them both to pass, for a brief, painful splinter of time, through the door to their past.

"He was a wonderful animal," Dorothea concedes, her voice softening. "His name was Brandy."

"I remember you rode him every day for six months one summer. He understood everything you said to him."

"And you had a handful at that time—that wild young mare Lucy. You were so good with her."

"Brandy was very jealous."

"I was, too. You and Lucy were inseparable."

Iris laughs and shakes her head. "What a glorious creature."

The twins are sitting very close now, shoulder to shoulder in the cart, just as they used to sit in their four-in-hand in the park. As they continue to talk about their beloved horses, their voices sound almost indistinguishable, and their language becomes telegraphic, full of unspoken meaning from long years of intimate understanding. Like a retired song-and-dance team, they have begun performing the old, familiar routines again, for an empty stage.

"Oh, Dorothea," Iris murmurs, "will we ever—" But her question is rudely interrupted. The horse has suddenly started back, rearing and jerking his head sideways in fear. Dorothea snaps to attention, pulling on the reins.

"Hush," she says to the horse. "It's nothing. Hush."

Iris points into the darkness ahead. "Look. That's what frightened him."

A group of soldiers takes shape in front of them, the men staggering, hardly able to lift their feet. They push one another forward weakly, muttering among themselves, cursing.

"We have come to bring you water," Dorothea calls out to them, trying to calm the horse. "Quick, Iris, get the cups." Iris jumps down from the cart and starts pouring water out of the barrels in the back. "Here, drink this." The barrels are heavy and the water sloshes recklessly over the sides of the cups. "Can someone help me?" she cries.

The men seem not to hear her, and lurch past the cart, some holding on to it for temporary support. It is impossible to tell whether it is mud or blood that sticks to their faces and hands.

"Water?" one of them groans in a rusty voice. "Water?" The others pick up the word, and they grab the cups that Iris offers them, drinking the dirty liquid greedily. Dorothea has run to help, and she seizes the cups back from them, pushing them away. "Go on," she says. "Keep going. You're nearly there. We need this for others farther ahead."

Iris packs the cups back into the cart, and the soldiers move off reluctantly, their boots barely clinging to their feet as the muddy ground envelops them. *Suck, pull, suck, pull.* The sound of the squelching boots sinking into the quicksand of wet earth and being pulled out again provides an eerie counterpoint to the grinding of the cart's wheels as it draws away.

Suddenly the twins hear a scream. But it is not a human scream. Human screams they know by now. They look at each other in dread. As the cart continues to move, they see ahead a sight like no other so far in their experience of war. Out of the gray darkness, a large crater looms, formed by an exploded shell. It is filled with water and mud. In the crater, enmeshed in a slow-motion death struggle, is a horse. It has sunk deep into the hole, evidently having strayed from the path. Soldiers surround it, shouting. They have detached its cart, which stands to one side, almost tipped over. The horse is hurling its body against the relentless weight of the mud. Its eyes are wide and glassy. Its mouth and nostrils are flecked with a white foam that sprays the onlookers like snow as the animal rears and twists its neck in desperation. As though for energy, it bellows each time it makes its lunge toward the rim of the crater, its neck increasingly covered in slime, its head slipping farther and farther beneath the black, viscous liquid.

"Find sacking," someone shouts. "For God's sake, sacking or planks. Something."

But there is nothing at hand. The soldiers have tried everything, tossing in sticks, twigs, tree branches—even their bayonets. Frozen, Dorothea and Iris stare at the plunging animal, then Iris begins to cry out, her voice almost matching the cries of the floundering horse.

"Help!" she screams, jumping down from the cart and racing to the perimeter of the sinkhole. "We must do something. Quick!"

"Take the water," Dorothea calls to the men hovering helplessly nearby, directing them to the cans in the cart. "Drink the water and get back to the road."

"That's right, *mes enfants*," one of the soldiers says. "Nothing to be done now."

Iris turns on the soldier. "What do you mean?" she retorts, eyes blazing. "Of course we can do something. Get me some rope."

The soldier laughs and shrugs. "There ain't no rope, mademoiselle," he says. "We've tried, but there's nothing we can do now. Usually they can tell a hole like this instinctively and step around it. But this dumb pony's been at the front too long. Lose their senses, they do."

"Like us, eh?" another says, and they laugh raucously.

Iris stares at them, her fists clenched. "How can you be so heartless?" she shouts wildly. "We must do something! The horse will die!"

"Iris!" Dorothea's voice is icy. "Get back here and help with the water. You're needed here. At once. We've got to get the water to these men. Iris, do your job." Dorothea pours water into the cups. "Iris," she summons her again. "Get back here."

"How much longer, then?" a soldier with wide, feverish eyes asks her as his comrades gulp down the water and start trudging back to the rutted road.

"The hospital is only five minutes away," Dorothea tells him. "Keep going. Good luck."

Iris slowly returns to the cart, holding her hands over her ears. The horse's screams are quieter now.

"How can you?" she whispers. "How can you, Dorothea?"

"Collect all the cups, please, Iris," Dorothea orders her brusquely. "We'll need them again." Iris stares at her sister as though not comprehending. "You can take your hands down now, Iris." Dorothea goes over to her and pulls her sister's hands off her ears. "There. You see? Take these. For God's sake, Iris, pull yourself together."

She shoves a pile of cups into Iris's hands. Iris stacks them and automatically puts them in the back of the cart.

"Thank you. Now see if you can find any others."

Dorothea returns to the driver's seat and urges their horse, sweating with panic, away from the convulsing crater and back onto the trail. Iris climbs up beside her, leaving a distance between them. Clinging to the side of the cart, she stares fixedly down at the road. Dorothea does not look at her or speak to her. Her face is set in stone. There is no intimacy now. No singing. Only the nagging ache of disconnection.

The piteous peals of the horse fade away. Everything is quiet except for the creaking of the cart and the *suck, pull, suck, pull* of the soldiers' boots vanishing into the darkness.

Chapter 16

Dear Adeline,

Thank you for your letter. I am not sure how to respond, as there is not much time for reflection. There was a push—that's what we call an offensive—which means that more than the usual number of casualties are brought to the hospital. That was the situation a month ago, so the work load has been heavy. There were so many stretchers that they had to be propped up vertically and the yard looked like a stockade. Indeed the work was so arduous that the directrice softened her normally rigid stance and allowed us a day of rest. We could hardly believe it! I think she sensed that Iris was close to breaking down, not having slept since the push and having to address some of the worst injuries that we have yet seen. There was also an incident with a poor horse—but I cannot describe that now, except that it, too, affected Iris most distressingly.

So on this unexpected day of freedom, we managed to get a ride to Rheims, which is not far from here. In some ways, we did not wish to go, as people had told us of the devastation done to our favorite city. For a whole month this time last year, the Germans bombarded it every day, all day, without stopping. And they have been back several times since then. Do you remember mention of a film about the burning of the cathedral in 1914? It had some provocative title,

Rheims Cathedral Set Alight by the Barbarous Hun! Typical wartime propaganda, we thought at the time.

It is worse than anyone could possibly have imagined. Whole streets have practically disappeared. The rue Buirette is in ruins, with only the brave Subé Fountain still standing, surrounded by rubble, in the place Drouet d'Erlon. The hôtel de ville is a hollow shell. The church of Saint-Jacques has almost entirely disappeared.

There is worse to tell. Our beautiful cathedral is in ruins. Those marvelous buttresses and gargoyles, the magnificent nave and transept, are all dreadfully damaged. The roof, spire, and caryatids all burned to the ground. But the worst ravages are to the stained glass. Those resplendent rose windows we so admired are almost totally destroyed. We walked around, our feet crushing the shards of broken glass covering the floor, our hearts equally crushed by what we were seeing. I can hardly bear to write these words. Thirteenth-century masterpieces of incomparable delicacy and artistry, which had lasted for seven hundred years, smashed to pieces in a senseless act of rage. I think it was seeing this savage destruction of one of the most noble monuments in all of France that brought home to me that there can be no future for us, no redemption from this tragic time in which we live. The buildings, even more than the people, speak to me of what we have so wantonly lost.

We remembered with deep sadness our visit with you that summer of 1912. How ironic that so much of that trip was inspired by Mrs. Wharton's lyrical prose. You know, of course, that all she writes about now are the "wounded and dishonoured" cathedrals with their "torn traceries," words better than I could ever write—assuming, indeed, that I ever wanted to write again.

I apologize for sounding so melancholy. It reflects a loss of spiritual confidence that will no doubt dismay you. But you cannot have any idea of what it is like here. I often feel isolated and alone. I am envious of the camaraderie the men feel for one another. The friendships they have made on the front line or in their platoons uplift them. They have total loyalty to one another. Perhaps I feel this because my own loyalties have been sorely tested recently. I am reluctant to admit this, but Iris seems to have gone away from me in some way. We do not share each other's thoughts and feelings as we used to. She is on a different path, one where I may not accompany her. Of course it is possible to attribute this to the strain that we are both under all the time. No doubt when the war is over, we shall recover our former harmony.

I am so pleased to hear you are to receive a medal from Saint Mary's. Nobody could deserve it more. And we beg you to banish any anxiety about the future (please inform me if the bank is still following our instructions with regard to your account). Your health is a priority and you must respect it. I trust you are avoiding those rich chocolate desserts to which you are so partial.

We eat chocolate here but it is not quite the same.

Loving wishes,
Dorothea

~ NEW YORK ~

Chapter 17

GEORGE CROSBY AND ADELINE WETHERALL were sitting in the drawing room of the Crosby apartment. George looked diminished, his bald head marked with brown spots, his eyes watery. For a man still hovering on the borders of middle age, he looked as though he had already emerged on the other side. Miss Wetherall, in contrast, looked positively youthful. She had a perky black feathery hat on her head, gleaming black leather shoes, and a smart cashmere shawl. Whether it was the twins' generous income that had so enlarged her spirit, or simply a period of fulfillment discovered in retirement, for Miss Wetherall, June 1918 was an exceedingly promising month. George poured his guest some tea.

"What beautiful china," she murmured, lifting the delicate cup to her lips.

"Sèvres," George said automatically. "From my mother's family."

"Ah, your mother," Adeline said, replacing the cup on its saucer. "First of all, Mr. Crosby, I must congratulate you on the magnificent news." George shifted in his chair uneasily. "Why, the new addition to the Crosby family, of course," she went on. "At least this child will not suffer what the twins suffered. I always felt that was such a tragedy for the girls."

George was silent.

"For you, too, of course," she added generously. "A boy's losing his mother is always tragic. But I feel that Dorothea and Iris suffered most deeply from the lack of a mother's love."

George mumbled agreement.

"Of course, I tried to do my best when they came to me at Saint Mary's. I feel that our fine school was one of the most serendipitous choices you made for them."

George bowed his head.

"The friendship we forged there was not only educational and spiritual but also, I like to think, in some way a replacement for the loss of their poor mother."

"I'm sure you're right," George said.

"Our trips to Europe were perhaps the most significant events in their young lives," she continued. "To be able to instill in their innocent minds a sense of the greatness of France and its contribution to Western culture was an honor for me. Their sensitivity and intelligence made it a pleasure to travel with them, and together we experienced some of the most elevating moments that life could offer."

"Indeed," George agreed. "You were an incomparable companion, Miss Wetherall."

"I'm so gratified that you think so. Young people are so restless these days," she went on. "I have observed this in many of the girls I see graduating from Saint Mary's. There is a lack of discipline, of values. Our traditional sense of morality is under attack. The war seems to have unleashed some dogs, if I may paraphrase a great playwright." She cast a coy eye at her companion to see if the cunning reference had made its mark.

"On the contrary, for some it gives a focus, I believe," George exclaimed with sudden asperity. "War unites people against a common enemy. I, for one, wish I could be of more service to our Allies overseas."

"An admirable sentiment," Adeline asserted imperturbably. "Of course, we are all trying to do our little bit here at home."

"I am sure you are doing your part, Miss Wetherall. I suspect, however, that we fall short." He paused. "But most of all, I worry about my dear sisters." He said this quietly, as though talking to himself. "I fear daily for their safety."

"I do, too, I assure you," the teacher agreed. She sipped some more of her tea. "That is why I requested this meeting," she explained, looking down at her admirable shoes.

"Yes? What is on your mind, Miss Wetherall?"

"Your sisters are very talented, as you know, Mr. Crosby. Before they left on this unfortunate venture abroad, they had produced quite a considerable body of poetry. Most of the work, I believe, was done by Dorothea, whose gift is exceptional. Iris shows her own special artistry also, however. Their poems are of the highest quality, in my opinion."

"I'm very interested to hear you say that," George said cautiously.

"It came to me one day as I walked in Central Park, thinking, as I always do there, of the delightful sight of your sisters trotting by in their carriage, that we should publish these poems. They deserve to reach a wider audience, Mr. Crosby."

"Publish their poems?"

"Just in a small, simple edition, of course. Nothing elaborate. I would write a short introduction and perhaps include a few verses of my own, to set the scene, so to speak. Then the best of Dorothea's and Iris's work would follow. I truly believe they are worthy of public attention."

"Well, indeed." George stroked his chin. "It's not exactly war work, Miss Wetherall, but if you think my sisters . . ."

"Oh, I can assure you they would be delighted." The tip of her nose blushed pink. "I think I can speak for them with confidence on this matter."

"Hmm. Of course, I know nothing about publishing."

"I could assist you there," Adeline assured him. "I am able to call on the school printers to make a preliminary draft, and then we could go over it together. As you see, I have already taken the liberty of making inquiries. I am extremely eager to carry out this project."

"I see." He glanced at her. "I suppose you have no idea of the financial commitment it would entail, Miss Wetherall?"

"Not at the moment, Mr. Crosby," she murmured, fluttering her eyelashes. "But if you will allow me to pursue the matter, I may be able to come up with an estimate without too much difficulty."

"Very well." He stood up and held out his hand. "Thank you very much, Miss Wetherall. I am grateful you keep the interests of my sisters so close to your heart. If you think this would please them . . . As you know, I would do anything for them, including bringing them home if it were possible. But they would never agree to that. I've tried."

"I've tried, too, Mr. Crosby. They seem unable to think of anything except their work over there. It's most regrettable. Our world back home seems to hold very little appeal for them now, sad to say!" Adeline gave a self-deprecating laugh. "But we must simply soldier on," she said, smiling briefly at her choice of words. "I'm quite certain this proposal will please them."

"By the way," George said as he summoned the butler to show her out, "was Henry David Thoreau one of the writers you encouraged my sisters to read?"

"Thoreau? Wasn't he a transcendentalist?" Adeline Wetherall looked shocked. "Oh, dear, no. We devoted all our time to the romantic French and English poets, with one delightful exception—Emily Dickinson, whose work is so wonderfully elevated, I find, compared to that of her contemporaries. And one of our sex, too! Indeed, you might call her a transcendentalist in a completely different sense of the word!" She expelled a little laugh at her conceit.

"Yes, of course. I see," George muttered untruthfully. "Well, thank you for coming, Miss Wetherall."

She put her hand on his arm.

"I do believe they will be greatly enamored of our little plan, Mr. Crosby. Although they are both charmingly modest about their achievements, I suspect Dorothea in particular has a little flame of ambition that has been temporarily extinguished by her experiences over there. I think this news will bring her back to herself. She seems at the moment a little, shall we say, remote from us."

"Really? You don't say so!" He looked sharply at her.

"Well, of course," she said hastily, "you know them both much better than I do." George sighed and shook his head slowly before answering.

"I don't think I know them at all."

After Miss Wetherall had left, George sat down again and took a letter out of his jacket pocket.

"Thoreau," he said to himself. "Yes, she definitely said Thoreau."

He got up and walked reluctantly along the corridor to his sisters' suite. Gathering fortitude from the gallery of horse paintings, he noticed a rim of dust along their gilded frames. When had he last been down here? he wondered. It was difficult for him to think of the empty rooms, but it was even more difficult to imagine what everything would be like when his sisters came home. They would no longer be young; their looks would be faded, their chances of marriage even more unlikely. And how easy would it be for them to adjust to their old life here on Park Avenue? Would they still be able to enjoy the picnics in Newport, the ballet in New York, the hunting parties in Far Hills? War veterans often suffered mental disturbances, he knew. Evidence from the Civil War and the more recent Spanish-American War documented in ever more distressing detail the long-term consequences of these conflicts on the survivors.

Would Iris and Dorothea be considered war veterans, he wondered, or did that only apply to men? The word *veteran* sounded so old. Would his sisters really be old maids?

None of this could he discuss with Lavinia. The twins' long absence had not, in the optimistic truism, made her heart grow fonder. When he tried to talk about them over dinner (normally a congenial time), she would remind him how upsetting they had always been to her, spying on her, doing mysterious ("Well, what *were* they doing?"), time-wasting things in their back quarters that she, Lavinia, was never allowed to see. She would castigate George for indulging them by allowing them to participate in this disagreeable undertaking abroad, particularly since it clearly postponed ever longer their ability to do their family duty by marrying. Her objections hit a nerve, and more recently he had ceased to mention the twins' names to Lavinia at all, either at the dinner table or elsewhere.

Now, with Lavinia pregnant, George knew it was even more important to keep his wife in a calm frame of mind. She was not young, and thoughts aroused by Miss Wetherall's earlier insinuations haunted him as he thought of Lavinia's tense face and blossoming belly. A son would be wonderful, of course. The Crosby name had some importance still, and he wished it to be continued. But he dreaded the possible cost to his wife's health — or to the unborn child. Miss Wetherall was right about that. His sisters had been affected perhaps more than anyone knew by their loss.

George went into the twins' drawing room. It smelled musty. He missed the flowers they always had on the table. He missed their presence in the chairs they always sat in. He even missed the piles of handwritten manuscript lying on the floor. The room felt like a museum. He walked quickly to the fireplace and began looking through the volumes in the left-hand bookshelf. He soon found the book Iris had requested. He pulled it out, admiring its leather binding and gilded lettering. He opened it at random, and his eyes fixed upon the lines on one of the pages: "*This is a delicious evening, when the whole body is one sense, and imbibes delight through every pore.*" He snapped the book shut, suddenly flushing and finding it hard to breathe. Reassuring himself that it was the room's stale air that had affected him, he quickly put the book under his arm and left.

Chapter 18

MONDAY, JUNE 10, 1918,
531 FIFTH AVENUE, NEW YORK

Bring her to me, Willis."

"Very good, sir."

Everett Grayfield was in the living room of his apartment. The air was warm and the windows were open. The red damask curtains swayed slightly, as though waiting for a play to begin. Everett was at his usual post looking out over Central Park, smoking a cigarette in a long black holder. The park looked wonderfully green this afternoon, in spite of such a severe winter. Life is very insistent, he thought. He was dressed in white trousers and a light blue shirt, almost the same color as the pale spring sky tenting the park. A blue and silver silk foulard was tied loosely around his neck.

"This way, madam."

Everett turned and watched as Willis ushered his guest into the living room. She was short, stocky, with a well-upholstered body and surprisingly tiny ankles and feet. Her businesslike suit was dark and well tailored, French obviously, Everett thought. Her face was the least appealing part of her appearance. Long in nose and brow, with flat cheekbones, a generous chin, and a halo of tightly curled blue-tinted hair, he decided that she resembled a sheep.

"Miss De Wolfe, sir," Willis said.

"Thank you, Willis. Please bring the tea. You would like some tea, Miss De Wolfe? Or would you prefer something stronger?"

"Tea is perfect, Mr. Grayfield, thank you. Something stronger might be appropriate a little later."

Everett liked that.

"Please sit down, Miss De Wolfe. I trust you have not come far?"

"Indeed, no. I have just been visiting the apartment of Mr. Condé Nast. It is a little farther up the avenue. Perhaps you know it?"

"But of course. He gives excellent parties. One meets such a fascinating mixture of people there."

"That is because he is always thinking of his magazines. His parties are carefully planned to provide good copy for *Vogue* or *Vanity Fair.* I am not sure he really enjoys them himself."

"Indeed." Everett thought for a moment of the austere, unsmiling host of the glamorous parties at 1040 Park Avenue. "You may be right. He always seems off to one side, an observer rather than a participant."

"Precisely." She paused, stroking one of her white gloves. "You have, of course, observed the decor of that apartment."

Everett bowed. "I believe he owes it all to you, Miss De Wolfe." (At a not inconsiderable price, he refrained from adding.)

"Well," she said, "I like to think I have given him the proper backdrop for his entertainments. That Chinese wallpaper, you know, was extremely difficult to obtain."

"People admire it enormously."

"Yes, I believe they do."

During this exchange, while Willis brought in the tea and began setting it up on a table near the fireplace, Miss De Wolfe had been taking a subtle measure of the living room.

"If it is not impertinent," she said, "may I ask where you acquired those screens?" Everett and she looked together at a pair of Coromandel screens that were placed at the far end of the living room.

"Evidently not from Elsie De Wolfe," he said with a smile, pouring her tea. "A little lemon?"

"That is your loss," she said briskly. "I'm sure I could have found you a better price. Lemon will do perfectly."

"And what do you think of my chairs?" he said, pointing at his eighteenth-century French fauteuils.

"They are very fine," she said. "But I believe they are not all authentic." She put down her teacup, stood up, went over to one of the fauteuils, and tipped it over on its side.

"You see," she said, "this one has been repaired—and not so long ago, either." She returned to her seat and sipped her tea.

Everett laughed. "Oh, dear," he said. "You are now going to examine every detail of my modest apartment and reveal its imperfections."

"I should enjoy that very much," she responded. "One should always know one's faults, so that one can correct them. I speak only of the decorative arts, of course."

"Naturally."

"But that is not why I came, Mr. Grayfield. You know that."

Everett put his cup and saucer back on the tray and indicated that she should continue. "I'm certain you had no intention of discussing my interior design flaws on this occasion, if that's what you mean," he said smoothly.

"Of course not. I believe you are aware that I spend a great deal of my time in France. I own a villa in Versailles, with Anne Morgan and Bessie Marbury. It is now a hospital, of course. Until the war started, I made much of my living in association with the top Paris dealers, purchasing French furniture and fabrics. The results of that, of course, can be seen in Mr. Nast's apartment." Everett inclined his head.

"Like all of us, I have been haunted by the terrible devastation in France. Many of my friends have been called to duty or have offered their services for the glory of France. In my humble way, I am trying to do my part."

"How admirable," Everett said. "Have you by any chance encountered Mrs. Teddy Wharton in your good works over there? She is an old friend of the family's and I hear she is making a wonderful contribution to the cause."

"Edith Wharton? The authoress?"

"I believe she writes books, yes."

His companion turned and looked out the window. "Mrs. Wharton used to visit Miss Marbury and me when we lived on Irving Place," she said coolly. "But her set is distinctly literary, whereas mine . . ." She paused. "Mine, shall we say, is more *demi-mondaine*."

"Perhaps." Everett agreed. "And I would wager, much more amusing. I'm sure I should much prefer your circle of friends." He lifted an eyebrow suggestively. "Your salon on Irving Place was the envy of us all."

Elsie De Wolfe gave him a sharp look. Not a sheep, he thought. A wicked old goat.

Willis knocked at the door and entered, and Everett waved away the tea things. "Is it time yet for something stronger, Miss De Wolfe?" he asked.

"I would consider a drop of bourbon," she replied demurely.

Everett told Willis to bring a bottle of his best vintage bourbon and two glasses. "I have a cousin who lives in Charleston," he explained.

"Southerners have such good taste," she observed.

"Indeed. And now please proceed." He lit a cigarette and fixed it in his holder. "I do not expect to hear good news."

"I do not have good news to relate, Mr. Grayfield. What I have to tell you is not pleasant. One of the most severe problems faced by the French and American medical teams over there is treatment for burns. Burns are a persistent threat to the soldiers—from shell attacks, from incendiary bombs, from explosions in the trenches. Our airmen in particular suffer from being trapped in burning aircraft." She paused meaningfully and stared at Everett, who perceptibly flinched. "And burns are a particularly difficult condition to treat."

Willis brought in the glasses and the bourbon decanter. Everett poured a generous amount into both glasses and handed one to his guest. "Please go on."

"The skin is partially sheared off by the burn, so that it is exposed, raw, oozing pus, and—most problematic—very vulnerable to infection, which is a constant danger, as you might imagine, in the primitive conditions of the hospital wards. To protect these open wounds and allow them to heal at the same time requires a complex form of dressing in combination with certain ointments, which has been only partially successful. Some patients are lowered, screaming, into baths; then an antiseptic acid is applied to the burns, frequently causing as abrasive an effect as the original fire. Others are exposed to equally violent attempts at healing. Meanwhile they are in excruciating pain and find it hard to endure what is, frankly, horribly clumsy and ineffective treatment. Yet this is all that is currently available."

Everett took a deep drink of his bourbon. Miss De Wolfe had risen and was standing in front of him, giving him a performance that she knew would appeal directly to his emotions. He remembered that she had once been an actress. He closed his eyes as though in pain as she continued.

"Anne Morgan and I have been working for a year with doctors on this problem, and recently a French physician, Dr. Barthe de Sanfort, came up with a revolutionary new treatment for these poor, suffering creatures. His invention is a waxlike substance that resembles petroleum jelly. If you heat it and pour it over the burns, it hardens and creates a covering like artificial skin, which both relieves pain and helps to prevent infection. The hospital where Dr. de Sanfort works is in Issy-les-Moulineaux. It is called the Ambrine Mission, and that is the name of his treatment. I have seen for myself how effective it is." She did not add that while admiring the innovative technique, she had several times almost passed out at the stench of the burned flesh that she had been invited to witness.

"But that is splendid, Miss De Wolfe. I congratulate you." Everett's admiration was genuine. "Perhaps you would like to smoke?" He held out to her a slim gold case, and she took a cigarette. "How intuitive of you," she said. "You must have guessed that most of us who spend time at hospitals at the front begin to smoke. I do not think I need tell you why."

Everett shook his head with a mild grimace. "Please continue," he murmured.

"We are very encouraged by the ambrine treatment, Mr. Grayfield. But of course the treatment is very expensive." She paused, taking deep inhalations of smoke. "We wish so much to be able to help our boys who have been so brave on our behalf," she went on, looking him in the eye. "Anyone who loves France as much as you evidently do must feel the same way. We have had major support from Baron Henri de Rothschild and his wife, Mathilde, and I have traveled throughout the United States in the past year to encourage others to support the mission. I am here to ask for a substantial contribution."

There was a small silence. "You are experienced in the ways of the rich," Everett observed. "I like your candor."

"Thank you, Mr. Grayfield. I see no point in being obscure. My dealings with Mr. Nast, Mr. Frick, and my other clients have confirmed my opinion that the very wealthy are like everyone else. They like straight talk." She darted a quick look at her host and smiled slightly. "And now, if I might be permitted, I should like very much to see the rest of the apartment."

"By all means." Everett finished his drink and put the glass on the table. "I hope, however," he added with a cautionary glance at her, "that you will be kind. As you will see, I am horribly allergic to — what is it called? Taste."

She laughed merrily. "Oh, set your mind at rest, Mr. Grayfield," she said. "Taste will not be an issue here, I assure you."

They walked amicably along the corridor, while Elsie examined the flooring ("fine Carrara marble"), the console tables ("from England; I saw some just like this at Mr. Duveen's country house"), the paintings ("You must spend a considerable amount of time in the auction rooms"). They entered the master bedroom, where she approved of the four-poster bed but commented less favorably on the fabric used for the hangings. "Yellow is very unflattering. I would suggest a shade of rose."

"Should I be taking notes, Miss De Wolfe?" Everett inquired.

"A pier glass on the far wall would greatly enhance the light in the room," she continued, ignoring his remark. "As you know, I am a great admirer of mirrors."

They passed back into the corridor and arrived at the closed door to Harry's room. Here Miss De Wolfe paused expectantly. "Not in there," Everett said sharply. "It's just a box room." Elsie glanced at him in surprise, but he volunteered nothing else and they walked on.

The tour ended in the conservatory, which was granted high marks from the famous decorator. "My design for the Colony Club reflected this idea of creating an outdoor room," she informed him. "They were all dismayed, but it was a beautiful place, with trellised walls and carved niches for fine statuary. Quite daring for its time, you know. Now it, too, like my beloved Villa Trianon, is being used as a hospital for the war wounded." She paused. "The Colony Club itself has moved to a new building," she added in disparaging tones.

"What a pity," Everett said.

"Their loss," she said dismissively. "We don't mourn the past. It's a wasteful pursuit. The present is all that matters."

She walked around the conservatory with narrowed eyes, feeling the upholstery fabrics, stepping daintily on the Persian carpets, looking up at the molded ceilings. She paused near a French window. "You could use a sculpture in this space, Mr. Grayfield. That is the only thing the room lacks. And I know exactly the one for you. It is a charming small torso of a Greek discus thrower, dated circa fifty-four BC, acquired in a remarkable coup by Mr. Duveen. I could have you view it immediately."

They walked back to the living room. "I've enjoyed this enormously," Everett said, raising his glass to her. "I'll arrange to send a check for your burn unit at once."

"I am most grateful to you," she replied, raising her glass in return. "I shall leave the address with your butler. And you will be hearing from me shortly about the discus thrower. I assure you that you won't regret the purchase. It will retain its value, even in these difficult times."

Willis came to the door and she turned to follow him. "By the way," she said as she withdrew, "next time you redecorate the living room, which I trust will be in the very near future, I suggest you call in a furniture expert. I believe we could avoid some of the more egregious mistakes committed here if someone of my experience and knowledge were consulted."

Everett bowed. "Miss De Wolfe, as always your advice is beyond reproach," he said. Giving him a graceful smile, she left the room.

Moving to his desk, Everett opened a drawer and took out a

checkbook. Changing his mind, he went over to the French fauteuils and examined them as the decorator had, tipping them over. With a rueful shake of his head, he returned to his chair. He picked up a small photograph of Harry in an oval frame that stood on the desk and gazed at it for a moment, then suddenly put it down as though it were burning him. Lighting a cigarette, he lifted his pen and started to write.

The donation to the Ambrine Mission would be generous.

~ FRANCE ~

Chapter 19

Darling Isabel,

This is a follow-up to our conversation on the telephone last evening. I cannot imagine anything more wonderful than your wanting to be my wife. Your beauty, your energy, your liking sports, your laughter, your bobbed hair, are all things I love. I know I haven't been much fun recently. I am so keen to do well for my squadron, and so much is expected of me, that I do not have time to think much about romance and all the right things to say to a girl one's crazy about. Anyway, I never was any good at that sort of thing. As you gathered, my mother wasn't the kind of person to teach her son anything, and at college there were really no girls around to get used to them and find out what they really liked to hear. So if I bore you with my talk about planes and getting victories, it's really the only stuff I know how to talk about.

It's hard to describe what you mean to me. I'm not even sure myself. Of course, I worry about how I'd look after you when this damn war is over. Your people are so very well off, and you are accustomed to things I am afraid I shall not be able to provide for you. I fear you'll feel cooped up in some small apartment in New York, instead of living in a fine country house, playing tennis and buying clothes from Paris and going about in the latest roadster. Can you imagine it, while I'm working in some damn bank, longing to be outside somewhere, feeling instead that I'm in a prison, stuck in a useless occupation?

So I think we should take this slowly—give ourselves time to get used to it. By all means let's get engaged, that's the important thing, and maybe later we can think about getting married—when the war is over. Things will look different then. Marriage is certainly on the minds now of many of my friends, including Maurice. He seems really to be making a fool over himself over one of those Crosby twins—damned if I can tell them apart!

Hell, I am terrible at expressing myself. If I could get ahold of a large highball, then perhaps I could do the whole thing justice. It's just that I don't know how everything will work out between us. I can't really see our future clearly. The only thing that's clear is when I climb into my dear old Spad and fire off a few rounds of ammo. Then, I feel as though I know what I'm doing and can actually do something worthwhile.

You are a swell girl, Isabel, and I know you will make a fine wife. I just hope I'm going to be up to it all. When I next get leave, I'll call you to arrange a meeting in Paris. I am sending to New York for a ring. You'll have to help me do this right, it's not at all my sort of thing. Frankly, I'm pretty rotten when it comes to Real Life. That's not much recommendation for the future husband of Isabel Lexington—but I know you'll see it through for me.

We have a mission tomorrow if the weather holds. Fingers crossed!

Your Harry

Chapter 20

THE WHOLE OF PARIS seems to have turned out for Independence Day. French and American flags wave everywhere. The avenues are packed with American, French, and British soldiers, all cheering and laughing and throwing their caps in the air. Whole regiments have been assembled for the parade through the center of the city. Doughboys and poilus march side by side down the avenue du Trocadéro — renamed, for the day, avenue de Président Wilson — eyes right as they salute the statue of George Washington. Many carry bouquets of flowers. Marching with them is a group of American Red Cross nurses, their long skirts billowing in an ocean of dark blue serge. As they stream into the Champs-Élysées and file past Red Cross headquarters at the corner of the place de la Concorde, the noise is deafening.

The balcony of the Hôtel de Crillon is crowded with Americans. The stone balustrades can barely hold the press of people, who lean over to watch the thrilling scene below. Rubbing shoulders with top military and political personnel are luminaries such as Eddie Rickenbacker, the flying ace, and Edith Wharton, who later writes to her sister-in-law Mary Cadwalader Jones that it was the "greatest Fourth in history — only slightly unreal from its sheer beauty, & the extraordinary weight of associations, historic, symbolic & all the rest, added to the aesthetic perfection of the setting."

Iris and Dorothea are thrust together, bemused by the sights around and below them. Their brother has wangled them an invitation to this most exclusive of expatriate celebrations, and they are both daunted and excited by its glamour.

"Of course, it was glamorous before," Iris observes to Dorothea as they push their way through the gilded salons.

"But glamour with Adeline Wetherall is slightly different from glamour with Edith Wharton," Dorothea points out.

"Oh, I don't know. The ceilings! The decoration! We stood right here and listened to the history of the comtes de Crillon for the umpteenth time!"

" '*Ô, France, quoique tu sommeilles, / Nous t'appelons, nous, les proscrits!*' What was she thinking?"

"And what about the champagne in Épernay! The Bordeaux in Biarritz!" Iris gesticulates wildly, knocking back an imaginary glass of wine. People watching think she is entering into the spirit of the occasion and smile kindly at her. Iris smiles back, abashed. "It all seems so long ago," she murmurs in Dorothea's ear. "How little we knew about anything then."

They are jostled apart by a group of people pushing their way to the front of the balcony to attract the attention of a contingent of British nurses passing beneath. The leader of the group is a tall, handsome woman dressed in pink chiffon, with a white satin turban, and diamonds and emeralds at her throat and wrists. A large wolfhound stands guard next to her. Moving Iris aside, she calls down in a commanding English voice, "Veronica! Harriet! Diana! Up here!" A group of nurses look up, beaming. She waves down vaguely, turning toward the twins. "That wasn't them, of course," she explains to Iris. "My nieces, I mean. They must be somewhere down there. Diana is supposed to be meeting me later at the Ritz. But heaven knows if we'll ever find each other."

"Here, Lady Grenville, over here!" someone at the balustrade calls to her. She leans across to get a better look, stepping on Iris's foot.

"My dear child, I'm so sorry," she cries, taking Iris's hand. "Are you hurt?"

Iris shakes her head. "No, not at all."

Lady Grenville looks from her to Dorothea with momentary concentration. "Twins, I say, how unusual," she observes. "My brother Bertie has twin daughters. Both of them perfectly ghastly, and you can't tell them apart to give them a good spanking, which, frankly, is exactly what they need." She raises two perfectly arched eyebrows. "I do hope you don't wear the same clothes," she goes on. "I always thought it was so unfair for my sister-in-law to put the girls in matching smocked frocks all the time. A terrible mistake."

She looks at the twins' identical Red Cross uniforms. "Never mind," she pushes on blithely, "I suppose in wartime those kinds of things don't matter." Iris laughs and leans down to stroke the dog.

"Poor old Lambchop, he's not really used to this," remarks his owner. "Prefers a nice stretch of Sussex Downs. But the poor soldiers love him, so I can't send him home." The dog licks Iris's hand. "Well, I can see you're a dog person," she says approvingly. "Lambchop won't do that for just anyone, will you, love?" She kisses the wolfhound's nose and starts to move back from the balustrade. "Isn't this amusing, darlings," she exclaims. "But oh, so exhausting. I've not seen crowds like this since dear Eddie's coronation." She checks a diamond-studded wristwatch. "Time for a teeny gin, don't you think?" she says to the dog. She leads the obedient animal back into the main salon. People make way for her. "Lady Grenville, over here!" English voices call out. She embraces people extravagantly. "Darling, how wonderful to see you!" Dorothea and Iris watch her in amusement. "I feel we must be at a Newport garden party," Dorothea remarks. " 'Smocked frocks?' Is this really happening?"

Later that day, the twins walk through the jardin des Tuileries toward the rue de Richelieu, stepping over the heaps of wilted flowers fallen from the marchers' bouquets. They pause for a moment at the fountain in the center of the garden, where couples in uniform sit in locked embraces, mothers distract their fretful children with American flags, and groups of French and American soldiers slug back bottles of beer and wine, hugging one another, drunkenly singing, intoxicated more by the wild demonstrations of encouragement expressed by over fifty thousand supporters who have filled the city than by the cheap liquor that they recklessly pour down their throats.

At the Union, the scene is not very different. The lobby and public rooms are decorated with streamers and banners and American flags. Balloons have been found somewhere and are fastened to the heavy brass floor lamps that illuminate the two rooms. A bar has been set up at the back of the lobby, loaded with spirits and wine. A gramophone plays loud jazz in one corner. American soldiers and airmen in uniform fill the two rooms, smoking, drinking, slapping one another on the back, laughing rowdily, consuming the free-flowing liquor like the soldiers in the park, with an unnatural urgency.

There is a muted quality, however, to the atmosphere of these Fourth of July celebrations at the Union. The clothes are all dark, khaki, brown, or gray. No bright scarves, colorful jackets, or sparkling jewelry to suggest a party. In spite of the flags and streamers, the dominant impression is of a room in twilight. It is as though an artist recording the event has chosen a monochrome palette for his painting *Americans in Paris on Independence Day, 1918.*

Isabel Lexington is an exception. She has found a scarlet ribbon somewhere and tied it around her waist like a sash. It draws attention to her slim figure, and several men eye her with wartime hunger as she swings through the crowd.

"Have you seen Harry?" she asks everyone as she passes. "Has anyone seen Harry Forrester?"

The twins greet her and admire her sash. "Oh, I'm glad you like it," Isabel says. "I'm looking for Harry; you know we are engaged?"

"Engaged?" the twins exclaim in surprised unison.

"Yes, he did it so romantically. He got a night's leave especially, came up from Toul, and proposed in the Café Napolitain. He hasn't got a ring, of course, but he promises to get one sent from New York as soon as he can."

"That's marvelous, Isabel," Iris says, embracing her.

"And now I must find him," she says eagerly. "He is so elusive, the darling!"

"Excuse me, Miss Lexington." She is stopped by a small, stout person with fluffy blue hair and an elaborate black-and-white silk bow tied under her chin. With her is a tall, thin, austere woman with dark circles under her eyes, dressed, like her companion, in a black silk gown with embroidery that could only have been stitched in the finest Paris houses.

"Yes?" Isabel looks at her in puzzlement.

"I'm Elsie De Wolfe," the small woman says. "And this is Miss Anne Morgan."

"Oh, I know you," Isabel squeals. "You decorated my aunt's apartment in New York."

"Indeed I did, my dear. Mrs. Penniston has very good taste. And what an agreeable person to work with. I recall that I was able to find her the most splendid console, a little piece from the Marie Antoinette auction in London a few years ago that went perfectly in her bedroom. We were greatly satisfied with the purchase."

"And you are working here in Paris?" Isabel asks her politely, searching all the while for Harry.

"Well, not at interior decoration, my dear. This poor city is hardly the place for that at the moment. Anne and I are working with the Ambrine Burn Unit."

"Oh, yes," Isabel replies vaguely. "I believe I've heard people talk about that."

"I'm here looking for people who will come with me to put on a presentation at the Children of Flanders Rescue Committee party tomorrow. I saw you and thought at once you would be perfect. Finding that red ribbon is so creative, my dear. Just what the boys need. Don't you think so, Anne?"

Miss Morgan eyes the scarlet sash with distaste. "Quite," she murmurs.

"Well." Isabel looks doubtfully at the imposing couple.

"Here's my address. If you could call on me tomorrow morning at nine o'clock, we can discuss it further. I know you want to help all you can. Now, who was it you were looking for?"

"Harry Forrester. My fiancé."

"Really? So optimistic of you at such a time. I believe I know a very close friend of his, Mr. Everett Grayfield."

Isabel looks at her distractedly.

"So he hasn't mentioned Mr. Grayfield to you? That's odd. I had heard that Mr. Forrester lives in Mr. Grayfield's apartment. I recently visited it, 531 Fifth Avenue. Mr. Grayfield has quite a fine collection of French furniture."

"Ah, there he is!" says Isabel, relieved. "I see him now. Please excuse me."

"Nine o'clock tomorrow morning, then. Thank you, Miss Lexington. It was delightful to meet you. Please give my regards to your aunt." Elsie De Wolfe turns now to the twins, who have been standing by in polite silence. "And you are . . . ?"

The twins introduce each other as they always do. "This is Dorothea Crosby," says Iris.

"And my sister, Iris."

"Twins, yes. Let me see . . ." Miss De Wolfe's efficient filing cabinet of a brain kicks into action. "Now I remember. You girls worked for the Red Cross during the Triangle Shirtwaist disaster a few years ago."

Iris looks at her with wide eyes and puts her hand to her face. "Of course," she whispers. "What a tragedy."

"You invited us to tea," Dorothea adds.

"Did I? Well," the decorator goes on, "that's ancient history. We have more pressing things to think about now. Perhaps I may invite you to something a little more than tea next time. We'll be in touch." The twins shake her gloved hand, and the two women turn and begin walking stiffly toward the front of the lobby in their elaborate couture dresses, one tall, one short, like an unmatched pair of black widow spiders.

"The other one is Anne Morgan," Iris says. "She was a suffragist."

"I wonder what she is now."

"What are we all?"

"At war, obviously," Dorothea says impatiently. "Really, Iris, do snap out of it. Miss De Wolfe is right. There are more important things to think about now."

"I thought Miss Morgan looked a little like Anna. Those eyes . . ."

Dorothea looks at her in shock. "Anna? Don't be ridiculous. Miss Morgan is tall, middle-aged, American, and very rich. Anna—well, there's no comparison."

But Iris has broken the spell. She is suddenly back there with the burning smell in her hands, eyes, hair. How do you numb your mind? Inject it with anesthetic? Cauterize it?

"Sorry," she mutters to her sister. "It was a stupid thought. There was just something in the eyes, the expression . . ." Dorothea brushes her aside and starts walking toward the bar to catch up with Isabel in the throng of officers in pilots' uniforms. Harry and Maurice are smoking and drinking with them.

"Harry!" Isabel calls out breathlessly.

Harry looks up as Isabel rushes toward him, waving madly. "Darling, I've been looking all over for you." She throws herself into his arms. He touches her briefly, then disentangles her like a vine, smiling sheepishly at his friends.

"So who's this, Harry?" one of his companions says. "Where have you been hiding her?"

"Isabel Lexington," Harry introduces her. "She's been in Paris awhile. We knew each other in New York."

"We're going to be married," Isabel announces. "Imagine. You can't imagine how difficult it was to persuade him!"

Harry looks at her and grimaces. His friends whoop and laugh.

"So you've snared the legendary Harry Forrester!" one of them exclaims. "The greatest punt returner anyone has ever seen!"

"Fastest man on ice in the history of university athletics," another one chimes in.

"Oh, quit it," Harry says, turning away. "Just let it go, will you?"

His friends look surprised at the edge of anger in his voice. "We were only kidding," one says to him. "Hell, we'd all heard about you. You kept Harvard on top for years. What's wrong with that? I speak as a Yale man myself." Everybody jeers.

"So how's he doing now?" The questions keep coming. "What's his victory count?"

"The Boche never has a chance. Harry's relentless. He's even got Eddie running scared."

" 'Ace of aces' up for grabs, eh?"

Harry is looking more and more uncomfortable. Isabel gazes at him adoringly.

"Leave him alone, fellas," Maurice says, intervening. "Let him be."

"Excuse me," Harry says suddenly. "I've seen a pilot from the squadron over there I need to talk to. I'll be right back."

He pushes his way through the crowd and disappears in the smoke. Maurice almost starts after him, then checks himself. Isabel looks down, her face red, then turns back to the group with a defiant toss of her head. The music has become much louder. "Hey," says one of the airmen, "since he's left you to us, how about a dance?"

"Sure," Isabel says boldly. "Why not?"

"My name's Charlie," he says, "Charlie Longstreth. I've watched you. You're good. Let's see how it goes."

He takes her hand and they move to the small space cleared for dancing. A few other couples are on the floor, shuffling and swaying in a random fashion. When Charlie and Isabel start dancing, the electricity between them ignites instantly. They move together in a quick jazz step that soon has the others stopping to watch. Charlie whirls her around, brings her close, swings her out, and pulls her back to him again. Isabel's eyes are half-closed, her supple body and quicksilver feet moving in sensuous rhythm. As the music intensifies, they smile delightedly at each other, bodies swaying, hands touching, hips twisting. Their voluptuous performance infects the other dancers until they, too, lift up their arms and gyrate and tumble into one another in an avalanche of pleasure. It is as though the dance has released these young people from the fetters of—what? Convention, sexual hunger, danger, death. The way Charlie and Isabel dance is the way people are going to dance after the war is over.

Iris watches them with parted lips. Maurice looks at her and then at the dance floor. Dorothea turns away and starts to smoke a cigarette. Harry has returned and watches with the others, an enigmatic expression on his face. The four friends seem not to know one another, standing apart as they drink in the rapturous scene in front of them, estranged from one another like guilty viewers at a peep show.

The spell is interrupted by Charlie Longstreth, who sees Harry and lets Isabel go, offering her back to his friend.

"Your turn, Harry," he says, breathing hard. "Thanks for not cutting in. That was something, Miss Lexington. Thank you. You're a lucky man, Harry."

Isabel runs into Harry's arms, panting, flushed. "Oh, let's go on doing it," she cries. "I don't want to stop."

Harry shakes his head. "I want another drink," he says. "It's going to run out, the way everyone's going at it. I need to tank up before going back to the squadron."

Isabel jerks her head back as though he has strangled her. She turns around to look at Charlie Longstreth, who is gazing at her with undisguised lust. He throws up his hands in disbelief at Harry's rejection, salutes Isabel, and turns back to the group.

"But Harry, it's fun." Isabel turns again, taking his arm. "Don't you want to enjoy yourself just for a little while? You make it seem like a crime. What should we be doing in this damned war except dancing?"

"I just want to fly," he mutters. "I can't explain it. We want to win this war, don't we?"

Maurice, who has been listening, turns away, shaking his head. His eyes meet Iris's. "Will you dance with me, Iris?" he asks.

"I can't dance at all," Iris says, blushing. "But I'll try."

The music has changed. The syncopated beat is now smooth and creamy. Several couples are on the floor, dancing close together, heads turning sideways sometimes to inhale smoke from cigarettes. As Iris steps into Maurice's arms, she gives a placating wave to Dorothea, who watches from the sidelines. Dorothea does not wave back. Iris glances anxiously at Maurice, who firmly draws her farther into the center of the dance floor. Trying to find Dorothea again, Iris notices Isabel tug at Harry's hand. He pulls it away.

"Why is he like that?" Iris asks Maurice. "Why is he so cold to her?"

"I think he's afraid," Maurice replies.

"Afraid? I thought he was this wild, heroic character who killed Boches at the drop of a hat."

"That's in the air. On the ground, things look different. He's afraid of what's going to happen after the war. Married life. Finding something to do back home. Earning money. Making a living when you've lived like this."

"Poor Isabel."

"Isabel is in too much of a hurry."

"How can she be?" Iris protests. "All the men are disappearing. I can hardly bear to read the lists on the bulletin board anymore. Carpe diem. Everything here is heightened, intensified . . ." She pauses. "I can quite understand how she feels."

"Can you, Iris?" He looks at her intently.

"It's hard for Isabel," Iris repeats, avoiding his question. How dare she tell him that she understands her friend's need to make a connection, any connection, in this relentlessly disconnecting war? "Imagine. Isabel and I having something in common!" she exclaims. Maurice laughs.

"That's what war does," he says. "It's full of ironies. Haven't you noticed? Look at Harry. The war seemed at first to have liberated him, but now it has trapped him."

"Do you feel trapped, Maurice?"

"Iris!" He speaks her name with sudden passion. "If only you knew. If only I could . . ." She hurriedly puts her fingers to his lips.

"Shhh, Maurice." She pauses, then says in a low voice, "I think I do know."

His face lights up at her lovely revelation. They dance more slowly, watching each other's faces. He takes her fingers, kisses them one by one, and rests them on his cheek.

"I believe you do. For a woman with such a sheltered background, you have suddenly become very wise."

Iris laughs. "Well, I'll take that as a compliment."

"You want a better one?" He pulls her closer to him and kisses her lips. *This mustn't happen,* he thinks.

"Mmm, that was a lot better," Iris murmurs through his kiss. *This mustn't happen,* she thinks.

"You are so full of life," he whispers.

They kiss. They kiss again. The music resolves itself into a slow, winding coda, wrapping them in a cocoon of attenuated sound. They gaze at each other for a long time, studying each other's eyes, cheeks, lips, hair, each composing the precious contours of the other's face for a score that they will later play alone.

"There's no full moon," Maurice says apologetically, "or soft music, or sound of nightingales in the garden . . ."

"But 'The "Tune is in the Tree—" / The Skeptic—showeth me— / "No Sir! In Thee!"'"

Maurice looks at her questioningly. Iris laughs.

"Emily Dickinson. Our old English teacher used to quote it."

"Women's stuff. What did she know?" Maurice rolls his eyes and Iris punches him in the chest. Their little intimacy is interrupted by Harry, who comes up to Maurice and takes him roughly by the arm.

"Let's go," Harry says abruptly. "Let's get out of here. I need to get back to base. I just learned we're getting some new planes in."

Isabel runs up after him.

" 'The base,' 'the planes,' " she repeats impatiently. "You only want to be with your comrades on the base. That's the only time you're happy. Darn it. I don't think this is going to work." She gives his chest a flick of her finger.

"Where's Dorothea?" Iris asks, looking around guiltily for her sister.

"Come with me," Isabel says. "We'll find her." She grabs Iris's arm. "Let's leave the boys to themselves. After all, they don't want us."

"I'd better go with Harry," Maurice whispers to Iris. She nods. They separate slowly, as though it hurts. "I'll see you when I get another leave," he promises her. "I'm sure I can get away in a week or so. Write to me."

Iris nods. "Please," she says, "please come back to me soon."

"Come on." Isabel pulls Iris away. "Stop these sentimental scenes. They're not going to go anywhere, so what's the point?" She starts to drag Iris through the dwindling crowd. It is getting late. The dancers are now quiet, making seductive motions to one another in time to the music, as though they believe that for another day, at least, they have a future. Iris looks back and watches Maurice as he and Harry make their way through the lobby and into the rapidly emptying place de la Concorde.

"Men are pitiful, aren't they?" Isabel observes.

Iris glances at her. "But aren't you engaged to one, Isabel?"

"I don't think so," Isabel replies. "That was last week." She gives a short laugh.

"Oh, Isabel," Iris exclaims.

"Don't worry about me, darling. I can take care of myself."

Dorothea is finishing a glass of wine. The bar is strewn with cigarette butts, empty glasses, bottles, torn streamers, and paper flags.

"Has Maurice gone, too?" she asks cheerfully. "Well, it's still the Fourth of July. Who shall we drink to?"

"Wasn't it a wonderful day?" Iris says eagerly. "The scene at the Crillon, the crowds, the cheering down the Champs-Élysées . . ."

"Harry told me that a French aviator crashed into the Champs-Élysées earlier this year and broke one of the wrought iron lamps on the corner," Isabel announces. "He was killed, of course. The plane had to be removed by truck and sand shoveled over the place to hide the blood."

There is an appalled silence.

"Sorry," Isabel says lightly. "But that's the kind of thing you hear around here. Harry's full of aviator stories. That's why I'm leaving this boring place. Charlie said he'd take me to the cinema next week if I can get off. At least he seems like fun. Good dancer, too. I'm still young, darn it." She puts her face up to the light and tweaks the skin beneath her eyes. "No wasting time for Isabel Lexington." She blows a kiss to the twins and walks off, her head high.

"Poor Isabel," Iris murmurs. She rubs her fingers gently over her lips and turns to her sister. "I guess that only leaves us to drink to," she adds with an attempt at heartiness.

"Us?" Dorothea scoffs. "There is no 'us' anymore."

Iris braces for the onslaught. "What do you mean?" she asks carefully.

Dorothea barks out a laugh. Iris takes a deep breath and moves closer to her sister.

"Don't be angry with me, Dorothea," she begs, putting a hand on her twin's arm. "I can't explain it, but it is something magical. Something I've never felt before. Ever. We used to read all that lyrical poetry and never had the slightest sense of what the words meant. I wish you knew what I was talking about."

"I'm delighted that I don't." Dorothea exhales a stream of smoke. "One of us had better remain sane. I have no wish to be where you are. It's destined for disaster—you will be blown up just like our poilus in the trenches. It's madness, Iris. I can only watch and salute you as you go." She gives a violent wave to the air, piercing the cloud of smoke in front of her like a machete.

"Stop it, Dorothea. You know we're in this together. Just us. As always." Iris takes a deep breath as she starts the journey to bring her sister back to her.

"Just us?" Dorothea mocks her.

"Of course," Iris insists in a stronger voice.

"You mean that?"

"You know I do. There was never anyone else."

"Really?" Dorothea gives her sister a penetrating look. Iris returns the look without flinching.

"Really."

"Even now?"

"Particularly now."

"Well, at least that sounds like the old Iris." Dorothea utters a mocking cheer.

Iris puts her hand on her sister's cheek. The skin is rough from the long months of exposure in the hospital. She takes Dorothea's hand and puts it on her own cheek. "Feel it," she says. "We once had such soft complexions." Iris strokes her sister's face, smoothing it like a piece of linen. As she had hoped, the physical contact between them retains its old power, the strained wires reconnect, and gradually Dorothea's eyes grow less distant and her mouth relaxes. They smile with relief at each other.

"There, darling. We are back now, aren't we, Dorothea? Even without daisy chains, remember? Let's drink to that. To us."

Iris takes her sister's wineglass and drinks greedily. She sees in the ruby liquid Maurice's pale, dark face smiling sardonically at her. Maurice. Her body grows hot at the memory of their dance together, their enraptured lips, their entwined hands. She keeps her gaze fixed on the bottom of the glass, afraid that Dorothea will see the guilt in her eyes. But Dorothea is not looking for a further breach. She takes back the glass and, without looking at Iris, raises it.

"To us," she says triumphantly.

Carefully turning it around, she places her lips on the rim of the glass where Iris has drunk and drains it to the dregs.

A LITTLE OVER A WEEK LATER, the nurses so wildly cheered along the Champs-Élysées are back at the front, and the soldiers celebrating that great Fourth of July in Paris are engaged in a deadly new German attack launched from Château-Thierry to the Argonne. With Bastille Day passed in a fury of disillusion and despair, the place de la Concorde is once again silent.

Chapter 21

HARRY IS LYING in a corner of the airfield, wearing only his shorts. The place is quiet, with a few rumblings now and again from engines being tested. There is a lull in the action, as though the heat has suppressed for a while the momentum of the battlefield. The hot summer sun beats down on the young American aviator, and with no trees to shade him, he sweats. But he does not seem to care. Propping his head on his arm, he begins reading a letter. Sometimes he puts it aside with an impatient sigh, then picks it up again.

My dear Harry,

So you are engaged to be married! What a surprise! Your news was totally unexpected. Indeed it was the last thing I had imagined. You seemed so caught up in the romance of flying that to find time for any other kind of romance seems inconceivable.

I must confess that it seems to be an uncharacteristic move on your part. I am quite concerned that you may be making a very considerable mistake. It is clear that you do not know Miss Lexington very well (even though her family is highly respectable, of course) and that you are getting to know her under very difficult and unnatural circumstances. Emotions tend to be unreliable at such times.

I am also a little vexed about another, more delicate aspect that presents itself. This sudden decision of yours reminds me most unfortunately of your dear mother, who was sadly afflicted with impulsive behavior all her life. (As you know, my own mother was not perfect in this department—a bond between you and me that we have always valued.) I wonder if you are perhaps not rushing into this engagement because of an emotional weakness that is inherited from your mama, whose ability to make one disastrous marriage after another must set a world record for stamina, if not for discrimination. As the ineffable Dr. Johnson said, "Marriage is the triumph of hope over experience."

I strongly urge you to reconsider your decision, Harry, or at least not to allow it to progress any further for now. I am sure Miss Lexington is a person of good character and will understand if you wish to postpone any preparations for marriage. You are both young and living under extremely testing circumstances, when decisions are made in the heat of the moment and regretted later. Meanwhile I shall not convey the news to anyone here. If someone mentions it, I shall simply say that nothing has yet been settled.

I have to confess that the war is beginning to wear upon even the most optimistic of supporters. The very goals for which the Allies entered into it seem now blurred and confused. The imperial need for victory is beginning to look more like aggression than altruism, and the endlessly escalating death toll does not seem to justify the marginal pieces of ground gained—or lost. I am certain that when the war is over, the world will have to be realigned in a very different fashion. I fear the next generation in whose hands your future lies will show us up as terrible bunglers. Assuming, of course, that there is a next generation. (You can see how the mood of disillusion is infecting us here!)

By the way, I read the Alan Seeger dispatches that people are talking about. His claims of encountering the sublime in the embrace of death and other such high-flown rhetoric about heroism now seem pathetic in their immaturity. I recall that you told me your friend Maurice shares my opinion. These essays are being used simply as propaganda. I hope you are not becoming influenced by such self-indulgent bombast.

The city had become oppressive, so I came up to Newport early this year. Mrs. Oelrichs is organizing a big war benefit at Marble House next weekend. Mrs. Belmont is also putting on some show for French orphans. I believe Mrs. Wharton is outdoing everyone in Paris with her Refugees and Rescue committees. I even had a visit from Elsie De Wolfe asking for money for her Ambrine Mission. Quite an amusing competition between these war widows, don't you think? I have decided that for Mrs. Oelrichs's event, I shall wear the white silk suit I purchased when you and I visited Rome before the war. It still seems in excellent condition and is the right weight for the very warm weather we are experiencing here. Such issues as these pass for distractions these days.

I have just mailed you a small package. I know you do not like me to send you anything valuable, but I saw a pair of cuff links in Cartier before I left for Newport that I feel sure will please you. Keep them in their box for now, and if you find time occasionally to look at them, I trust that you will think of me. Your room, as I have frequently assured you, remains untouched, just the same as you left it a year ago.

It's been quite warm here, but I do not expect you are interested in the weather.

With you always in my thoughts,
Everett

Harry folds up the letter and uses it as a fan to cool himself. Then he lies down and puts it over his face. He blows on it a couple of times so that it floats up and then lands again. A few minutes later he sits up, takes the paper, and folds it several times until it is in the shape of a plane. He throws it into the air, where it hangs for a second before doing a rapid nosedive into the ground. With a laugh, he crumples it up, stuffs it into a pocket of his shorts, and lies back, closing his eyes.

Chapter 22

It is the strange twilight of a hot summer evening in northern France. The twins are seated in their small cubicle, and Iris is brushing Dorothea's hair. The noise from the tent is less insistent tonight. The heat seems to have served as a sleeping potion for all but the most desperate of cases. The twins luxuriate in the momentary lull.

"I wish you would do some writing," Iris says. "I know you would like to."

"Like to? I don't think so. I don't know why I ever presumed to call myself a poet."

"But before, you had nothing to write about. Now . . ."

Dorothea shrugs. "Now I couldn't possibly find the right words to express it."

"I know what you mean. Remember Adeline's praise for 'the private shrines of thought,' 'the glorious words of youthful dreams,' 'the beauteous spirit withheld from worldly view'?" They laugh at their foolishness in once savoring those words.

" 'If I should die, think only this of me: / That there's some corner of a foreign field / That is for ever England.' " Iris declaims the lines with theatrical intensity, putting her hand to her breast. "Now that's 'beauteous.' "

A high, long wail comes from the tent.

"*Aidez-moi, aidez-moi, mes camarades!*" The wail stops, then starts again. "*Le sifflement, vite, vite!*" The poor boy has heard the whistle again, and like roosters waking each other at dawn, another patient picks up the sound, then another, and suddenly the tent is alive with men crying. Perfidious sleep has abandoned them.

"'For ever England,'" Iris repeats sarcastically as she puts the hairbrush down. "He should have been here."

"Who?"

"Rupert Brooke."

"Another of Maurice's favorites, I suppose."

Iris pretends to throw the hairbrush at her sister but instead tosses it onto a shelf, where it dislodges a small package. Iris quickly covers it up with a scarf.

"What is that?" Dorothea asks sharply.

"Nothing." Iris backs off from it.

"Iris!" Dorothea is shocked at the guilty look on her sister's face. "What is it?"

Iris sighs and gingerly unwraps the package. Inside is a book. It is Thoreau's *Walden*.

"What is that doing here? Isn't it mine? How did you get it here? Who is it for?" As Dorothea fires off her questions, Iris quails, then recovers.

"It's for Maurice," she announces firmly. "I know you didn't particularly care for it, and he is a great admirer of Thoreau."

"It's for Maurice," Dorothea mimics her. "Lucky Maurice. A lover of Thoreau now?" She tries to grab the book, but Iris snatches it away from her and opens it.

"Listen to this." She finds the page and starts to read as quickly as she can, the words running into one another, as though the book will explode before she finishes.

"'In any weather, at any hour of the day or night, I have been anxious to improve the nick of time, and notch it on my stick too; to stand on the meeting of two eternities, the past and future, which is precisely the present moment; to toe that line.'"

Dorothea says nothing. The noise from the tent invades their silence. "We must go," she says shortly, tying her kerchief around her head. "Put it away."

Iris puts the book down and ties her kerchief like her sister. "Why don't you like him?" she asks in a resigned voice.

"Thoreau? Or Maurice?" Dorothea bends down to lace up her boots. "Not that it makes much difference. They are very similar in mentality, I gather." She laughs suddenly. "But I don't think Thoreau was Southern."

"Or Jewish." Iris laughs, too. "Really, Dorothea, this is ridiculous."

"That's precisely what I mean. It's ridiculous to be reading Thoreau or attaching yourself to Maurice here at this time. Anybody could tell you that."

"But we are still human," Iris argues. "We feel things."

"That's not our job. Look at the directrice. How could she go on if she 'felt' things?" Dorothea moves toward the tent, to the source of the anguished thrashing sounds of young men trying to outlast the war.

"Dorothea." Iris looks at her sister reproachfully.

"So when are you seeing him again?" Dorothea opens the flap of the tent and strides ahead, not wishing to hear the answer.

"I wish I knew. Whenever he is free. I know there is some big offensive going on in the north."

Dorothea whirls around and grabs Iris's shoulders. "That's what I mean, Iris. Feelings—invitations to grief. I only want to protect you."

"Oh, Dorothea. Please try to understand. We are trying to improve our 'nick of time.' Isn't that beautiful?" Iris tries to embrace her sister, but Dorothea pushes her away.

"It's no good," Dorothea says again, tight lipped. "Please. We have work to do. This is our 'foreign field.'"

They check their armbands and enter the tent together. The usual rotting smell engulfs them. The sultry night heat it seems stationary, waiting for orders to move. The twins tend to the patients, calming them, redressing wounds, speaking in soft voices. Some call out to them, "*Aidez-nous, où sont les anges, les anges . . .*"

Les anges. The angels. When the soldiers return to the front, that is the name they give to the two identical nurses who treated them in the field hospital, and as in a fairy story, by now the story has spread, and the twins' double image has been exaggerated and embellished so that new arrivals call for *les anges* and believe they are lucky. It is felt that there is something superstitious in the twins' mysterious duality. With their pale kerchiefs veiling their unfathomable faces, they remind the soldiers of the Virgin Mary, that image of female virtue to whom they used to pray as little boys during Sunday Mass in their village churches before the war. How much better for them is this, to be exposed to the remote caresses of *les anges* rather than be reminded of *les autres,* the girls back home with moist lips and warm thighs, who would inflame them with desire and drive them to madness? Even the directrice, who has no truck with things spiritual, understands the usefulness of the twins' sexless power, and she excuses them from some of the more quotidian tasks her nurses must undertake, such as washing the floor and cleaning out the latrines.

The smell in the tent is sickening. Iris almost chokes over one of the patients; Dorothea brings out of her pocket a lavender bag and hands it to her sister, who quickly puts it to her nose.

"How wonderful. I thought we couldn't get them anymore."

"While you were playing at romance with Maurice, I got a small supply from an English nurse at the Union."

Iris ignores her sister's sarcasm. She doesn't care anymore. The present is all that matters, all that will ever matter now. She is at the meeting of two eternities. She can see Maurice in the faces of the soldiers as they look up trustingly at her. Radiant with sudden happiness, she waves the bag of lavender in the air and beams down at them.

"It's all right, *je suis ici*. I'm here." She goes along the row of beds, wiping a brow, stroking a hand. Her warmth transmits to the wounded men, and they turn and move their broken bodies toward her. Dorothea follows her with water on sponges for those who can still feel thirst.

"*Combien de temps, mes anges?*" one soldier asks. How long? Iris glances at Dorothea. The boy will be dead before the night is over. She holds up five fingers.

"*Peut-être cinq heures,*" Dorothea tells him. The soldier grins at her. "*Merci,*" he mumbles. "*Je l'attend.*" He raises his burned fingers to his eyes and closes them, then folds his hands over his chest. He has laid out his own body for death.

The twins look at him in admiration.

" 'The lone couch of everlasting sleep,' " Dorothea murmurs. She brings another lavender bag from her pocket and passes it gently over his still form. The faintest hint of a smile touches his lips.

As the two nurses continue their rounds, heralded by the scent of lavender, the soldiers stir. As they catch a delicious whiff of their country's beloved plant, they call out, demanding it for themselves. "*Ici! Pour moi! La lavande! Ici!*"

Dorothea and Iris laugh and tear open the lavender bags, sprinkling the dried flower heads with abandon all about the beds and floor of the tent, as though sowing seeds. Suddenly the tent is transformed into a field of purple scented blooms. The fresh herbal smell pervades the men's starved senses. The twins' feet skid in the mixture of lavender and straw, and they kick it up into the air, holding hands like farmers' daughters doing a country jig. The soldiers who are well enough sit up in their beds, clapping and cheering. One of the young poilus starts singing.

Auprès de ma blonde,
Qu'il fait bon, fait bon, fait bon,
Auprès de ma blonde, Qu'il fait bon dormir!

Others pick up the song, their reedy, childlike voices out of tune but vibrant with forgotten joy: *How sweet it is to sleep next to my fair one!* The twins clap along with them, joining in the simple ditty. "*Qu'il fait bon dormir!*"

The directrice appears, looking annoyed. "What is all this noise?"

The twins freeze. "*Pardonnez-nous.* It was the lavender," Dorothea says, trying to catch her breath. The directrice looks down at the floor and inhales.

"Mmmm." Even she is momentarily seduced by the associations aroused by the pungent aroma. "Oh, this takes me back . . . ," she begins, with an unexpectedly youthful smile.

A soldier starts coughing up a trough of phlegm. She breaks off, her expression hardening. "Back to work," she orders the twins. "And sweep up this stuff. It's bad for their lungs."

The twins continue checking on their patients. On their way back to find brooms for the floor, they pass the soldier who has not moved from his position with closed eyes and hands clasped across his tattered uniform. "*Les anges,*" he whispers again, as though sensing their scented presence.

"I think he likes it," Iris says. "You must get some more lavender. If it's bad for the lungs, it's good for the soul."

"It's not the lavender he likes; it's you."

"Us," Iris corrects her automatically. "That was fun there with the lavender, wasn't it?"

"If George could have seen us."

"Or Adeline."

The shared moment does not last. They move to opposite ends of the tent and begin sweeping up the lavender. The heady perfume is beginning to fade, but one of the soldiers still hums the song quietly to himself, *"Auprès de ma blonde, / Qu'il fait bon dormir . . . ,"* until he, too, falls silent and the distant mortars can once more be heard, contributing their relentless obbligato to the familiar night sounds of the hospital.

Chapter 23

My dear Mother,

Thanks for your latest package of letters. I loved hearing from little Tommy. He's growing up fast. I'd better get back before he starts beating me at chess. Tell him there's a huge new bomb called Big Bertha that the Germans are aiming on Paris, and it's more powerful than anything he could possibly imagine. Its range is something like seventy-five miles. That's a longer distance than from Madison to Atlanta! Tommy would love it! Parisians are pasting paper over their windows to deflect the blast — but guess what? They cut out the paper in patterns to make it look prettier! Typical French!

We were given leave to go to Paris for the Fourth of July celebrations. I've never seen anything like it. The whole of Paris had become American. Flags, music, marchers, flowers, all to salute our boys' arrival here. The joy and relief on the Parisians' faces made one want to weep. Thank goodness we finally did the right thing. It took long enough. There was a big party at the Union, and lots of friends showed up. I even danced — me, can you believe it? All right, we were drunk, but we were also letting off steam after all the pent-up strain of these last months. I don't remember feeling like that since my first year in college.

So you see, we'll get through this somehow, and don't let the neighbors tell you otherwise. They are just living in the past and can't see further than Sherman. Sure, I fly over French towns that are burned to the ground just as Atlanta was, but now with American forces taking over, the Boche is definitely on the run. I believe people are really resilient and will rebuild. Remember how we threw out a jasmine that had been smashed to death by a fallen rock, and then we found it two weeks later with fresh green leaves sprouting from its stem? Boy, didn't we feel bad about giving up on that plant!

Speaking of the future, you have asked me if I'm thinking about what I want to do when the war is over. Since they say it's the war to end all wars, the one thing I know is that I don't intend ever to sign up for combat again! I know several fellows who are keeping journals, and that's one way of staying sane and being productive at the same time. But I don't trust myself at this point to write anything that would ever get published. Seeger's stuff in the *New York Sun* may have impressed people, but it was really a lot of hot air. I expect you'll say I'm just jealous. And you're right, as always, Mother dear.

My ambition is that sometime I'll find something about my experiences here that I can write about honestly, with some perspective, and I'm sure that the only way to do that is to come home to Georgia. There'll be nothing in Europe to keep me here, believe me. If I never see another boarded-up café saying "Closed indefinitely," that'll please me mightily. And New York doesn't look that inviting, either. Harry and I talk about this a great deal. He's got himself engaged, the fool, to some pretty thing without a brain, but he is not sure about that—he's not sure about anything. People are doing stupid damn things all over the place these days. Harry seems really blue about the idea of returning to New York after the war. He hated his time there before, and now he's really worried about Life after Spads and whether he can afford to provide properly for Isabel.

I have to admit that's on my mind, too. If one wanted to marry a girl, it would be an enormous responsibility, particularly if she's rich. And all the girls over here seem to be rich. I guess that's why they can afford to come to France and work as volunteers. What's a poor writer to do? It's odd that we should think of such things when bombs are going off all around us, but somehow emotions get blown up (so to speak) here. We find ourselves longing for things we never knew we wanted. And we want them in a hurry. In the words of an obscure German (sic!), "Life is a fight with Fate."

I tell you, Mother, Madison begins to look mighty good from here. I think of the glorious camellias on the back veranda, Granddaddy's whisky, your corn bread. I even yearn for your flu remedy—raw egg with sugar and a teaspoon of rum, three times a day. That would cure me of everything right now!

But I ramble. The air has a Southern feel to it tonight. Tomorrow they say it will be clear. That means we should get some action.

Much love to all, and especially to you,
Maurice

Chapter 24

B<small>UT HE SAID</small> it was clean."

Iris is alone in the twins' cubicle next to the hospital tent. She is sitting on the bed, her eyes swollen with weeping. In her hands is Thoreau's book.

"Maurice said flying was clean. Don't you remember? He lied." She repeats the phrase over and over as she fiercely, and with intense deliberation, tears up page after page of the book. The process is arduous. The pages are thick, and there are a great many of them. After destroying several handfuls of paper, she seizes the binding and, like a dog with a bone, begins to shake it violently. She tries several times to rip up the brown cover with its gilded letters. She pulls at the cloth, but it will not give. She throws it down, then picks it up again and clutches it to her chest.

"He lied."

Friends from Maurice's squadron have told the twins what happened. Maurice was in a dogfight over a heavily manned region in the western Argonne, not far from Verdun, and he took a round straight on, a direct hit into the cockpit. His German opponent had come racing through a cloud from behind and executed a brilliant maneuver to surprise the American. The subsequent crash produced one of the most devastating sights witnesses had ever seen. When they ran to the smoking ruins of the plane, they found a burning mass of steel so mangled that they could not identify the pilot until later, when a comrade from the base recognized Maurice's wristwatch.

Long after the wreckage of the plane was brought in, the image of the charred metal continued to burn in Iris's mind. Now she doesn't see Maurice at all. However desperately she tries, she can't summon him up in her imagination. His grave face, his olive skin, his tender voice, his ardent touch, are all crushed together in a heap of compacted steel, so there is nothing left for her to picture, other than a scorched cemetery in a French field. She wants to go there at once, to place a flower on the wreckage, but of course that is impossible.

"The war in the air? *'A glorious thing'*?" She reproachfully shakes the book again, as if it has made the error. Torn pages cover the floor, some crumpled, some ripped into tiny pieces, some almost undamaged. She looks at the desecration. "It's my fault," she declares to herself. "Somehow, I helped him to his death. I weakened his resolve, made him care, and that was fatal. You must never care. They all say that." She picks up a sheet of paper from the book and neatly tears it into strips. "No, it's his fault," she argues aloud. "Not mine. He became attached. Terrible mistake. Inviting disaster. How could we have let it happen?"

She throws herself on her cot and pushes her face hard into the pillow as though burying it deep in the ground.

"Iris!"

Dorothea comes into the cubicle and runs to her sister. "Iris, you must stop this. The new directrice is about to arrive. We are needed still. Remember that. There are our poilus out there who need you, darling."

She strokes Iris's rigid back, whispering words of comfort. "You

are needed, Iris. You are precious here; we cannot do without you."
She pauses. "*I* cannot do without you."

At this, Iris sits up. Her cheeks are reddened by the abrasive texture of the pillow.

"It was my fault," she concludes. "It was my fault. He once said
I was like all the Southern girls he knew, overprotected and dependent. We laughed. It was so funny! I was just learning to be with
him on my own, as Iris. He was so proud of me. I let him down."

"Please, darling. There is no blame. Except of course for those
who continue to keep this horrible war going." Dorothea holds Iris's
shoulders and looks deep into her eyes. "We are still here," she tells
her sister. "You and I, we must continue on together. Remember, you
and I are still together."

Iris stares at her. "You and I," she repeats vaguely. "Yes, that's true.
How fortunate we are. We have each other." She gives a confused
glance at the mutilated book cover, then lifts it up and shows it to
Dorothea. "I'm sorry," she says. "It was the first edition. I never got
to give it to him. He didn't even know I had sent for it." She drops
the book on the floor. "That's good, isn't it?" she implores. "So he
wasn't disappointed?"

She falls back on the cot and closes her eyes. She seems to be going
to sleep. "I was just learning to be Iris," she whispers. "He was showing me the way to be myself. It was so—freeing. I'd never felt like
that, to be me and yet not me—outside myself, outside you, outside
both of us. Just in a safe place with him. When I looked at him, I
saw who I was for the first time. He showed me who I was. It was so
funny, really!" She begins to laugh but chokes with tears instead.

Dorothea shakes her violently. "Iris. Please. We must go. We're on
duty. Maurice has gone."

Iris pulls herself up again. She gazes at her twin sister, so tall and
beautiful against the backdrop of stained canvas and rusting tent

poles. She sees herself, too, the mirror image. That is my face, my body, my hair, my lips, my eyes, she says to herself, counting off the items of the identical reflection like an inventory. All present and correct. Dorothea is also me. How strong she is. How lovely. When one falters, the other stands firm.

"Maurice has gone," she repeats. "Maurice has gone." She looks down at her hands and then to the floor. "Look at the book," she exclaims. "Did I really do that?" She looks at Dorothea nervously. "You don't care—about the book, I mean?" she asks.

Dorothea takes Iris's face in her hands and kisses her. "I don't care about the book," she responds. "All I care about is you."

Iris nuzzles her head in her sister's shoulder. "I think you will save me," she says.

"We shall save each other," Dorothea replies. "We always have, and we always will. We'll make a daisy chain." She pauses. "Remember?" Iris nods and smiles serenely. "Even without daisies," Dorothea goes on. "Now go and see to your patients."

She watches as her sister, obedient, disappears into the hospital tent. After Iris has gone, she brings out a letter from her apron pocket and with a sigh of resignation, begins to read.

Dearest Dorothea,

I'm sorry to be writing you some Bad News, but I have recently had to spend a little time in the Hospital. Nothing serious, I assure you. Just a little problem with my interior workings, the usual Penance we Women have to endure from time to time. But I had the most splendid care, the Nurses were so helpful, & I had several Guests who brought food and wine, & Miss Goddard (our wonderful mathematics teacher, now retired, like me) even brought her little Suzette to cheer me up. As you know, I do not care for Dogs, but Suzette is quite an unusual creature, and one can't help liking her.

Sadly, I fear other aspects of the School are less rosy. A new Headmistress has been installed, replacing the incomparable Miss Allington. Her name is Miss Fortenbaugh, and so far her performance has been, let us say, disappointing. I fear she seems unimpressed by some of the Traditions so treasured by Miss Allington and myself. For some reason I was not consulted about the Appointment, a Mistake that naturally I will overlook. But it was quite a Shock when I received notification of Miss Fortenbaugh's arrival, and I had to take several medical tinctures prescribed by Dr. Elsinore before I felt strong enough to pen a Note to her, introducing myself and offering my Services. So far, I have not received a Reply.

I was so sorry to hear about Rheims. I vaguely recall the film you mention, and your Description is, of course, a thousand times worse. I can see that the Fate of these great Monuments has affected you more deeply even than your Work with the wounded. That shows your sensitivity to our Higher Calling, Dorothea.

Dorothea throws the letter away from her with a groan and starts pacing the little hut back and forth, back and forth, her arms crossed in front of her chest. Then she sighs and picks up the letter again.

Speaking of Verse, it has been a great Disappointment to me that so far you have failed to pick up your Pen again, in spite of the newly acquired Insights into the Human Spirit that you have gained over there. After much earnest Cogitation, I recently presented to your Brother a modest Proposal that perhaps will encourage you to do so. However, I feel that in the interests of Discretion I should let Mr. Crosby be the one to impart the exciting News. Let it merely be said that you may find yourself after all a Published Poet!

On that inspiring note, I send you my Fervent Prayers.

Adeline Wetherall

She's talking of publishing our work, Dorothea says to herself. How absurd. This must be stopped. She starts to go find Iris to tell her and then holds back. She must protect Iris now, more than she has ever protected her. This silly idea of Adeline Wetherall's might make her sister laugh, but she fears that at this moment it would more likely make her weep.

Dorothea picks up the torn chunks of the Thoreau book and puts them in a large paper bag. The broken cover goes in separately, its gilded lettering gleaming in the candlelight. She takes Adeline's letter and puts it to the candle, letting the flame curl the paper into ashes. Then she scrapes up the ashes and puts them in the bag. Folding over the top of the bag, she walks to a large disposal bin outside the tent. As she opens the lid, the smell of rotting gauze and stale blood fills her nostrils. A fitting grave. Making a face, she throws the paper bag with its sad remains into the bin and turns away.

Chapter 25

Dearest Brother,

Thank you for all the gifts and books you have sent us. I cannot tell you what a difference they make in the long nights here when we cannot sleep and are too weary to talk to each other. As usual we have been very busy at the hospital, as the soldiers come and go in this seemingly endless war.

I am sorry to have to tell you that Iris has received terrible tidings. She had become friendly with a young airman named Maurice Aronsohn. He was a Harvard man, in Harry Forrester's class; perhaps you remember his name. Aronsohn was shot down and killed a week ago, and Iris has taken it very badly. Of course, everyone had warned us that we should not make attachments and that any romantic liaison conceived in these uncertain times would almost certainly lead to sorrow, but Iris chose to close her ears to this excellent advice, and now she is suffering the tragic consequences.

I was not an intimate of Maurice's, but I understood Iris's attraction to him. He was one of those people I think of as scholar-soldiers, like that teacher from Maine who joined the Union army and was so courageous at Gettysburg. (What was his name? I fear I forget. It is difficult these days to remember anything that happened more than a few hours ago.) We have met similar young men here, most of them English, who left Oxford and Cambridge at the beginning of the war to come to France, abandoning their studies for the cause, and who are now using their literary gifts to immortalize this very mortal conflict. Some of their works get printed up and passed around to us; others are posted in the Union reading room in Paris; still others are published in newspapers that perhaps you have seen. Maurice gave Iris several of his (unpublished) poems, and they were of as high a standard as any of those that I have read, but I suspect they would not mean a great deal to you, so I shall refrain from forwarding any of them on to you.

My own work has no place here among these anguished documents, so Adeline Wetherall's kind proposal to publish any of it seems not only inappropriate but insulting. Please do not continue with this project. It would only be an embarrassment to me—and no doubt to the family, too. Perhaps one day I shall be able to return to poetry, but it seems now a very remote possibility. "One day" sounds to me a perfectly futile expression. "One day" is only today, this day, this life. There is no future that I can see.

My concern must be, of course, for Iris, whose fragile emotional state has been badly damaged by this recent loss. I'm not confident that you would recognize her, George, she is so thin and pale and her temper so frayed and highly strung. How different she is from that easygoing and carefree sister you used to love to go riding with in Far Hills! It used to be me whom you would castigate for being irritable and self-absorbed. Now it is Iris we must watch as she sits in feverish silence on her bed and reads poems from her dead aviator. It is as though we both wear blinkers now, she and I, like overwrought racehorses, trying to get to the finish line without stumbling into each other and breaking limbs or bones irreparably.

I apologize for this rather gloomy letter, particularly when I know you and Lavinia must be in the final preparations for the arrival of the baby. From where I walk in these poppy fields of death, the notion of birth seems nothing but a sad anachronism, I'm afraid, but I wish for you that it becomes your greatest joy.

With very much affection, dearest Brother,
Dorothea

Chapter 26

THIS MORNING, THERE IS a different atmosphere in the hospital. The old directrice has left. She has been sent home to Lille for an indefinite leave. She will not return.

By the middle of August, Dorothea and Iris had begun to notice that the directrice's normally ruddy face had taken on an alarming pallor. Her temper was even shorter than usual. She forgot instructions she had given only minutes before. One particularly hot day, when sweat rolled down the nurses' cheeks and it seemed nothing could be done fast enough, the directrice suddenly abandoned her station and walked out of the hospital tent. She had never done this before.

"Perhaps she has the grippe," Iris whispered to Dorothea. Rumors of a flu epidemic had reached the hospital, and the nurses were being alerted to a very different kind of enemy, one that had already accounted for a frightening number of fatalities, among both civilians and fighting men.

Dorothea shook her head. "I don't think it's that," she said. "She doesn't seem to have a fever. But something is terribly wrong."

The directrice returned to work, but the atmosphere was so strained that even the patients began to complain.

"What's going on? *Vite, ma foi!*"

"I didn't get my medicine this morning."

"*Elle est folle aujourd'hui!*"

"I need the directrice! *Qu'est-ce qui arrive?*"

Dorothea and Iris did their best to fill in for their embattled leader, but late one afternoon, Dorothea heard a terrible cry emanating from the directrice's private quarters. She ran into the usually off-limits cubicle to find the directrice lying on the floor, beating the dusty sand with her hands. "I cannot do it," she screamed. "I cannot make my body whole again. I, the healer, cannot do it now. I am lost. *Je suis perdue.*"

Dorothea was shocked to see the directrice so overtaken by her demons. She tried to lift her up onto the cot, but the two almost came to blows over the maneuver. The directrice was a big, heavy woman and resisted the younger woman's attempts to aid her. "Leave me alone," she ordered. "I don't need your help. Leave me. Leave me." The directrice kept referring to the incident with the lavender, somehow connecting it to her own mental decline. "I have lost myself," she kept saying in a hoarse voice. "I was once fifteen years old. *Je suis perdue.*"

Dorothea tried to calm her, but to no avail. "I must get away from here," the directrice told her. "I am no use to you anymore. *Je vous en prie,* get rid of me."

A month later, on a warm September morning, Iris and Dorothea watch in sorrow as two orderlies help the directrice to a waiting ambulance. She has at last become one of those she has tended for so long, a casualty of war.

"What can we do without her?" Iris asks. "We depend on her. She is the only one here with the skills to run this place. Dorothea, how can we possibly go on here without her?"

Iris is angry at the directrice's abandonment of them. She is afraid to be without the older woman's strength and guidance. She was too stern to be a mother, but she provided the attention and care of a mother, and now she was walking away from them. There is also another reason for her anxiety. If the directrice, their sturdy overseer, has ultimately been driven to despair by the nightmare in which they are living, how can they possibly survive it? Iris sees in the directrice's departure another death, another loss. How much more can they stand?

"We'll be all right," Dorothea responds. For her, the abdication of the directrice is measured by more complex considerations. The directrice was the twins' first witness. She had validated their presence, stamped their *cartes d'identité*, so to speak, as participants in the war. She was the one person who could confirm that they had played their part from the beginning without flinching. Their self-doubt coming into the war, their fear of being judged as dilettantes, passive onlookers, or thrill seekers, had been effectively eradicated by their grueling work at the hospital under the directrice's iron rule. The tough, demanding, unsentimental Frenchwoman bequeathed to them their legitimacy and, perhaps more important, kept them together. Now she has gone, and the twins must reestablish their bona fides within themselves, alone.

"She inspired us," Iris says. "She made us work."

"Only the directrice knew what we did," Dorothea says in agreement, " — that we could do our job."

"She was our nurse, our governess," Iris wails. "She told us what to do."

"We'll have to grow up," Dorothea says. "We'll have to do things ourselves."

"Grow up?" Iris looks in mock horror at her sister. "But I don't want to grow up. I liked being told what to do. She taught us everything!"

"She didn't teach us table manners. Or how to ride horses. Or understand poetry."

"Completely useless things. She taught us what we needed to know here."

"And now it's up to us, Iris."

"Yes, I suppose it is." Iris looks at her sister. "Soon there'll be nobody left," she says quietly. "Just us."

She turns over the battered body of a new arrival. His lips are clamped together with dried blood; he talks with his eyes instead, weeping tears that glint like glass on his swollen, cracked lids. Iris bends over him with exceptional attention. In the face of every soldier she is assigned to now, she looks for the face of Maurice. Although it is impossible for her to conjure him in her own mind, she examines each patient with meticulous care, in case she sees a likeness that might reawaken him for her and thus make her feel again the grinding hunger of loss.

"I'm here, darling." Dorothea knows what Iris is doing and lets her go through the process without attempting to divert her. There is almost no chance that any of the poor French conscripts who stumble into the tent could remotely resemble Iris's American, and Dorothea understands that it seems to give her sister some paradoxical satisfaction that, however often she repeats the performance, none of the poilus bears any similarity to the person for whom she so faithfully searches.

Dorothea glances at her sister across the soldier's bed. Iris's face is tired, the luminosity of her skin faded to parchment, her warm mouth framed in tense lines. Dorothea knows she herself looks just as worn and fractured. But Iris's deep brown eyes convey a kind of somber glow that reflects a flame within. Do Dorothea's own eyes burn as steadfastly?

"I'll get some more gauze," she says in a matter-of-fact voice. Iris touches her sister's hand. Their fingers intertwine for a brief moment before separating.

"You see, we don't need a governess anymore."

Iris laughs. "If you say so." She shakes her head. "But I'll miss her."

"I shall, too." Dorothea briskly smooths down her apron. "What would she say to us now?"

"*'Courage'*?"

"Yes. *Courage.*"

THE NEW DIRECTRICE, Sister Waddington, is English. It is a temporary appointment. She has been sent from a neighboring hospital to cover for her predecessor until the French Red Cross can find a permanent replacement. She has arrived with a new nurse, Diana Naylor, who is also English.

"This is the Honorable Diana Naylor," says Sister Waddington, introducing her to the twins with that special emphasis on the title that is the sure indication of a snob.

Diana looks disgustedly at Sister Waddington. "Oh, for heaven's sake," she says. Dorothea laughs. She and Iris like her immediately.

When the English matron has gone, Diana turns toward them excitedly. "You're so lucky," she exclaims. The young Englishwoman is looking admiringly at the twins' clothes. By this time, the Americans have mostly abandoned their Red Cross uniforms and wear loose-fitting smocks and aprons, with kerchiefs on their heads of various faded colors, which they have been sent or have purchased in the village. Diana explains that the British are famous for their rigidity about uniforms. Their nurses must wear outfits of stiff gray flannel, with no decoration or extra flourishes allowed, on pain of a serious "ticking off" from their matron.

"I once wore a scarf with a tiny yellow stripe in it to go into Sois-sons," she tells them, "and Matron passed by in a car. The next day, she brought me into her office, and said, 'Miss Naylor, I believe I saw something rather odd round your neck last evening.' I explained that it was a scarf. She said, 'Miss Naylor, I greatly dislike my girls beat-ing about the bush. You are beating about the bush. Miss Naylor, it was not *just* a scarf.' So I had to admit it had a yellow stripe in it, and she said, 'If I catch you in that . . . thing again I shall have to severely discipline you.'"

The twins laugh.

"Well, while you're here, you can wear whatever you like," Dorothea consoles her. "Our French directrice always looked the other way. I think she thought a little color cheered up the patients."

"I wish I could," Diana says doubtfully. "Sister Waddington looks a bit of a wet blanket to me."

Dorothea finds a pink scarf that Isabel once gave her, and Diana wears it on her rounds. Sister Waddington eyes it but says nothing. Diana then hitches up her skirt a little, again inspired by the twins, whose ankles are now often visible, to the delight of the soldiers (another concession from their old directrice, whose French soul was pragmatic on such issues). Sister Waddington again says nothing. But when Diana cuts off most of her long hair, as the twins have done, Sister Waddington draws the line.

"I don't know what you're playing at, Nurse Naylor," she says to her, "but I will not allow bobbed hair or short skirts in my hospital, whoever you are." She stares meaningfully at her victim, then adds darkly, "We're not American, you know."

One of Diana's first patients is a badly wounded soldier whose body is racked with small seizures. She tries to comfort him as he moans and twitches.

"I think it's shell shock," Iris comments, coming to assist her.

"He reminds me of a golden retriever at home called Holly," Diana tells Iris as they change his dressings. "He always has terrible dreams."

"We had one like that, too," Iris replies. "He was one of George's hunting dogs, and he would twitch and whimper just like this, obviously dreaming of chasing a rabbit. I used to have to wake him up to stop his nightmares."

They exchange a sympathetic glance. There is no point waking up this poor, trembling creature on the cot in front of them. He is already awake. The two girls sigh and continue their tasks.

Diana is a good nurse, but her French is poor and she often struggles with the soldiers' delirious ramblings.

" '*Je demande ma mère,*' " she quotes to the twins as they work on their rounds. "He's asking for his mother, isn't he?"

"They always ask for their mother," Dorothea explains.

One of Diana's patients is very young, probably not more than seventeen. Half his face has been shot off, leaving a dark red, brackish crater, one eye that can still see, and a mouth that is little more than a hole through which liquid food is painfully and unsuccessfully passed. His head has been shaved; infection has swollen his brow to such an extent that dressings slide over the constantly oozing pus and have to be reapplied almost hourly. The rest of his body is beautiful — slim, graceful limbs, a marvelously sculpted torso — and miraculously unmarked.

"Look at him," Diana says to Iris as she is passing with a roll of soiled bandages. "He's so beautiful."

"Michelangelo," Iris murmurs, stopping to admire the boy's body.

"Vandalized Michelangelo," Diana adds. "God, how unfair it is." Her voice begins to break.

"Don't." Iris puts a hand on the English nurse's arm.

Diana nods. "Sorry."

They smile at each other, and Iris moves on down the tent.

"She's a good friend," Diana informs Michelangelo. "She stopped me making a fool of myself just now."

The poilu begins to speak through black, cracked lips. He talks fast, in a thin, feverish whisper that Diana cannot understand. *"Je suis, j'étais, je suis, j'espère . . . ,"* he mutters. *"Priez pour moi, où sont les anges, les anges . . . Voilà, les barbelés sont pas coupés!"* She presses a wet compress on his chest to cool his fever. *"Les anges,"* he says. *"Vite, pour moi, je suis, j'étais . . . perdu . . . Les anges, LES ANGES . . ."* His voice rises in agitation. Diana looks down the tent.

"What is he saying?" she calls out frantically. "Where are *les anges*? Does he think he's in church?"

Iris runs to the bed. "Don't worry," she says hurriedly to Diana. "He's saying the usual things—'they haven't cut the barbed wire,' 'I feel lost,' you know the sort of thing." Iris takes the boy's hand. *"Regardez-moi,"* she says in a commanding voice. *"Ouvrez les yeux.* Open your eyes. *Nous sommes ici. Voilà."* Dorothea appears at the other side of the bed, pushing Diana out of the way. She takes his other hand.

The boy opens his working eye. It is an astonishing deep blue, with green lights in it. He looks up and sees the twins, one on each side of him. The jeweled eye widens as though in a smile. *"Voilà,"* he croaks. His body stills. *"Voilà."* The eye closes, and he falls silent.

"Quelle beauté," Dorothea says, lifting up his hand and placing it on his chest. Iris rests his other hand over it. The poilu lies in peace, carved in stone like a medieval saint. "I think he may sleep for a while now."

Diana has been watching Iris and Dorothea in awe. "Angels," she says. "You are *les anges*. I might have guessed. I've heard people talk about you. Thanks."

The twins say nothing and return to their tasks. Sister Waddington, who has observed this scene, orders them over and informs them that in her hospital, nurses don't double up on duties. It is against the rules. Moreover, it is a clear case of wasted personnel. She says she trusts that while she is in charge here, the Misses Crosby will remember that.

"Silly old boot," Diana comments on hearing this chastisement. "She's no *ange,* that's one thing we can safely tell the soldiers. By the way, I hope you'll come to Paris with me on your leave next weekend. I've been invited to a first-rate party and I'd love you to come with me."

Later, in their cubicle, Iris brings out a piece of paper from her pocket. It is crumpled from much folding. She smooths it out and says, "I want to read this to you, Dorothea."

Dorothea shakes her head. "I don't want any more words," she says. "Words are very unreliable these days."

"It's Wilfred Owen," Iris persists. "Maurice wrote it down for me and gave it to me. I think you should hear it." She begins to read, her voice dry and emotionless.

What passing-bells for these who die as cattle?
Only the monstrous anger of the guns.
Only the stuttering rifles' rapid rattle . . .

Dorothea suddenly runs to her sister and seizes the paper from her hand. "Stop it!" she shouts. "Stop it! I don't want to hear it!"

Iris stares at her sister and makes a movement toward the paper as though she is afraid Dorothea will destroy it.

"I'm sorry," Dorothea says in a quieter voice. She sits down on the bed, still holding the paper. "It's good, I'm sure. But you shouldn't be reading this sort of thing. It doesn't help, you know. It just makes things worse." She pauses. "Is he dead yet?"

"Owen? I expect so." Iris looks at the piece of paper for a moment, then crumples it into a small ball and throws it into a wastebasket.

"We seem to spend a damned amount of time throwing letters and papers away. Best place for them, I suppose."

Dorothea raises her eyebrows but says nothing.

Iris turns to her sister and takes a deep breath. "There. I think we should go to Diana's party," she declares in a cheerful voice.

"Good girl, Iris," Dorothea says approvingly. "I think so, too. I suspect it will be full of her grand English friends."

"Diana's fun, isn't she?"

Dorothea shrugs. "I don't think she's going to be here long."

Iris looks at her and laughs. "Nobody is," she says lightly.

There is a small silence. A few late summer crickets chatter in the darkness. Then a sudden low wail of panic floats out from the ward. Another journey to the barbed wire. Another push over the top. Another hallucination. More voices pick up the sound, and the wailing becomes a lamentation. This night, the soldiers seem possessed. The twins quickly pick up candles and enter the tent, the flickering light casting uneasy shadows on the stained canvas walls. They bend over the beds, one after another, with their kerchiefs falling over their shoulders, two veiled sisters of consolation standing watch over the souls of the dead.

Chapter 27

HARRY SITS IN HIS HUT. He has shorts on and a towel around his neck. He has been running and is panting slightly. Beads of sweat rim his brow. He rubs his hair with his towel, making it stand up, prickly like a field of cornstalks. He picks up a letter from his bunk and flips it between his fingers. I've had so many letters here, he thinks. More than I've ever had before. From Everett, from his mother, from college friends, from old teammates, some now dead. Gone, like the letters. He hasn't kept any. What is the point? Who will be interested? People don't like being reminded of unpleasant things. They'd rather forget. They want to move on. Like Isabel. He unfolds the letter and reads it slowly.

"I know you'll understand, darling," Isabel writes. "I don't want to wait. Who knows when this horrid war will end? Charlie wants us to get married right away, and we'll have a big party back in Philadelphia when we get home. Of course, you'll come!"

He won't keep this one, either. Oddly, he feels little regret. He is not surprised that Isabel wanted more than he could offer. She saw through him. Good for her. And she was in a hurry. Fair enough. He understands her feeling of urgency. Everyone feels that way these days. It won't be easy to break the news, however. She's made him look something of a fool. He had told quite a few people about their engagement. It made him feel good, on the right track. He was pleased he had managed to get even that far with her. She was the closest any girl had ever come to capturing his interest. He liked her slender body, her grace of movement. Dancing, she looked quite spectacular. But she was an expensive proposition — that was obvious. How could he have given her what she wanted? He could not have come close to satisfying her demands. "But darling, I *must* have a swimming pool." "I have to have a horse." "*Everyone* goes to Newport in the summer." He could hear her high-wire voice now. It was impossible right from the start.

Would it always be impossible? Would he ever find a way to marry someone? He had liked Isabel more than most, but even she fell short. Quite apart from her rich background, she was too fast. All that flirtatiousness, that suffocating attention. Frankly, he preferred the coolness of the Crosby twins. Maurice had it right, as usual. Lucky Maurice. Lucky in more ways than one.

Harry crumples the letter up into a ball and tosses it over his shoulder with a shrug of relief. He turns around automatically to see if it fell close to its intended target, the wastepaper basket. It has landed right in it. "All right!" he exclaims. Not lost his touch in that department, at any rate. Immediately above the basket, on the wall, hang his skates. Harry rests his eyes on them, then gets up and examines them, feeling the blades, testing the laces, stroking the scarred leather boots. He won't be here this winter when the pond near the airfield ices over, as it did last December. The war will be over by then. He is sure of it. Everyone is sure of it.

Harry leaves his hut and walks toward the airfield, where a few Spads and Libertys are parked. Instead of giving the impression of dangerous fighting machines, they look like toys — as light and dainty as baby carriages with their spoked wheels lined up neatly. Only the painted wood of their wings, chipped and blackened by gunfire, gives the lie to their artless pose. Perhaps they are toys,

Harry says to himself, and I am just a child asking to be allowed to play with them some more. He has read that many people regard aviators as schoolboys who have never grown up, flying blithely through the air like Peter Pan. Yet we kill the Boche, Harry would argue. Who else is going to do it, if not us? Don't we want to score? Don't we want to win?

The airfield is deserted. Most of the mechanics take days off now, instead of working around the clock as they used to. Harry misses the banter with the technicians who primed, nurtured, and cosseted the temperamental aircraft into action. Even after all this time, the planes remain perversely unreliable. Harry doesn't care. Their erratic behavior is part of the fun. The only thing he cares about is getting the Hun, and for this he has asked the mechanics to fix his guns more loosely on their mounts and to overload his ammunition, requests that are both illegal and dangerous.

He has no fear. Not in the air, that is. It's being grounded that makes him afraid — the ground, the dark, heavy ground that weighs on you, imprisoning you. It's on the ground that people ask you to do things, like earning money, going to parties, finding girls. Those are the difficult things, not combat in the air. He is afraid of his mother for always demanding too much of him. He is afraid of Everett because he can never live up to Everett's generosity. He was afraid of Isabel because he knew he could not fulfill her expectations. The world on the ground expects great things of Harry Forrester. He felt safe on the football field and on the ice rink, but he cannot go there anymore. That's over. He is on different ground now, where most people live. He kicks the stubble by the runway with his boot, as though somehow he can break through the earth's weight, its relentless pressure. It's the ground that pulls you down, sucks you in. What he craves is the release from gravity — that blessed never-never land he finds in the sky.

He starts nervously pacing up and down the runway. It's so damned unfair. Look at Lufbery, Luke, Rickenbacker. Lufbery and Luke are dead, but before they were killed they had flown many more missions than he. They have eighteen, twenty victories. He has only three. Not a chance to beat them now. He clenches his fists in frustration. As for Eddie—why hadn't Eddie invited him north to Château-Thierry earlier this summer? Why wasn't he in Gengoult now, attached to Eddie's "Hat in the Ring" Squadron? That's where the action is, where they go up in any weather, fog or rain, and blast the Boche out of the air and take them down with the skill of sharpshooters. Reckless? You bet! What sport! The more fighting, the more fun! How else would you win the title "ace of aces"?

The September offensive at Saint-Mihiel seems to have been decisive. General Pershing's troops seized 460 German guns and fifteen thousand prisoners with a cost of only seven thousand American casualties. The rest of the Allied forces moved into Cambrai and then started a new Meuse-Argonne push with huge losses but some major successes. This month the ground troops finally reached the Hindenburg Line, breaking it in several key places and convincing the German leaders that the war must come to an end.

As the news trickles in, Harry's friends listen to the radio and cheer at each new Allied triumph. Harry does not join in. No back-slapping for him. What is there to cheer about? While his colleagues in the squadron make plans for going home, Harry looks at them with disdain. Not for him the anticipation of war's end. He broods over the story of Wilbur White's brilliant performance during the Meuse offensive. Apparently White had been authorized to go home after becoming the 147th Pursuit Squadron's highest-scoring ace. But he decided to join one last patrol in his Spad. While engaging the enemy, he spotted a Fokker on the tail of a novice American pilot. Finding his own guns jammed, in a desperate move to save his young comrade, White intentionally drove head-on into the Fokker in a suicide collision and crashed to his death. One last patrol. It happened two days ago.

Harry leaves the airfield and goes back to his hut. He throws himself on his bunk and puts his arm over his face. The roster of the dead passes before his eyes. White, of course. There's Lufbery, who got his a long time ago, falling from his flaming Nieuport back in January while attempting to down a Boche north of Nancy. But he had achieved the coveted "ace of aces" with sixteen credited victories before he got killed. And David Putnam? Wrested the title off Lufbery with thirteen kills before going down a few weeks ago, deep inside German territory. He had only had the title for a short time, like Lufbery. So who's superstitious? Who cares? You get the title and go into the record books. What more could you ask? Before White, there was Frank Luke. The news of his death has only just reached Harry's squadron. He had become ace of aces with eighteen kills when his Spad was shot down by enemy fire. He fought the Boche on the ground till the end.

Now several of his comrades jockey for position. Harry compulsively goes over the list again. Gillet and Beaver are in the running. Kullberg is badly wounded, and Lambert was sent home with battle fatigue after crashing two Fokker biplanes. They have all equaled Luke's record and maybe will beat it. But Harry knows who the final ace of aces is going to be. Eddie. Eddie Rickenbacker. Eddie will win the most victories, and Harry Forrester will be nowhere. Harry Forrester will never wrest that title off Eddie, or anyone else, for that matter. The Allies may be winning the war, but he, Harry Forrester, has lost. A few more runs, goddamn it. He should have done more when he had the opportunity, when things were hot. A few more runs. And then, maybe at least ratchet up his score to something respectable.

He remembers with regret the legendary Boche Manfred von Richthofen, who died in a tough engagement with British Sopwith Camels, way back in April. The count isn't confirmed yet, but it is believed that his victories easily outnumber any of the Allies'. To have met this champion of the air in single combat! To have locked wings with that damned red triplane! Now, there would have been a dogfight!

But there is still an air war, Harry reassures himself. Lufbery and Luke have gone, but Eddie's still here. Gillet is still here. The competition is still alive. And there is still the Boche, lurking behind the clouds, waiting to be shot down. The war isn't over yet. Nothing has been signed. He knows that. Not yet. He can still fly his faithful Spad a few more missions.

He hears a roar from the mess room. Something's up. He looks outside. The night sky is crystal clear, without a cloud. His heart lifts. He hears engines starting up. Is it his imagination? The airfield is just as empty as it was earlier except for a colleague looking at the sky and smoking. The distant figure calls out to Harry, but Harry doesn't respond. That's no surprise. Harry is known as a loner. They know he's a great athlete, they admire his dashing exploits in the air, but he is not a club man and they leave him alone.

But something is up, all right. That night the squadron is told to be prepared. The weather forecast is excellent, and there are Germans in the vicinity. Harry doesn't think of sleeping. He pictures in his mind the air battles he has engaged in, revisiting them, judging them, correcting his performance. A feint here, a twist here, a spurt of acceleration there. He will do better this time.

The next morning, at six o'clock, a messenger comes to give him his instructions from headquarters. He is to take up a patrol at nine. They should be back by midday. Harry raises his fist in acknowledgment. Who said the war was coming to an end? He looks at himself in the mirror and smooths back his hair. His expression is self-contained, his eyes hard, his lips narrowed. His opponents on the field have often seen that look. It is the look of a student before an examination, a runner before a marathon, an archer before releasing the arrow. Harry has always had this gift of being able to focus, to concentrate exclusively on the immediate action. All the coaches and sportswriters said that about him. It set him apart on the playing field, and it sets him apart now.

He starts to put on his uniform with ritualistic care, slowly buttoning the buttons, lacing up the boots, and finally putting on the heavy black leather flying jacket that is so flattering to all the airmen. There is a price for such vanity. It is the only protection at a thousand feet against the freezing air—or an enemy bullet. He grabs at a chocolate bar on the table and starts to chew it. He walks out of the hut, tossing his leather helmet in his hands like a football. His breathing is deep and even. He waves to the rest of the men in his patrol. He checks the Spad, as he always does, wheels, rudder, wings, propeller, tail, guns, in preparation for flight. Saluting his comrades, he climbs into the cockpit and pulls his helmet and goggles over his head.

Engine roaring, the Spad gathers speed and swoops up, in an almost perpendicular lift, into the welcoming sky.

Chapter 28

"MAY WE TALK ABOUT home finally?" Dorothea asks her sister as they peek out of the tent at the late afternoon sun. It has been a beautiful day. While autumn in France is a gentle affair, not like the impetuous, flamelike landscape of New England that the twins once knew and loved, the golden light and long evening shadows cast over the tent remind them of their country in a way that nothing has done since they have been here.

"Home?" Iris makes a face.

"Well, other people are beginning to talk about it," Dorothea observes. "Haven't you noticed?"

The word "home" is on everybody's lips. In the hospital, at the Union in Paris, behind the lines, people are beginning to accept the fact that the war is finally coming to an end. The twins have been told the news about the Allied successes farther north, the big Meuse-Argonne offensives, and the failure of the Hindenburg Line. They have been assured that the generals are preparing to receive conciliatory communications from Ludendorff, and that President Wilson and Prince Max von Baden are having private conversations about conditions for peace.

The hospital is winding down. Most of the patients have been sent home—or to the morgue. There is no reason anymore to patch them up for further action in the trenches. The nurses' assignment now is to get them out of the hospital and back to their future, such as it is. The hospital aides are disposing of all the furniture and furnishings—amusing descriptions, as the twins point out, for the wretched wooden slats they called beds and the lice-ridden sheets they used as covering for the poilus.

"I shall miss the lice," Dorothea says, folding a threadbare blanket and putting it in a trunk. "They kept the soldiers company."

Iris laughs. "Clever little devils. Did you notice how they always stayed hidden inside the seams of the uniforms? You think you've laundered them out, and then *voilà*! There's a nasty little pile of black specks waving at you."

"Thank goodness we bobbed our hair before Sister Waddington came. Less for them to nest in."

Dorothea and Iris are awaiting their orders for departure. They walk up and down the tent, talking to the few patients who remain, taking their time over a dressing or rinsing out a basin. They scatter wet tea leaves on the floor before sweeping it, one of the many English tricks taught by Sister Waddington that make cleaning up easier. "If only we'd known about this earlier," Iris comments to Dorothea. "I hated that dust and dried mud flying around. I was constantly sneezing."

"Another household hint that we'll find invaluable when we get home," Dorothea remarks.

"That and the lavender," Iris adds. "I think that's what tipped the directrice over the edge."

"Mmm, the lavender. You see what memory can do," Dorothea says pointedly.

Iris stops her sweeping and leans on the broom. "Yes . . . It can catch you unawares," she reflects. "It can come at you in a thousand different ways, when you least expect it—by a smell of herbs, by the sound of a piano, by reading a poem . . ."

Dorothea darts a look at her. "Unless you are very careful," she declares.

"And that's not always possible, of course."

"No?" The question hangs in the air. "Anyway, keep sweeping. We have the whole floor to finish by tonight." Iris picks up her broom and sweeps energetically.

"How can lavender ever mean anything else to us?" Iris asks. "Even on Park Avenue?"

Dorothea harvests the dusty tea leaves into a heap. They look like a mound of dead beetles. She disposes of them tenderly in the incinerator.

"I once read that prisoners sometimes become attached to their cells and fear the world outside," she tells her sister. "I used to find that puzzling. I no longer do."

The change they notice most is the diminution of noise. Most of their time at the field hospital has been accompanied by an incessant din—of shelling, of mortar fusillades, of flapping canvas, of howling wind, of drumming rain, and of the relentless clamor of the wounded. At regular intervals, the earth under their feet would shake with a deep, thunderous vibration as bombs thudded down unnervingly close to their tent. They look down now at their peaceful shoes and are surprised at the stillness of the ground, a stillness that, oddly, seems more unnatural than the reverberation that kept up its deadly beat for so many of their days and nights.

Diana Naylor converses happily about going home. "My parents have this lovely house in Wiltshire," she tells the twins. "It's Georgian, with roses climbing up the walls, and a pond with swans, and an orchard with the most delicious peaches, and a vegetable garden where we grow cucumbers that win a prize at the local harvest festival every year."

The twins try to listen to her, but her words seem foreign. Roses?

Swans? Peaches? Cucumbers? They cannot summon up the images required to understand what she is saying. They have only one language now, and it belongs to their poilus.

"How do you think you'll get home?" Iris asks politely.

"I hope I'll meet my cousin when we get to Paris and I can get a lift back to England with her," Diana explains. "She's filthy rich and has all sorts of marvelous ideas of how to get us home—particularly since she has to transport Lambchop. That's her wolfhound. She was going to be at the party we went to, but she had to go and dine with some American generals."

Iris focuses on the young Englishwoman for a moment. "Wolfhound? Lambchop? I remember that dog. Wonderful dog."

"Absolutely. People always remember Lambchop."

"Is your cousin a duchess or something?" Dorothea asks.

"Well, sort of, yes, Lady Grenville. You may have read about her. She came over here as soon as the war started with some friends—and, of course, Lambchop. She was sent to some hospital near Belgium, where of course she hadn't the faintest notion about nursing, but she used to welcome the wounded soldiers when they came in from the trenches and get all their medical and personal information down on scraps of paper. At least she knew how to write French. She turned the whole thing into a garden party."

"We heard all about her," Iris says. "I remember that she insisted on dressing in full evening dress when the convoys arrived."

Diana laughs. "Of course. She'd put on her ball gown and tiara, even if it was nine o'clock in the morning, and make all her friends dress up, too. She said it cheered up the men."

They look around the dilapidated tent where so many sick men have passed through, trying to imagine such a bizarre and wonderful spectacle.

"The directrice would never have allowed it," Dorothea concludes.

"Anyway," Iris adds, "we left our tiaras at home." As she says that, she pauses and draws in her breath, as though hearing the faint echo of something else. "Fauré," she whispers. "The barcarolle. It was so cold and we talked about our sables . . ."

Dorothea hurriedly interrupts her. "We saw your cousin once, you know, Diana," she says, picking up the conversation. "On the balcony of the Crillon on July Fourth. With the dog and lots of jewelry."

"That would be Pamela," Diana says. "Her husband's madly unfaithful, but he's very generous with her account at Aspreys. I say, were you at the Crillon that day? You lucky things. I had to march with the Red Cross. I felt so idiotic with all those boring nurses from the provinces. I was longing to be up there with all my friends, drinking champagne."

"It seems a long time ago," Iris says vaguely, clutching her arms as though she is cold.

"I met a super chap later that evening," Diana prattles on. "He was Italian, terribly handsome, and an aviator to boot. They're always the most glamorous, don't you think? I would have married him right there if he had asked me."

Iris makes a sound that catches in her throat. Dorothea moves toward her, but Iris shakes her head.

"I'm going to clear out the big medicine cabinet in the back," Iris mutters to her sister. "See you later."

"That's the one problem about being over here," Diana goes on airily. "Every time I meet someone I like, he disappears and I never see him again. It's awfully annoying. When I get home, things will be a lot easier from that point of view, thank goodness."

Dorothea makes a noncommittal noise.

"It's the same with you and Iris. When we get back home, I don't think we'll ever meet again, do you? I mean, it's a pity and all that, but who would want to, and be reminded of all the ghastly things that happened in this horrible war? Not that that's your fault," she adds hastily. "Of course, I'd love you to come and visit us—it's not far from Pamela's house. Wiltshire's a lovely county, and you could get some riding in. But I just somehow don't think it's very likely. We'll all be wanting something new and different after this." Diana gesticulates derisively at the decaying tent, upsetting the patient whose face she is supposed to be washing. He takes her hand and stops her.

"Ooops, sorry, *mon cher*," she says. "I got a bit rough there, what?"

"'New and different.' You sound just like Isabel," Dorothea says.

"Isabel? Do I know her?"

"You should. You'd get along just fine. She works in Paris at Red Cross HQ. She wasn't much good as a nurse, and so they have her answering phones. She just got engaged to Harry Forrester, who's out at Toul."

"Lucky thing. An aviator." Diana rolls her eyes and makes kissing noises.

"Just drop it, Diana," Dorothea blurts out with rising irritation.

"Oooh, dear, I'm shocking Miss Crosby," Diana persists teasingly. "Mmm, airmen are the best, don't you think? All those gorgeous black leather jackets and goggles? Doing those wild acrobatics in the air, eh, Dorothea?" She raises her arms as though dancing with someone, then drops them impatiently. "Oh Lord, I'm longing to get out of here. Think I'll go for a smoke." Humming, she sashays through the tent. The soldier she has abandoned whistles as her swaying body catches his eye.

Later, in their cubicle, Dorothea informs Iris that they probably won't be seeing Diana again after she goes home, though of course they would be welcome in Wiltshire. Iris expresses regret.

"I felt so old, listening to her," Dorothea explains. "She's not much younger than we are, but she seems from a completely different generation."

"Isabel, too," Iris says.

"We must have missed something," Dorothea muses, "skipped a few pages of the calendar. Our life before 1917 seems to belong to another century. That's what Adeline says, of course. She's very concerned about it." Once again, she opens a letter resting by the side of her cot and reads in a solemn, scandalized tone of voice:

There has been some serious Trouble with three students in the Twelfth Grade, & the new headmistress, Miss Fortenbaugh, failed to take Action when things could have been controlled. I felt obliged to offer my Advice in this Crisis. Suffice it to say that all three Girls have been expelled, & the School is creating new rules about Access to the building from the Street. Most important, all interactions in the Washrooms are to be strictly monitored. My Feeling is that this should have taken place a long time ago. Times have changed, & Society is not the same now as it was when the School was founded. One cannot ignore the disgraceful Laxity between young men and women these days, behavior that would have shocked an earlier Generation. What is the World coming to?

"Good question," Iris comments. "If only we knew."

"Let's introduce her to Isabel and Diana. Talk about 'disgraceful Laxity.'"

"Heaven knows what goes on when *they* are in the washrooms."

"What is the world coming to?"

The twins fall on their cots, hooting with laughter.

"Thank you, Adeline. Little do you know how you've helped us get through this," Dorothea says through her laughter. "You're all right, then?" She looks carefully at her sister as they wipe the tears from their eyes.

"Well, all tears look the same, don't they?" Iris touches her cheek. "It's only water. I guess I'll never be all right. But I have to get used to it. There's no escape."

"Let's go for a walk."

It is almost night. There is a crispness in the air, presaging another winter, another season of frost and snow. The twins are unaccustomed to the steady darkness. Normally, brilliant red and yellow explosions churn up the evening horizon, along with streams of smoke and showers of black shrapnel. Now everything is quiet. It is as though the landscape has amnesia.

"Where shall we go?" Dorothea asks as usual.

"Where we always go." Iris suddenly shivers in the cold October night.

They follow the familiar path through farmland that once grew corn and wheat in fields lined with poplars. Now, its only crop is bones and fertilizing flesh, punctuated by blackened tree stumps that jut out of the ground at odd angles like vandalized headstones in a cemetery.

"I didn't mean now. We can't stay here."

"No. Of course not."

"Where would you like to go?"

They fall silent. The only sound is their shoes slithering along the path, succulent with mud.

"Somewhere where it never rains," Dorothea says.

"Havana?"

"Sounds good."

They look at each other doubtfully.

"We'd get sunstroke."

"We'll wear hats."

"I won't wear hats anymore."

They are silent again.

"Let's go back to the tent," Iris says. "It's too quiet here."

"*D'accord.* I think I heard Gaston calling us. He's the farm boy—loves telling me about his flocks of ducks. He's got a crushed leg. I fear he'll go home with only one."

"Ah, yes, sweet boy. He comes from the Périgord. He told me about the cathedral in Bordeaux. He says it's very big and very beautiful."

"I think the new one—Theo, is it?—will be needing us, too. Poor fellow. So close to the end. He keeps talking about the whistles. He doesn't understand there are no whistles anymore."

"That's all he'll ever hear now."

Animated by the hospital talk, the twins turn around and start walking briskly back to the tent. A small animal skitters across the path in front of them. The tent seems small and welcoming, its decomposing interior revived by eager candles. Here they feel at home. Here they belong. Here they are needed.

"I don't think we'll ever go to Wiltshire, do you?" Dorothea murmurs.

"It seems a long way away."

"No peaches," Dorothea comments happily.

"No cucumbers."

Dorothea quietly begins to sing, "*Auprès de ma blonde . . .*" Iris joins in, "*Qu'il fait bon, fait bon, fait bon . . .*" As they step up their pace through the darkness, striding together in time to the tune, the nunlike moon peeks through its veil and shines a blessing on the two young women before covering its face again in preparation for mourning.

Chapter 29

My dear Everett,

I am sitting here waiting for instructions as usual. So much of this war has been waiting and sitting around. But at least this time I have something to write to you about, instead of just complaining about the lack of action.

The first week of October, we were told that one of the companies involved in the Meuse-Argonne effort had been cut off for several days from the main battalion without adequate supplies of food or ammunition and that they were surrounded by enemy troops. Our job was to locate the battalion (77th Division) and attempt to drop supplies to them from the air. Their commander was a fellow called Charles (I think) Whittlesey, who went to Harvard Law School and was in partnership with Bayard Pruyn in New York when he joined up. You probably know him.

We had a lot of trouble with the information from the carrier pigeons, but after several failed attempts, our patrols finally managed to find the men, and we did in fact drop supplies to them. It took some cunning flying, but we did the best we could. During the reconnaissance, two of our pilots were shot down and killed by ground fire, so the situation was pretty sticky all around. But Whittlesey's men had their backs to the wall, and in the end we did what we had to do.

We learned later that the Boches demanded that Whittlesey surrender, and that he refused. Finally the Allies located the place where the company was holed up, and they were rescued. They are calling Whittlesey the hero of the Lost Battalion. It sounds like something out of Rider Haggard. I believe the fellow is back in the States now, covered in medals. Well, there are lots of ways to be a hero.

Frankly, I was annoyed at being asked to carry out this assignment instead of doing what we are supposed to be doing, getting the Boche. But I have to admit that it opened my eyes to something I had not fully realized before. We had to fly over several battlefields in our search for Whittlesey's battalion, and the sight of so much French countryside littered with dead bodies (from both sides) was quite impressive. If you think the war in the air is dangerous, those boys in the trenches never really have a chance. So you can be thankful I signed up for the air force!

Isabel and I have called it off. You will no doubt be pleased. It's an odd feeling to have made this big decision and then to have nothing to show for it. But I suppose that's how things are these days. I don't feel much either way. She was really just a prom trotter, I guess. I was beginning to worry how we would manage after the war anyway, on my nonexistent income. She was certainly more than I could afford. But it means that now I have fewer plans for the future than ever. There seems very little for me to go back to. So I just take the days here as they come, waiting for a chance to fly and get some fighting in.

I have been taking up some of the latest Libertys in recent weeks. Tremendously exciting. Using a new tomato crate (as the British call them) is always a challenge. The Liberty is a much heavier machine than the Spad, and it's got a bigger engine, so it's tricky to handle but fun when you get the hang of it. I think I'll always be loyal to the Spad, however. It really suits my style of flying. Now, just to take one up and chalk up a victory here and there—that's all I think about at the moment.

I expect you are pleased to be back in New York. The city must be looking great at this time of year, and I'll wager your mantel is packed with invitations.

All the best,
Harry

PS: I think I told you in my last letter about Maurice. It was too bad. He never really wanted to be an airman in the first place. He'd have been better on the ground—unlike me. Anyway, it's rotten luck all around.

~ NEW YORK ~

Chapter 30

SEVERAL NEWSPAPERS LAY on the large mahogany table in Everett Grayfield's library. Everett sat in his favorite maroon leather wing chair, wearing a smoking jacket and matching slippers, with a cigarette in its black holder resting in a nearby ashtray. He picked up a newspaper at random.

WAR COMING TO AN END! THE KAISER RESIGNS! OUR BRAVE BOYS WILL BE COMING HOME! The headlines, peppered with exclamation points, were spread over the front pages.

A paragraph in the *New York Times* mentioned a ceremony in recognition of Lieutenant Colonel Charles Whittlesey's forthcoming Medal of Honor. "We are proud of his service in 'the Pocket,' when many men lost their lives but many others were saved thanks to the leadership of Charles Whittlesey," a spokesman said. Lieutenant Colonel Whittlesey was not available for comment, but in a carefully worded statement he emphasized to reporters the bravery of the enlisted men who served with him, who were equally deserving of medals but who received no recognition for their courage. He was said by friends to be deeply embarrassed by the triumphal accolades accorded him.

Everett looked out the window, remembering a shy man who seemed both unworldly and impractical, whom he saw occasionally at the Union Club—an unlikely hero. He put aside the newspaper for Harry, who would be interested in the sequel to his assignment with the Lost Battalion.

Willis knocked at the door and came in.

"Lord Jarvis is here, Mr. Grayfield," he announced.

"Send him in, Willis."

Lord Jarvis was a big, rotund man with a face dominated by eyebrows and mustache made of the same thick reddish brown bristles. He looks like a military man, Everett thought, except that he hasn't ever been anywhere near the front.

"Ah, Lord Jarvis," he said, standing up and offering his hand. "Good to see you. Most gracious of you to come. What can we get you to drink? I have some good champagne up from the cellar."

"That will be capital, old man," Lord Jarvis said. "It's good to have some quality stuff after this long austerity binge."

Willis bowed and withdrew, returning with two champagne glasses and a bottle of Bollinger.

"Eighteen ninety," Everett said, examining the bottle's label. "This should be all right." They drank appreciatively, letting the sparkling liquid curl around their tongues. "I suppose we'll be getting back to normal now," Everett said lightly. "This war has been irksome in so many ways."

"My God, yes," Jarvis replied, smacking his lips. "Of course, it was much worse at home. You Americans have no idea. My place, Swaincourt, was requisitioned, you know. Poor Helen and Mary— that's the wife and daughter—had to move out and live in the gatehouse while the main house was filled with poor blighters sent home from the trenches in various states of disrepair. I never saw them, of course, but I gather some of them were in pretty poor shape. Mental cases, too, a lot of them."

"Indeed," Everett murmured.

"Helen told me the lower gardens were used as an exercise yard for all the chaps getting artificial limbs. They'd organize races with the amputees, dragging all the hospital beds out onto the lawn so that the other patients could watch. What a sight, all those crippled chappies with no legs or arms hobbling up and down the lawn on crutches or wheelchair contraptions, trying to bob apples or something. I should have thought they'd have all done rather better in three-legged races!" Jarvis guffawed loudly.

"How true," Everett said with a pleasant smile.

"I don't like to think what condition the lawn is in now. It's where we always played croquet. I'm pretty damned sure I'll have to get the whole thing relaid. I was reminded of that seeing all those lawns in Newport. Their gardeners up there do quite a job." Jarvis sighed, stroking his toothbrush mustache.

"Do you often spend summers in Newport?" Everett asked.

"Lord, no. It's a frightful dump really, don't you think? All those ghastly old women looking like boiled potatoes, giving huge parties with not enough to drink and too much to eat. And their houses! More like mausoleums, in my view. Nowhere comfortable to sit down. Have you noticed that? Bloody nowhere to sit. My feet were always killing me."

Everett stole a look at Lord Jarvis's oddly small extremities.

Jarvis plumped the cushions on Everett's sofa and lay back appreciatively. "Those old battle-axes must be made of steel to sit on that furniture, even if everything is worth millions of dollars," he mused. "The old battle-axes are, too, of course. That Tessie Oelrichs, now, what do you think she's worth?" He pursed his lips and savored a sip of champagne. "Mind you, she's too far gone on the sauce for my taste. Lord, what a nightmare. As for Alva Belmont—such a disappointment. Gone all suffragist, eh? Frankly, I was only up there because life in England is so difficult in the summer these days, if you see what I mean, with nowhere to go and nobody around to have an amusing time with. If one can't even get into one's own house, what's a chap to do?"

"I imagine things will be getting back to normal now," Everett repeated.

"Oh, yes, certainly. We all want to get back to normal. Even if it means relaying the croquet lawn, what?"

Everett stood up and poured more champagne into Lord Jarvis's glass. "Actually," he said, "that is really what I wanted to talk to you about."

"Ah, yes? Croquet?" Jarvis laughed. "Just joking, old fellow. What can I help you with?" He settled down into the sofa and composed his features in a serious expression.

"I have a . . ." Everett hesitated. "I have a ward, you might call him. He is over in France, a fighter pilot, doing marvelously brave things in the air war."

"An ace, you mean?" Jarvis interrupted.

"Precisely. He was also a great athlete at school and college," Everett continued. "Many people know his name. Harry Forrester."

Jarvis furrowed his brow. "Sorry, old boy. Doesn't ring a bell."

"Well, maybe his fame never reached England," Everett said. "But for many Americans, he is a legendary figure."

"Like a blue?" Jarvis asked.

"Indeed." Everett paused a minute. "The thing is, Lord Jarvis, that he will be coming back from the war soon."

"Jolly good," Jarvis said. "Conquering hero, what? Medals all around?"

"I'm worried about him."

"I don't see why," Lord Jarvis objected. "These boys home from the war, they're given everything—idolized by the press, with endless medal ceremonies, parades, memorial celebrations. Why, the country's so grateful to 'em they'd give 'em anything they wanted. When my little brother came back from the Boer War, Eddie gave him one of the royal estates and a seat in the House of Lords. I thought it altogether too much, frankly."

"I'm not sure that kind of gratitude is really what some of them want," Everett observed. "Adjusting to civilian life after exposure to war is known to be exceedingly difficult. There is quite a lot of evidence to prove this." He took a drink of his champagne and turned the stem of the glass around so that it picked up the light and reflected it like a diamond. "I don't believe," he went on thoughtfully, "that those of us who have not experienced the battlefield firsthand have any notion of how profoundly it affects a man's mind and spirit. I think we here at home should be prepared to greet the returning soldiers, not just with the victory parades that will no doubt pass under my windows, but with a great deal of patience and understanding."

Lord Jarvis stared at Everett with bulging eyes.

"I'd have thought they'd be happy to be alive," he blustered.

"Well," Everett said quickly, returning his attention to his guest, "I'm sure Harry will be happy to be alive. But he does not know what he will be coming back to. He had a position in the Morgan bank before he left for the war and was not at all comfortable there."

"In heaven's name, why not? Morgan was one of the best. Did some very satisfactory business with him myself in the old days. He's someone you'd not easily forget. That proboscis alone—it would have sat well on an elephant." Lord Jarvis tapped his nose in a jocular fashion.

"Perhaps so. But Harry is not interested in money matters or finances. He hated being behind a desk."

"Ah, the outdoor type," Jarvis said. "Like my son, don't you know. Couldn't wait to leave Cambridge and go to France. He had all sorts of wet ideas in his head about idealism and sacrifice. Such tommyrot. Luckily he got a leg shot off and was sent home. He kept wanting to go back, but of course we didn't let him. He's with his mother now at my brother-in-law's place in Scotland. It's a fifteenth-century castle he's got up there, great salmon fishing. You might visit sometime."

"I wondered, Lord Jarvis," Everett persevered, "if you have any thoughts about what Harry might do when he comes back. You know so many people both here and in Great Britain, in all sorts of professions. I was thinking maybe of the art market, publishing, even certain kinds of international trade. Harry's enormously charming and could do very well for himself in the right circumstances. I do not want to have to send him back to the bank, but at the same time I am not confident about the direction he should take or indeed whether I can help him at all." He paused. "To be candid, I do not know what to expect when he comes home."

There was an awkward silence after this, as though Everett's confession had introduced an unpleasant smell into the room.

"Yes, I see, old chap," Jarvis said finally. He looked at the ceiling, searching for inspiration in the moldings surrounding the chandelier. "You say he's a good sportsman?"

"Very."

"Has he a good seat on a horse?"

"Well, I am sure he has, although riding was not one of his specialties."

"I'll tell you what, Grayfield. We are always looking for good people to help run our hunt back home. It was difficult enough before the war, but now, with so many of our boys going overseas and so few coming back, we are disgracefully short of sterling young men to be grooms or whippers-in. You can't run an efficient hunt without good help in the stables. In fact, I was thinking of going out to Bedminster to see if I could do any recruiting. I've heard the Essex Hunt puts on quite a good show, considering it's a bunch of colonials, what?" Jarvis laughed heartily. "Anyway," he went on, seeing Everett's expression, "we really need a good class of chap to get things going again. By the way, let me assure you, our hunt is one of the best in the country. Perhaps you've heard of it—the Lamberton Vale. You can look us up in *Baily's*—page 101, I believe."

"Yes, I see," Everett said in a carefully controlled voice. "What an interesting idea."

Jarvis smiled proudly. "Jolly good. It came to me just like that." He snapped his fingers.

"But even if Harry liked the idea of working with horses," Everett said, "would there be any money in it?" There was a slight intake of breath from the sofa. "Excuse me for bringing it up, but I'm afraid Harry has not been fortunate in that respect."

"Really?" Jarvis gave a sideways look at Everett's opulent library. "I thought all you Americans were, shall we say, on easy street."

"Well, Harry's mother unfortunately had a series of husbands, and . . ." Everett shrugged tactfully.

"Ah, I see. A bolter. We have bolters all over the place back home. One can tell 'em a mile off—they have those rolling eyes," Jarvis guffawed. "Like poorly bred horses. But what about his father? I've always said it's a father's duty to straighten out a son, just as I did." He stroked his large chest in a congratulatory fashion.

"His father was an inventor. A failed inventor. I don't think I need say more."

"What a shame. I never knew an American who wasn't rich. That's why we English love 'em so much." Jarvis chuckled. "Look at Sunny Marlborough. He did awfully well with that little Consuelo Vanderbilt, didn't he? Mind you, it was Alva, the old battle-ax, who fixed it. Maybe we could arrange a reverse match with your war hero, if you know what I mean."

Everett finally flinched. "I don't think that would be Harry's sort of thing at all," he managed to respond.

"No indeed. Quite, quite." Lord Jarvis coaxed a fob watch out from its nest beneath his belly. "Good God, is that the time?" He stood up, swaying for a moment on his little feet. "Well, old man, let me think about it. I have to rush off now to some tiresome old bag's cocktail party. You probably know her. Frances Carnegie. If you're looking for a few millions, she's the one for you. Perhaps she'll find something for your ward. I'll mention it to her."

"Thank you so much, Lord Jarvis. I'm most obliged to you," Everett said as the two men shook hands.

"Not at all, Grayfield. Enjoyed our little talk. We'll get you up to Scotland when all this is over. Maybe my son and your Harry could do some fishing and talk about the war — that's the only thing he seems to want to talk about. Awfully boring for everybody else. Dreary subject, in my book. Time to move on. By the way, that Bollinger was first rate."

His expression inscrutable, Everett watched his guest leave. So that was why the war was fought, he thought. For our wonderful Allies. He took a cigarette out of a silver box on a small side table, fixed it into its black holder, and lit it. Only from the tremor in his hands could one guess how angry he was. Moving to the window, he raised his head as though hearing something, a distant brass band perhaps, proclaiming a victory celebration somewhere down Fifth Avenue.

With an impatient gesture, he began to draw the curtains to shut out the sound. As he pulled the lengths of heavy velvet together, he looked down and saw a large black chauffeur-driven car draw away from the sidewalk. Holding up his champagne glass, he smiled bitterly in a toast to its departure.

~ FRANCE ~

Chapter 31

Dear Adeline,

We have all heard the wonderful news, and here at the hospital we are already packing up. Sister Waddington has constructed a major military operation for us so we may close it down as efficiently and economically as possible, and we seem almost as busy as we were at the height of hostilities.

It's difficult to realize that the war is really over. At times we cannot believe it and expect any minute a new push to be announced or another barrage of explosions to tear up the night air. How thankful we are that the soldiers here now are the last ones we shall treat. No more new arrivals from the front. No more mopping up, no more dressings, no more screams for morphine (which we could rarely obtain).

So we are finally leaving this place where we have worked and laughed and cried for almost a year. The preparations fill our days. We say good-bye to our friends here in the village, who provided us with fresh eggs and vegetables whenever they could. We say good-bye to the farmers who offered us their carts to take water to the men trying to get to and from the trenches. We say good-bye to the little children who came to play with the horses and chickens in the yard.

They would sometimes proudly tell us that their beloved brothers Albert or Jean or Henri had gone to the war. We used to pray that none of them would be returned here to our care. Wouldn't it be wonderful if they were alive and might be coming home soon?

We listen to our French and laugh. Such a vocabulary we have acquired! You would be shocked to hear us. We are fluent in a language that is understood by the local people here in the countryside and of course by our poilus but would be totally unsuitable, I fear, for the salons and drawing rooms of Paris.

That is not the only aspect of us that might be "unsuitable" back home. I do not believe anyone who has not been here could understand what I mean. We are privileged to have been exposed to one of the most extreme tests of human endurance and — perhaps, in a modest way — to have passed it. And even more privileged to have gone through this test with others who have shared our joys and sorrows. Such a bond could never be replicated in normal life, of that I am sure. But now it is over, and we are left feeling stranded, at a loss. "Home?" Iris and I say the word to each other but cannot fathom its meaning. It is too distant. Too much has happened. We have traveled too far. Since Maurice's death, we cling to each other more and more, Iris and I. Her grief is terrible to see, but she is as brave as a lion. I respect her more than I can say.

Yet of course there is Life, even in Death. This currently fashionable cliché is inspired by the news we have just received from George that his son was born on November 4. Perhaps he notified you or you read it in the newspaper. Our first reaction was mixed — to bring a child into this world is an act of optimism that we find difficult to applaud. However, the next generation must come into its own and will perhaps make this a better place. It's now their turn. And of course we like being Aunt Dorothea and Aunt Iris! George says the baby looks just like us. Lavinia will not be pleased.

I must stop now, as there is still much to do. I do not know where we shall be this time next month, or indeed next week. It is a time of great uncertainty. We do not sleep at night, and our days are filled with ghosts. We ourselves now seem insubstantial, flimsy pieces of gauze, slowly unraveling.

This will be my last letter to you from France. What a strange sentence that is to write. We both send our good wishes and warm thoughts at seeing you again soon. I'm not confident that you will recognize us. We are much changed.

With affection,
Dorothea

PS: We trust that Saint Mary's will continue to benefit from your sage advice. The problems it faces are emblematic of a world that will be forever different after this war. Of that at least we are certain.

Chapter 32

THE DAY IS GRAY AND WINDY, with clumps of porridgelike clouds hanging over the airfield. The weather forecast is dismal: two days of storms and heavy rain, with fog a probability. Harry is walking back to his hut after picking up his mail. His walk is lazy, his body slouched; it is the gait of a man who has no interest in getting to his destination. No letters today, he notices. That, at least, is a relief. Instead, there is a package. Unwrapping it in his hut, he stares at a small jewelry box. He throws it to the ground, unopened, with an expression of distaste.

Why does Everett persist in these things? he asks himself. How many times have I begged him not to shower me with costly presents? What does he want of me? Harry is as uncomfortable thinking about Everett as he was about Isabel. Everett has been a father to him. That's what he always says when people ask him. But is that true? Harry does not want to pursue this avenue of thought, has never wanted to pursue it. When Harry was playing football and ice hockey, Everett was only one of many people who wanted a part of him. That was understandable enough. Harry was used to it. It had been the same ever since boarding school. But in New York, it was different. They were together under the same roof all the time. There were moments when Harry thought he must flee. Yet Everett was always kind, always tactful, always kept his distance. There was never any unpleasantness. Harry was racked — the right word — with gratitude, a gratitude that at times came dangerously close to hatred. He used to feel he could keep things going until he found a better place for himself. When he'd made enough money to pay for it. But as time went on, nothing better seemed to materialize.

Until the war.

Now the news is always the same — Boche troops withdrawing from all sectors of the western front, Boche delegates crossing the lines to prepare for the armistice, Boche spirit totally defeated, et cetera, et cetera. Harry and his comrades are not impressed. The more they sense the war ending, the more eager the pilots are to fly. Now is the perfect time, with the enemy retreating, they argue. They won't be expecting us. They're vulnerable. We can probe really deep behind their lines, do some lasting damage, wrap up the war with all guns blazing, and score a few final victories. The planes are ready, there's no time to waste, we can attack those last German fighters and show them who are the real aces of the sky.

Harry participates in this call to action. His hands itch to hold the rudder, to experience the reverberation as he fires his guns. He yearns to feel the wind against his goggles. He can think of nothing except the noise of the machine beneath him, its power pulling him ever higher as he searches for his target. He and his plane are a perfect team, moving through the sky in unison, waiting to strike. How can the war be over? He has not finished flying, he must get into the air again, give his Spad one more run, feel the exhilaration of the unknown! What else is there?

Harry looks at the jewelry box he has thrown on the floor and feels panic rising. He circles around it as though it were a scorpion poised to attack. He starts making mock feints at it, pointing his fingers to shoot it. *Pow! Pow!* He laughs and steps in closer, firing off rounds energetically. *Pow! Pow! Pow!* The box remains unmoved. He stops as suddenly as he started and hits his head despairingly with the palm of his hand. He goes to the door and stares up at the sky. Suddenly he makes a decision. Turning back into the tent, he grabs his goggles and helmet.

In the mess, a group of airmen are sitting around, playing cards. Harry comes in and calls over five of them. He knows them well and has flown with them on many missions. "I hear there are some Huns over to the west of Saint-Mihiel," he says casually. "Any takers?"

His comrades leap up, cheering. "We'll go in pairs," Harry says. "See how far we can get. We should make a good run."

"What about the weather?" one of them asks.

"What weather?" the others scoff. "How long do you want to sit it out? You want to wait for the baseball season? This is the best we're going to get until it's all over. Let's go!"

"We want to come, too," some of the other pilots call out. "Don't leave us out. We want some action, too."

"No!" Harry glares at them. "You stay here," he says curtly. "We only need a few to go." The remaining airmen sit back, muttering curses, knowing the reason for their exclusion. Harry wants to make the kills himself, without help, as always. Too many planes in the air would dilute his victories. Typical Harry.

The chosen ones sprint toward their machines, throwing on their jackets and helmets. Harry performs his usual ritual of checking his Spad. Everything looks in order. The engines roar and the six pilots take off, forming pairs as Harry has instructed. In pair formation, it is easier to lose the others, which is his intention. Saluting one another, they zoom up into the clouds.

This is it for me. This is where I belong, in the cockpit, hand on the joystick, plane juddering, guns ready, the open sky ahead. This is it. Harry leads his partner swiftly away from the formation, moving west instead of north, away from the others. If they are successful in finding enemy aircraft, he wants to deal with the Boche alone, without the others interfering in the engagement, just as his comrades on the ground suspected.

I'm on my own, fighting my own battle, my own dogfight, one-on-one, a duel to the death if necessary, but on my own terms. This is my playing field—limitless running room, cold, intoxicating air. Now he feels it in full, the madness, the exhilaration, the rapture of the sport. *Focus, Harry, focus, concentrate, allow the moment to absorb every muscle, every thought, every sense. I'm up here, thousands of feet up, and nothing on the ground can pull me back. I'm free, the past is gone, the future is this moment, everything else is a waste of time. I'm Harry, Harry, hurtling through the air to victory.*

His eyes rake the heavy sky, praying for the black speck of the enemy to emerge. He flies higher and faster into the clouds. He can no longer see his partner. He is entirely alone.

Suddenly he sees something behind his right shoulder. His heart races. *At last! This is my chance. No thinking now, just instinct. Don't even breathe. Eye on the target, body tensed, mind empty of everything except Harry in the air.* He shouts aloud in delight. His hand squeezes the rudder as he steeply spirals his plane toward the target hovering in the murky sky. The Spad responds beautifully. *There's nothing better, nothing to beat this, nothing will ever match this moment.*

The clouds make visibility difficult, but Harry remains supremely confident as he side-slips into a perfect position up and behind the enemy plane, gunning the engine to make as much speed as it can muster. He calls on every skill for the test he knows is coming. He recalls his instructor's words, "Exploit the element of surprise." Concealed in the cloud cover, he is cool, poised, ready to attack. *There's nothing better, nothing to beat this, nothing will ever match this moment.*

As he finally fixes the other directly in his sights and prepares to fire, he suddenly pulls up short.

"*No! Oh God, no!*"

The plane is French.

At the last minute, Harry banks sharply to avoid a collision. The planes are so close that the pilots can clearly see each other's faces. The Frenchman starts to wave cheerfully and then, seeing the stunned, disgusted expression on the American's face, shrugs and flies off into the clouds.

All the aviators return to the base without damage. Their flight reports are uninspiring. One engine gave some trouble, and a pair of pilots spotted a few antiaircraft balloons, but visibility was so poor that they soon gave up hope of any enemy encounters and agreed to call it quits.

Harry returns to his quarters. He speaks to no one, and his colleagues leave him alone. He is not seen for the rest of the evening. A day later, on November 11, the news comes through that the war is over. Hostilities have ceased. The peace has been signed in a railway carriage in Compiègne, outside Paris.

"The war is over!" goes up the shout from the mess. "It's over!" Amid an outburst of cheering and yelling, the festivities begin. Pistol shots are fired, searchlights strafe the sky, helmets are hurled into the air, bottles of beer and wine are broken and poured over heads as people shout and hug one another in wild abandon. With an effort, Harry smiles and ducks, taking a few hits from the exploding cascades of beer. He feels a familiar hollowness. It was like this at the end of football games, after a particularly hard-fought contest. He hadn't been able to enjoy it much then, either. But how much would he have given now for it to be one of those carefree college celebrations ending a football game rather than this dreaded one that ends a war.

He grabs a beer bottle and walks away from the mess toward the airfield. There, everything is unusually quiet. No repairing of engines.

No testing of propellers. No refueling of aircraft. The planes sag like weary birds after a long migration. Harry stands and drinks, listening to the distant din of the victory revels. He gazes for a long time at the grounded planes as a threatening storm slowly shrouds them in darkness. "It's over," he says aloud. "It's over."

Later, they hear that the day before the armistice was signed, one of Eddie Rickenbacker's pilots, a Major Kirby, shot down a German plane over the Meuse and has since been credited with having brought down the last enemy plane of the war. Not only was this an achievement that would make the history books for the young aviator, but it was also a personal triumph. He had only just joined the Ninety-fourth Squadron; it was his first victory.

~ NEW YORK ~

Chapter 33

MONDAY, NOVEMBER 25, 1918,
14 GREENWICH STREET, NEW YORK

Dearest Dorothea,

We are all thrilled here that the Allies have achieved this triumphant Victory over Evil. How proud we are of those fighting Men who made the Ultimate Sacrifice, & how overjoyed I am that my two Blessed Girls are safe. I was hoping to get a letter from you now that the War is finally over. Perhaps it is even now speeding its way to me with the glorious News of your Return.

I have spoken to your Brother, who is also delighted that you will be Home soon. He is planning a large Party in your honor, with all your Friends & Relations. I am honored that he has included me in this distinguished Company. How we look forward to hearing about all your Exciting Adventures overseas! He asked me what would please you and Iris most, & I told him that "we three" enjoyed Chocolate in all its forms. I hope you will forgive me for revealing our wicked Secret! (And yes, how soon "we three" shall meet again!)

During my Visit to your Brother to discuss your impending Arrival, I was fortunate enough to get a Peek at the new Scion of your distinguished Family. I believe his name is to be George, like his father. The child was sleeping, but I could tell at once that the fine Crosby blood is well represented in his noble little Form. A certain breadth of Brow, a hint of a Smile, and the long Neck so character-istic of his two Aunts were perfectly apparent in this new Blessing who has graced our World.

A small room has been charmingly refurnished to suit the Baby and his Nurse, & it occurs to me that you might like to have your Suite spruced up after your long absence. There is a highly regarded professional Decorator here called Elsie De Wolfe, who boasts such distinguished clients as Mr. Frick, & who, you may recall, did the striking design of the Colony Club some years ago—a most agree-able retreat. Although I understand Miss De Wolfe has been spend-ing much of her time recently in Paris, I am sure we could persuade her to take on this Assignment. I am certain that she, like all our brave Americans over there, must be longing to return Home. They say she likes to use Chintz, a floral textile very popular in England. That might look attractive on the Sofas in your Drawing Room. Or perhaps you would prefer Toile de Jouy, as you are so French in Spirit!

You will be pleased to learn that Saint Mary's School is also plan-ning a Celebration for all the Girls, present & former, who gave their Time and Money to the Allied Cause. You, of course, will play a major Role, & Miss Fortenbaugh hopes you will both make some kind of Presentation (in the form of an epic poem perhaps) to the School about your Experiences in France. (I have come to respect Miss Fortenbaugh more and more. She now frequently asks for my Advice & seems extremely receptive to my modest Suggestions for the successful running of our beloved Saint Mary's.) I believe Med-als are being offered by the Red Cross to those who have given Ser-vice to the War Effort, so that will be another important Ceremony in which you will participate. In fact, the list of Victory Celebrations and Parades gets longer and longer every day, so you will certainly be kept busy on your Return. How exciting it will be!

But as well as these well-earned Tributes, which will gratify your poor weary Souls, I'm sure what you are looking forward to is a good long Rest, with some excellent Food & Fresh Air. You will then be able to forget your time at the Front and put all these recent Sorrows behind you. (I refer to Iris's loss in particular, of course. But she is still young and, like all Saint Mary's girls, well trained to find solace in the curative powers of Art.) Reluctantly, I must reconcile myself to the fact that travel to Europe is probably not a practical Proposition for the moment, although returning to our favorite Places in France, now that Hostilities are over, will be an urgent item on the Agenda. (Perhaps not Rheims.)

I will write no more now. This letter is simply a Prelude to our Welcome Home Festivities. How glorious to contemplate the Possibility that we might once again celebrate the Christmas and New Year's seasons together. Let us give thanks to God and our victorious Troops that 1919 will truly be a "new" New Year for us all! "Fill high the bowl with Samian wine!"

In great anticipation,
Your Adeline

~ FRANCE ~

Chapter 34

THE TRAIN IS PACKED with Americans, men and women, many still in uniform. Most are standing, pushing and jostling against one another as the train sways slowly through the French countryside toward Bordeaux. It is a long ride from Paris, through Orléans, Tours, Poitiers, Angoulême. Cities whose names are set like jewels in the history of France pass by in the darkness, unnoticed by the passengers.

Most of them are thinking only of New York. The mood is one of almost hysterical elation and relief. *Going home* is in the minds of them all, that blessed phrase that they have longed to hear for so long. *Going home*—the mantra of the survivors.

Dorothea and Iris are squeezed into a compartment with twelve others, ten men and two women. The women, like the twins, are wearing Red Cross uniforms. All four manage to get a seat, but the crush is intense and the men's bodies, smelling of stale cigarette smoke, wine, sweat, and urine, press against them, almost suffocating them.

The twins stare with glazed eyes into the distance, like animals in a cage. Their extreme pallor contrasts with the ruddy complexions of their companions in the compartment. A muscle twitches compulsively in the corner of Iris's mouth as though a fly is resting on it. From time to time, Dorothea brushes her hair back in a mannered gesture, although it is cropped and severely drawn back from her face. Their grim silence is in striking counterpoint to the boisterousness exhibited by their fellow passengers on the crowded train.

"Hey, you, where're you from?" somebody calls out.

"Minnesota!" yells one.

"Ohio!"

"New York!"

"Oregon!"

"Louisiana!"

The places ring out like a roll call. To Dorothea and Iris, it sounds like the shouts of the aides checking off the hastily written labels attached to the stretchers coming in from the dressing stations: "Perforated abdomen!" "Head wound!" "Burned hands and feet!" "Blinded by shrapnel!" They stiffen as though on alert.

"North Carolina!"

"Georgia!"

"California!"

After each name, everyone cheers.

"Michigan!"

"New Jersey!"

More cheering. Someone starts singing:

If you want the old battalion,
We know where they are,
We know where they are,
We know where they are.
If you want the old battalion,
We know where they are,
They're hangin' on the old barbed wire.

They all shout and laugh, swigging down bottles of red wine, rum, and bourbon. They pass the liquor around, wiping their mouths with their hands, smoking, and coughing in the heat and steam.

"What about you two, eh?" A soldier leans over the twins, breathing heavily. "Two for the price of one, lads—look what we got here!"

Iris and Dorothea do not look at him. They are as rigid as statues. With their chalk white faces, black hair, and narrowed eyes, they could almost be back in their Kabuki poses, so stylishly photographed by Genthe before the war.

"Come on, darlins, loosen up!" says another soldier. "We're not going to a funeral, you know." He stares at them through bloodshot eyes. "Jeez, you really are identical," he exclaims, looking from one to the other. "Hey, boys, guess how you tell them apart in bed?" He leans down, licks his lips, and laughs, pouring foul breath over them.

THE TWINS GOT ON the train because they were told to by Sister Waddington, because every other American was getting on the train. Any train. People had been waiting for days to get on a train. Seats were like gold. Most trains going to the north coast were reserved long in advance and often failed to run. The twins were lucky to find room on this train going to Bordeaux. Bordeaux was an important international port, and there was a ship in Bordeaux that would take them home. George had pulled strings in New York. During the chaotic period following the armistice, all transatlantic crossings had become chronically overbooked with people trying to leave France, but George had somehow managed to get them passage on the *Provence*. He was delighted at his success. The twins were fortunate.

Iris didn't think so. She stood on the platform, rearing back from the steam-shrouded train like a horse refusing a fence. Where was the train taking them? They had no destination. Why must she leave the place where she felt she belonged, where she had been loved and cared for? She was so tired. All she wanted was to stay close to where Maurice rested—and where she could rest.

Dorothea tried in vain to get her sister to move. Desperate, she looked around in the throng of people for Sister Waddington. The English matron was seeing off her last group of nurses, making sure they had their tickets and paperwork to get them out of France. She saw Iris's distress and took her and Dorothea aside. "Listen to me," she said in the down-to-earth manner they had come to appreciate almost as much as that of their directrice. "You are like cancer patients. The treatment has been successful. It is called remission. You must now get on with your lives." She did not add the bleak corollary, that in her experience the fight for survival was often so all-consuming that when it was over, only a void was left. In many cases, the energy expended on the treatment was replaced by disorientation; exaltation, by depression. Sister Waddington knew the signs and closed her eyes in anger at the unfairness of it all.

"Get on the train, both of you," she ordered brusquely. The twins instinctively obeyed. The wise old woman watched them climb into the crowded carriage and waved good-bye with a heavy heart. She wished she had been able to arrange for Diana to travel with them part of the way, but Diana had left for England with Lady Grenville. The twins, as fragile as Sister Waddington knew they were, would have to make the journey on their own.

"Two for the price of one, eh?" the soldier repeats now. He raises his fingers as though counting money. "Perhaps you're deaf-mutes," he persists, getting annoyed at their stubborn silence. "You must have been a real help over there. Couldn't hear the shelling, eh? Aren't you the lucky ones. Ha!"

He makes a noise like an exploding mortar and puts his hands over his ears. The twins flinch.

"Stand to!" someone calls out. Everyone groans.

"Hey, you," another one shouts. "We aren't in the trenches now. Dry up, will ya?"

The first soldier brays with laughter and lifts a bottle to his lips. "Anyway," his companion protests, "it doesn't sound like that, you goofer." He tries it himself. The other soldiers join in, and soon the compartment is filled with roars and explosions—*kaboom! crash! brrrm!*—the noises little boys make when they are playing at war.

Dorothea and Iris avert their eyes, staring fixedly down at the soldiers' worn and cracked army boots, still caked with French mud. The twins' boots are new, recently sent from home, high and well-fitting like their riding boots, the expensive brown leather burnished with polish. Iris and Dorothea push their feet under the seat and pull down their skirts.

Suddenly, one of the soldiers nearby turns a livid green. His forehead beads with sweat, and he vomits violently over Iris's lap. The stream of liquid is a lumpy reddish purple color, a compote of the wine he has drunk. The glasses he was wearing fall to the floor.

Iris springs up. "*Vite! Vite!*" she screams, galvanized into action. "Bleeding here! Bring gauze! *Eau de lavande!*"

Dorothea looks up, horrified, and begins to hunt for a handkerchief. The other passengers are trying to get out of the way, putting their hands over their noses, making choking noises amid laughter and jeers.

"You wanna leave everything behind?" somebody jokes to the soldier, who is still vomiting in short, jerky eruptions. "Don't blame ya, pal."

The two other nurses in the compartment find handkerchiefs and hand them to Dorothea. Iris remains standing, swaying, her face white, her lips parted. "Where's Madame la directrice?" she demands in a loud voice. "We need help here." The mess on her lap begins to trickle down onto the floor. Iris flicks at it absently and pushes her way toward the sickened soldier. He has black hair, longer than most. His skin is flushed now, as the color returns to his face. A nurse hands him his glasses and he puts them on, peering at Iris with wide, shocked eyes.

"Gee, ma'am, ah sure didn't mean—," he stutters apologetically in a strong Southern accent.

"Dorothea! Look at him!" Iris interrupts, trying to seize hold of his arm. "Doesn't he look like—"

The soldier shakes her off, alarmed at her tormented expression. "Hey, look, ah'm mighty sorry, ma'am," he repeats, pushing her away. Iris stumbles back, staring at him wildly. The compartment is in chaos. The doors open and close as people try to get out, away from the stench, groaning loudly in disgust.

"You couldn't have waited, could you, buddy?" one snorts. "I mean, you've managed to keep your guts in this long, eh?" More howls of laughter.

Dorothea tries to soothe her sister. "Iris, sit down, let me wipe this away. Please sit down and be calm." She searches in her bag for a lavender sachet, knowing there is none.

Iris sits down and begins to sob bitterly. The soldiers in the compartment try to escape, but the corridor outside is jammed with yelling passengers. "Move down, make room, move along, for God's sake . . ." Others push back in, only to inhale the sick-smelling air and struggle to get out again.

"It's only the dregs of your iron rations, Charlie," one says. "Stale hardtack and sugar water! What else could there be in your little ole belly?" Soldiers cheer raucously.

"Maurice." Iris continues to weep, her head in her hands. "Maurice, I saw him, he's here."

"No, darling, you didn't see him," Dorothea replies, efficiently cleaning the mess off Iris's skirt. She knows the drill. "It's your imagination. Maurice is not here. He's dead."

"Dead." Iris repeats the word, savoring it on her tongue, nodding. The passengers remaining in the compartment stare at her nervously.

"Of course, dead, like André," she agrees, brightening. "Remember, Dorothea? One of the earliest. He died of gas gangrene. That was the first time I saw it, that puffiness like a huge bubble with pus in the middle. Never smelled anything like it. Well, why would we? We'd only smelled daffodils and English soap and freshly laundered sheets." She laughs loudly. "Oh, innocent little us! We got to know some more smells, all right. That's when we first used the lavender." She cups her palm over her nose and mouth. "Mmm, it really helped, didn't it?" She inhales, closing her eyes.

"Do you remember the one who smiled," she continues, her voice muffled. "Luca, was it? And Jacques. There were several Jacques. One had both arms off, one got an infected chest, raw like meat, one died of bleeding through the stomach. Then Armand—do you remember Armand, Dorothea?" She opens her eyes and looks at her sister. "He told me his mother was a teacher. And Félix, didn't we like Félix? He kept apologizing for wetting the bed. Imagine! He sang a song for us before his lungs filled with blood and he couldn't catch his breath . . ."

Iris breaks off and gazes out the window. She points to spectral faces she sees in the black glass, reflections in the darkness of the night outside. "Ah, there's Alain—and Gaston." A pinpoint of light flashes by. "Look, there's Pierre, at least one of three Pierres, a common French name like Joe, I suppose. One Pierre looked rather like George, we thought, only thinner, of course, and his eyes had been burned out. They were black with flies, remember? Another Pierre had shrapnel in both hips, his legs had to come off . . ." Iris's voice is high and breathless. Dorothea tries to hush her. The other passengers are listening in embarrassed horror. The two nurses look at each other and roll their eyes.

"Balthazar, *quel beau nom,* I told him he was one of the three kings, he liked that, but he died, not like a king, it was an infected head wound, oh, the pain, like Jacques, yes, another Jacques, his leg had been amputated with a dirty knife . . . no morphine available. How often we had to tell them that . . ."

Iris continues to concentrate on the darkened window, her fingers touching the glass as though tracing the faces she sees so clearly. She speaks now in a soft, rhythmic tone, like a chorister singing plainsong. "Antoine, so young, the youngest, the really young boys never smelled quite so bad, almost sweet sometimes, weren't they? But his flesh was all rotted anyway, so it didn't make any difference. I'm not sure he was even sixteen. Alexandre and Jean, they came in together, they came from the same village—was it Vallentières? Died a day apart . . ."

The ghastly litany continues. "Jean, another Jean, yes, I remember, he was vomiting blood so often we had to empty his basin every ten minutes. Georges, remember, Dorothea, that operation to take out the bullets in his chest went on for hours and his face was so white and he died screaming, and Henri, remarkable, you never get over it even when you've seen it a hundred times, his fracture was all putrid, it was the old gas gangrene again, if you touched it, it exploded like a squashed cockroach . . ."

She stops and turns away from the window.

"Have I forgotten anyone?" she asks, her brow furrowed in thought. "I hope I haven't forgotten anyone."

"We don't forget." Dorothea's voice is gentle. "Don't worry, Iris. We remember all their names. We always will."

"Of course we will," Iris says, looking pleased. "Of course we will." She sits back and closes her eyes again.

"Your sister should get some rest," one of the nurses says. "It looks like brain fever."

Iris mutters some more names to herself. "Felix, Simon, Alphonse . . ."

Dorothea looks around despairingly.

"You did your best, you know," the nurse says, patting her on the knee. "We all did."

"We all did," Dorothea echoes her. "Yes." She, too, looks out the ghost-ridden window. All she can see is her own face reflected in the glass. She watches her lips move as she speaks. "We went to a bull-fight once. It was a mistake. Adeline Wetherall didn't realize . . ." Dorothea turns to the nurses. "She thought since it was in France, it would be different. We watched the bull being attacked by the picadors' lances, blood dripping down its sides like black paint."

The nurse again pats Dorothea's knee, and says, "There, there, dear." Dorothea smiles and continues to speak to her pale reflection in the window.

"And then, when it was mortally wounded, the matador held up his red cape and sword and once again the bull had to stagger up and respond, going back over the top, charging into certain death." The two nurses give each other knowing glances and sigh.

"Poor Adeline," Dorothea suddenly laughs merrily. "She had no idea. I thought she would never recover. We had to use our whole supply of smelling salts that day. Do you remember, Iris?" She pauses. "Or was it lavender? Damn, I can't remember! Iris, I can't remember!" She begins hitting her head with her fists.

Iris tries to stop her. "It doesn't matter, Dorothea," she whispers. "Don't get angry. You told me yourself just now. We remember everything."

Iris turns her attention back inside the compartment to the soldiers, scrutinizing their unshaved faces and red eyes as though seeing them for the first time. They ignore her, bored by her hysterical behavior, which is nothing out of the ordinary to veterans of the trenches. Most of them are occupied with complaints about the stench and the heat and the crush of bodies in the compartment and in the corridor.

"Might as well still be at Château-Thierry, eh?" one says, strangling the French name with careless abandon.

"Or how about Belleau Wood?"

"Don't forget our favorite—Verdun!" Waves of hilarity greet these witticisms.

Château-Thierry. Verdun. Names like clubs beating against their brains. Dorothea looks anxiously at Iris, but she is talking to herself again, immune to these new blows. Dorothea holds her throbbing head, then leans back and closes her eyes. "They come back and back," she murmurs to herself. "An endless flood. We can't remember? We only remember." She shakes her head as though to clear it. "Yes, we only remember."

One of the nurses offers her a drink of water, and Dorothea drinks greedily.

"We'll arrive in Bordeaux soon," the other nurse says encouragingly. "Then you can get to the hotel and clean up. I think the Red Cross has taken over a *pension* right near where the ship is docked. They'll be able to give you something for your sister. She definitely needs a sedative. Frankly, I think you both do."

Dorothea nods, exhausted. Out in the corridor, they have started singing again:

If you want the old battalion,
We know where they are,
We know where they are.
We saw them, we saw them,
Hangin' on the old barbed wire.

Dorothea glances at Iris, who tosses in her seat, having fallen into a feverish doze. The train whistles as it enters a tunnel, temporarily drowning out the sound of the song.

Chapter 35

IT IS ALMOST MIDNIGHT when the train arrives in Bordeaux. The troops swarm off with whoops and cheers, throwing their luggage onto the platforms and calling for cabs, buses, carriages, and cars, anything on wheels that will take them to their lodgings.

Dorothea and Iris accompany the two nurses from their compartment to a small bus that is waiting for them. It is already filled with other Red Cross personnel, who greet them warmly. Seeing Iris's and Dorothea's distraught expressions, they find seats for them on the crowded bus. "You'll soon be home," one of the nurses says comfortingly. "Just hang on a little longer."

The twins find their bedroom in a small hotel near the harbor that has been requisitioned by the Red Cross. The room is tiny, with acid green walls and linoleum floor, a slender barred window, and just enough space for two small single beds and a table. On the table is a gas lamp that gives out a greasy yellow light. There is also a metal basin and water jug; both are stained. Iris takes off her foul-smelling skirt and puts it in the basin. There is no water in the jug. She opens her bag and finds clean clothing. Dorothea takes the skirt, rolls it into a ball, and stuffs it into a corner of the room.

Then they sit on one of the beds and look at each other in numb silence.

"Awful." Iris shudders. "I'm sorry."

"Don't be. This is what life is for us now."

"Life?" Iris asks ironically.

"Well, you know . . . Some people call it that."

Dorothea reaches into her bag and brings out a letter.

"Adeline, for instance," she continues brightly. "I haven't even had time to read it yet. Our letters must have crossed. Shall I read it aloud?"

Iris lies down on the bed and puts her hand over her eyes. "By all means," she murmurs.

Dorothea puts the letter under the lamp and starts to read. Her hands tremble in the murky light. "'We are all thrilled here that the Allies have achieved this triumphant Victory over Evil. How proud we are of those fighting Men who made the Ultimate Sacrifice . . .'"

Iris gives a small moan. "Oh no," she says. "No more, *je t'en prie.*"

Dorothea stops reading and lets her eyes run down the page. "I think you should hear this," she says. "You'd like it."

Dorothea reads the rest of the letter to her. There is a small, incredulous silence.

"Chintz?" Iris stammers after a moment. "Toile de Jouy? *Toile de Jouy?*" But this time they do not laugh. Iris flings herself back on the bed, covering her eyes. "It's no good. I can't find it amusing anymore."

"Neither can I." Dorothea looks sadly at the letter. "There's nothing left to read."

Suddenly there is a bang on the door, and three Red Cross nurses come bounding into the room. "Hello, there," one says. "We're planning to go to a café around the corner and get something to eat. Want to come with us? You look as if you could use a bite of something, even if it's French."

Dorothea and Iris look displeased at the intrusion. The nurses become aware of their strange demeanor. "Oh well, I guess not," they say hastily. "Sorry we interrupted you. If you change your mind, you go left out of the hotel and there's a little place that's open on the street opposite. Imagine getting a cup of real hot coffee finally!" Continuing to chatter to one another excitedly about coffee and pastries, they leave the room.

Dorothea retrieves a notebook and pen from her bag. "Don't you think I should reply to Adeline?" she asks.

"Indeed you should," Iris says listlessly. "I think you should explain to her a few things. About life, for instance. And how much we're looking forward to all those ceremonies and tributes. And the medals at Saint Mary's. I can't think of anything more gratifying, can you?"

Dorothea starts to write, but before a few words are down, she tears off the paper and crumples it up into a ball. She begins again on another page, then stops suddenly. She tears it up into tiny strips.

"It's no good," she bursts out. "What's the point? I can't think of anything to write that would make sense to her. The hospital? The poilus? What we saw? What we know? You try."

Dorothea hands Iris the writing pad, but she pushes it away. "I'd do no better," Iris demurs. "It's probably good she doesn't know. None of them do, you know. How could they? It's not their fault."

"It's not their fault," Dorothea echoes.

"Poor Thoreau. Poor Owen. Poor Adeline. Poor everybody. Reduced to shreds on the floor," Iris exclaims, half-laughing, half-crying. "No more writing. No more letters. No more journals. No more poetry. Say good-bye to words, Dorothea. 'Writ in water,' our favorite epitaph."

Dorothea looks down at the bits of paper lying scattered at her feet.

"It looks like the artificial snow we used to sprinkle at the bottom of the Christmas tree, doesn't it? Imagine, Iris, snow! To think it was Christmas a week ago."

"Christmas." The word sounds like tinsel in Iris's mouth. "That's gone, too. No more Christmases."

"Nonsense, Iris!" Dorothea exclaims. "George and Lavinia would insist upon it. We've always been to church at Christmas. Remember how she always thought our clothes so unsuitable?"

"Lavinia thought we had an ungodly upbringing. She'll certainly be making amends with her own offspring. 'The baby comes to church, George.' I can hear her now."

"The baby? I had forgotten about him."

"Forgotten?" Iris asks in a shocked voice. "The son and heir?"

"The son and heir," Dorothea repeats. "I'm grateful to him, for George's sake."

"Yes. There will be more Crosbys. We should give thanks to God for that at least." Iris sits up briskly. "That's it. Of course. We must find the cathedral at once. He said it was very big and very beautiful."

"Who did?"

"Gaston. The one from the Périgord. Such an angelic boy. Don't you remember?"

"Yes, of course." Dorothea takes Iris's hand and pulls her off the bed. "Let's see if he is right. Anything to get us out of this room."

They leave the hotel and start walking down the quai Louis XVIII. It is lined with handsome eighteenth-century buildings. "Like Paris was once," Iris observes in a matter-of-fact voice. From these quays, Dorothea tells her, the incomparable local claret that Adeline so enjoyed was exported to thirsty Englishmen for three hundred years. "And from here," she adds, "the fruits of the Caribbean once made their way through Europe and on to us in America. Isn't that a splendid thought?"

"Does it make you hungry?" Iris asks.

"No."

"I don't think I'll ever be hungry again."

They continue to walk down the street. "Edith Wharton loved this part of the city, with its sculptured pediments and stately doorways," recalls Iris. "She called it 'a great decorative composition' — remember, Dorothea?"

"Edith Wharton." Dorothea lingers over her name. "She'll never know the part she played in our lives."

"We'll say a prayer to her, too, when we get there."

They walk on past the customhouse and the place des Quinconces. Bordeaux appears strange to them — so clean and healthy, unscarred by the catastrophic injuries that for four years have afflicted her fellow cities to the north. On the corner of the allée d'Orléans is a café called La Belle Époque. The twins look at it for a moment, admiring its exuberant art nouveau decoration.

"What a carefree period that was," Dorothea muses. "What innocence, what gaiety."

"Don't you wish we'd lived then?" Iris enquires.

"Don't be silly, Iris. We did."

Their laughter echoes off the old stones as they walk around the place de la Bourse, with its lovely fountain, then leave the harbor and find the church of Saint-Rémi, desecrated during the French Revolution but still standing. Pressing on through the cobbled streets to the place Gabriel, with its display of pale gray facades, they finally reach the cathedral of Saint-André, showing off under a gibbous moon in all its eleventh-century glory.

Here they stand, gazing up at the twin towers with their slender pinnacles, the flying buttresses, the rose window, the traceries of sculpted stone above the arches, and finally the fearful tympanum of the Last Judgment above the *porte septentrionale.* The basilica is open, and they go inside, awed by the vast nave, the dizzying Gothic choir and transepts, the vaulted ceiling, the grand altar.

"Very big and very beautiful," Iris murmurs. "Just as he described it."

They pause for a moment at the chapelle du Saint-Sacrement, where a vagrant ray of moonlight illuminates the stained-glass window depicting the Holy Family. Mary, Mother of God, pray for us sinners, now and at the hour of our death.

The twins walk slowly to the front of the cathedral. Guttering candles lit by the faithful flicker over the flawless contours of the building. Bordeaux's cathedral is in one piece, its soaring Gothic frame preserved from the bombardments that struck at the heart of its sisters Rheims, Soissons, Amiens. It stands tall before them, a triumphant exemplar of the Western ideal.

But to the twins, its beauty is corrupt, a sham, a trick of the light. They see the ghosts of soldiers with bayonets and tin helmets crowding the nave, praying for a miracle that will save them from the trenches. They hear the tolling of bells from the towers, announcing the latest casualties to grieving families in neighboring towns and villages. Like a pentimento to this treacherous masterwork, their beloved Rheims appears before them. Rheims is the architecture of their memories — the "bare ruined choirs," the splintered windows, the gutted vaults, the crippled spires. For them, the perfection of the cathedral in Bordeaux is an anomaly, an obsolete relic of a civilization in ruins.

This bleak epiphany draws the twins together. They study each other's faces as they studied the cathedral, like archaeologists, examining the fine lines now appearing around the eyes, cheeks beginning to sink like small caves under the high bone structure, lips damaged and dry, all rosy plumpness vanished. Each sister sees herself in the other as they have done all their lives, bare, stripped of artifice. Now they face each other in this moment of crisis, tracing the lost land-scape of their future in the shadows of the basilica.

" '*What is going to happen when people notice that there isn't any more sun?*' " Iris murmurs.

"Don't. It's too sad."

"I can't remember who wrote that," Iris says. "Who wrote it?"

"I never knew, Iris. You knew more than I ever did." Dorothea's voice sounds high, like a child's, in the vast emptiness of the cathedral.

"Oh, Dorothea, we're past all that now." Iris pauses. "All I know is that we can't stay here."

"No." Dorothea looks questioningly at her sister.

"And we can't go home. We can't go forward and we can't go back."

"Where shall we go?"

Iris takes her sister's arm. "Listen." She recites from memory, the lines floating sweetly through the lofty cavern of the nave:

We are the happy legion, for we know
Time's but a golden wind that shakes the grass.
There was an hour when we were loth to part
From life we longed to share no less than others.
Now, having claimed this heritage of heart,
What need we more, my comrades and my brothers?

"*Voilà,*" Dorothea says. "Who wrote that?"

"An English poet called Sassoon. Another of Maurice's favorites. I learned it from him. He said it might be helpful."

"He was right. Dear Maurice." She frowns. "Is Sassoon dead?"

"I expect so."

Iris glances up at the high, pointed arches ranged along the tran-septs toward the main altar and flings her arms wide in an impulsive embrace. "Sassoon . . . Sassoon . . . Sassoon . . ." She begins to dance down the aisle, aspirating the sibilant name through her lips, as though calling up his spirit. "Sassoon . . . Sassoon . . ." The vaulted ceilings respond with whispered hisses. She whirls around and runs back toward her sister.

"We're free," she exclaims. "Don't you see? We don't have to go anywhere, be anybody, remember anything. *'What need we more?'*"

"What do you mean?" Dorothea suddenly sounds afraid. "Are you certain?"

"Certain? Of course. Never more so in my life." She stops. *"In my life."*

"How?"

"We'll know."

"But I must think, Iris. I must think!" Dorothea looks desperately at her sister's calm face. "Please, let me think!"

Iris is silent. A rustling noise from high in the rafters breaks the heavy hush of the cathedral. The twins look up, startled.

"Les anges!" Iris cries. "The real ones this time! It's their turn to summon us at last, where we have seen so many go before!"

"No!" Dorothea fires back bitterly. "It's me. Alone. Scuffling in the dark. Confused, frightened, trying to think." Her voice breaks. "I'm so tired, Iris."

Iris laughs cheerfully. "Don't worry," she says encouragingly. "I'll bring you down safely." She begins to call up to the heavily shadowed roof. "Dorothea! Come down! You are needed here, with your sister, your twin, your Iris!"

The rustling sound comes again, more agitated this time. "Don't be frightened," Iris calls again, her voice confident. "I am waiting for you, just as you have always waited for me. Dorothea, come here to me!"

The cathedral is silent. They wait a few moments, but nothing now breaks the stillness. Iris turns to Dorothea, beaming.

"There, you see?" She cups her hands together as though enfolding a wounded bird and places them on Dorothea's heart. "There. Now you're safe."

Dorothea laughs reluctantly, shaking her head. "But I liked it up there," she protests. "You can see the stained-glass windows so much better."

"No, you can't. There's no light there. You were lost. Alone. Down here is where you belong, with me. We only know this life, this place, this moment, you and I together. Darling sister, '*What need we more?*' Don't think, Dorothea. Just imagine! We've lived our lives, finally. It's perfect. Remember? Wasn't it wonderful, being *les anges*? *Oh, there was nothing like it!* And there will never be anything like it again. We wanted so much to really live, didn't we? Now we have. Think of it. Nothing could ever match it now. Not ever."

"But what about George . . . the baby?" Dorothea stumbles over the words.

Iris laughs delightedly. "Oh, you funny one!" she exclaims. She thinks a minute. "Do you remember a game we used to play as children? 'What if I wear a blue hat?' "

" 'I'll wear a blue hat, too,' " Dorothea responds automatically.

" 'What if I sing a nursery rhyme?' " Iris goes on.

" 'I'll sing a nursery rhyme, too.' "

Iris looks into Dorothea's eyes. "Good girl."

Iris is radiant. She reaches for Dorothea's hand, her touch transferring the light from sister to sister, from flesh to identical flesh. Now each slender body becomes a perfect reflection of the other, each delicate head carved by the same sculptor, luminous skin blending seamlessly into a single alabaster effigy.

"Still tired?" Iris whispers.

Dorothea raises her head and stretches out her arms, as though embracing the mighty cathedral. "I know," she announces suddenly. "Adeline gave us the answer once. 'The "Tune is in the Tree?" "No,

Sir! In Thee!"'" She looks at Iris. "I never understood it until now. We must pray," she goes on in a strong voice. "We came here to pray, remember?"

"What prayer shall we say?" Iris asks, spurring her on.

"We can pray as we prayed for our poilus. That came to us easily enough. It's the only prayer we know."

They take each other's hands, the two angels of mercy, and say what they used to say over and over to the dying soldiers in the tent.

"Courage."

"Courage."

The twins walk out of the cathedral, stopping to look up once more at the Last Judgment, its grandeur tempered by the dark shadows of the night.

"It looks different now," Dorothea declares. "It's not frightening anymore."

Iris nods and squeezes her sister's hand. They retrace their steps back along the quay, finding the pier where the huge transport ship that is waiting to take them to New York is at anchor. Its immense gray hull is streaked with rust. It pitches in the oily black water until the hard-worked decks creak, complaining at being disturbed from their slumber.

"Will you still need a sedative, *chérie?*" Dorothea asks.

Iris shakes her head, smiling. "What about you?"

They gaze up to the top deck of the steamer. A lone sailor stands near the prow, looking at the sky. The moon is covered now with clouds. Rain is forecast. That means more work for the crew. He shakes his head and moves away, whistling.

A few seagulls wail. Distant drunken voices cry shrilly before falling silent. The twins stand motionless, listening to the waves slap against the ship's impassive hull. They are like sentries, guarding their secret. It will soon be morning.

TWO DAYS LATER they board the ship, along with a hundred or so Red Cross nurses, doctors, administrators, and other American war workers going home. It is about five thirty in the evening, and twilight is falling as the ship prepares for departure. It groans like an angry beast as the engines shake it awake to begin the long journey to the New World. Ropes are unwound and hurled from the bollards, iron machinery clangs from deep within the body of the hull, steam hisses from the smokestacks as seagulls whirl and scream above them, waiting for scraps from the human cargo that will supply their dinner.

Dorothea and Iris look down from the upper deck, finding the spot where they stood two nights earlier after their visit to the cathedral. Wrapping their heavy Red Cross cloaks more closely around them, they stare at the spray churning behind the ship as it slowly lumbers out of its watery cave. Someone on deck calls to them, but they do not answer. They do not hear. Bound together, they are lost in the ecstatic moment of release from France, from the war, from the world, from everything they have known.

"Good-bye," Iris whispers. "Say good-bye, Dorothea."

"Good-bye."

The shoreline gradually recedes. The port workers, becoming smaller and smaller, complete the procedures with the hawsers, closing down the pier until the next ship steams in, demanding a mooring. Some of them linger on the quay for a few moments to honor the sight of a great ship moving toward the open sea, before turning away to go home to their families.

As the twins stand together, the night air is ruffled by a gusty wind.

"Are you cold?" Dorothea asks her sister.

"Not a bit. Are you?"

Dorothea shakes her head. "It's not sad, is it?" She indicates the disappearing horizon.

"*Au contraire.* We've done it all. We've said it all. Everything else is meaningless."

"Yes. Nothing to remember or forget. Isn't that right, Iris?"

"We pulled it off, Dorothea. Now we can rest. We've earned it. The two of us together. '*What need we more?*' What bliss. What relief. What freedom."

"Yes." Dorothea repeats her sister's words. "What bliss."

The sisters turn to each other and touch each other's face, lips, hair, like blind people performing the familiar ritual of recognition. The connection has never been as strong as it is now. They do not need to see each other anymore.

The ship's engines suddenly kick into a higher gear. Losing their balance, the twins are thrown together by the sudden jolt of speed. Their bodies tangle and they laugh. Leaning over the side together, they watch the dark water racing far beneath them. They say nothing more but clutch the railing tightly, as though testing this last barrier that keeps them from their heart's desire.

A sailor comes by and calls them to dinner. The twins exchange a quick nod of agreement and turn away, following him below. It is not yet time.

Another passenger, looking over the side in the same place a few moments later, finds the railing still warm where the twins had gripped it.

~ NEW YORK ~

Chapter 36

EVERETT GRAYFIELD WAS IN Harry's room in the New York apartment. He had almost finished dressing to have luncheon with his aunt Marjorie, who, although in her late eighties, still retained a firm grip on the family affairs. Every year after Christmas, she invited Everett to the Colony Club and urged him to marry. "You wouldn't have to *do* anything," she would say, looking archly at him through her pale eyelashes. "You would only have to give dinner parties and spend weekends in the country. That house you have in Bernardsville would be greatly improved with a woman in it."

Everett walked around the room slowly. Everything was as it always was, expertly cleaned by the housekeeper, who after her dusting duties carefully put back every trophy, every picture, every book, as it had been originally placed by its owner. Harry was always very meticulous about that. He hated things to be moved. A set of brushes aligned at the wrong angle in the bathroom would put him out immensely. "Call out the National Guard," Everett liked to say, teasing him for his fetish. "Harry's been measuring again." Even the clock on the mantel, with Harry's name engraved on it in honor of a Harvard football victory, was kept wound and set.

Everett stood before the displays of photographs of Harry with his teammates at school and college and examined them as he had so often examined them before. Through the smoke of his cigarette, he gazed intently at the rows of athletes in their team uniforms. He had greeted so many of them after Harry's games and had them up to the apartment, but now all he could see was a question mark by each one's name. *How many of them were dead?* Those young faces gazing straight into the camera, optimistic, bold, gallant, representatives of a privileged generation ready to take on the world. Who was left? Where would those who came home find that confidence again? He looked more closely at the pictures of Harry. Despite the artfully nonchalant poses created by the photographers, Everett now noticed that Harry's expression seemed to impart a melancholy that belied the youthful spirit so cheerfully communicated by his companions. Harry was not thinking of posterity then, but which of them were? Were they all dead? Were these pictures memories, or memorials?

Everett closed his eyes briefly in a spasm of pain and then moved on, picking up a small portrait of Harry's mother, painted at the time of her debut, when she was the beauty of the year. He saw a silver key on a shelf and turned it over, wondering what it unlocked. He sat down on Harry's bed. The coverlet—a relic of Harry's childhood—had a pattern stitched into it of knights in armor, perhaps going off to the Crusades. Everett had never really looked at it before. How charming, he thought, stroking it with his hand. How appropriate for Harry. A fine epitaph.

He brought out of his pocket a letter and a small Cartier jewelry box. The men had found the box in Harry's hut when they came back with the body.

It was still unopened.

Everett put the box on the bed and slowly unfolded the letter, which he had read many times. Harry's friend Ken had written it.

We were all waiting to go home. We had been celebrating for days and were all but worn out. Harry's old Spad was having engine trouble and the mechanics had just reported it fixed, and that morning Harry said he wanted to take one last flight in it. Of course, one never says that in the air force, and we all told him to take it easy and stop being such a fool. But he wouldn't listen to us. He went out to the airfield where the Spad was parked, and we went after him and called him several times to come back and join us. Who cared about the damn plane at this point? But he ignored us. We were all feeling pretty unsteady with all the partying and so on, and so I think we just said to hell with him. I regret that now, of course. But he could be pretty darn stubborn. Well, a few minutes later we heard the crash. It was so close you couldn't help hearing it. We ran outside and saw the smoke. The motor had given out immediately. There was nothing he could have done. Nothing anyone could have done. There was no chance. The Spad was completely wiped out.

Forgive the poor writing, but I'm not much of a correspondent and I don't know how to tell what happened any other way. We are all deuced sorry. He was one of the best.

PS: We had trouble locating his mother, but I think our flight commander has finally succeeded.

PPS: There was a girl. Isabel something. But I think she got married and is back in the States.

Everett folded the letter and put it back in its envelope. There wasn't a girl, he thought. There never was a girl. He picked up the Cartier box and turned it over in his hands. He sighed. Harry was an unopened man. That tense face, those strong hands, that athletic body—one of Michelangelo's prisoners, locked forever in marble. Could he, Everett, have done more for him? The older man was helpless against Harry's impregnable past, the glory years when football and hockey meant everything. He remembered how offended

Harry was when he first realized that in his new postcollege world, the word "sport" was simply a casual form of address used by men to men as a social greeting. All of Everett's lavish attentions, the parties, the trips, the champagne, could not release Harry from his mourning.

The war was to have saved him. How ironic, Everett thought. Life in death. The light in Harry's eyes had come back. He worked on his body and grew fit again. On that distant airfield in France, he was his old self, flying with the same daring and joy that so many had admired on the playing field. Even Everett could sense the rush of exhilaration Harry must have felt each time he took to the air. Leaving the earth for something intangible, some adventure in the clouds — that was pure Harry. But the war would end. Wars always did, finally. Even Harry couldn't keep it going single-handedly, although he tried. "One last flight." A phrase as riddled with superstition as the title of Shakespeare's Scottish play. One last flight. That eager plea for continuance, for a suspended sentence. But this time the gavel came down without leniency.

Everett opened the box and took out the cuff links, pretty things in gold with small pearls at the center. He had chosen carefully, as always, but he now knew it was absurd to think that Harry would have liked them. What use to him were cuff links? Or any other of Everett's expensive gifts? They were a cheap symbol of Everett's own vanity, the assumption that with them and the other material enticements he provided, he could somehow keep Harry's affection, perhaps even keep him alive. But Harry's vanity was of a different nature. Perhaps it was better Harry never opened the box.

Everett glanced at the clock. He did not wish to be late for luncheon with his aunt. He got up slowly and put the box in his pocket. He would find another use for the cuff links. After stopping to look one more time at a pair of old ice skates dangling on a hook behind the door, he pressed his lips together and walked out of the room, closing the door firmly behind him. He would call Miss De Wolfe to come in and redecorate the room as a guest bedroom. There would be no more Harrys.

Chapter 37

TRAGIC DEATHS REPORTED FROM FRANCE

ALMOST EIGHT WEEKS AFTER THE ARMISTICE

THEY SAID IT was a very cold night as the French transport ship the *Provence* began to steam out of Bordeaux for New York. The ship was packed with American Red Cross nurses, aides, doctors, and other volunteers going home after heroic duty on the battlefield.

An ensign on watch that night saw them, two young women in Red Cross cloaks appearing at the top of the ladder from the lower deck. It was about eight o'clock in the evening, and the ship was inching its way through the narrow channel of the Garonne River, leading from the harbor into the Gironde estuary and out to the open sea. Most passengers by that time were below, either dining or retired to their cabins. The sailor said he didn't think anything of it at first. Why should he have? People often came up to the upper deck after nightfall to admire the lights sprinkled along the shoreline, or to get some fresh air, or simply to gaze at the dark water far down below being churned up by the ship's noisy propellers.

It was dark on deck, only a few lamps flickering to mark

the entryways and stairwells. The two figures suddenly started running, quite fast, holding hands, their cloaks flapping behind them in the night, like birds' wings. They ran faster as they reached the ship's rail. They did not speak. Then the first one freed her hand and quickly climbed the rail, balancing briefly before dropping over the side. The other followed her.

The alarm was sounded almost immediately. The ensign ran to the side and leaned over the railing. The water was murky and thick like mud. He could see nothing else. They were gone.

Afterward, it was said the ship could not turn around because it was in a narrow strait without any room for maneuvering. Anyway, the ship's staff explained to reporters, by the time the captain was alerted and able to do anything, it was too late. The water was below freezing. It was, as they said, a very cold night.

Sometime later, the ensign said he remembered that while the first one vanished beneath the surface of the water without a sound, he thought he heard the second one struggle and wave, briefly crying out before being sucked under by the voracious tide. "It was just an impression I got," he added. —*New York Gazette*

Chapter 38

M RS. WALTER STERLING STOOD in the drawing room of her Fifth Avenue apartment, surrounded by reporters who had crowded in with notebooks and cameras. Mrs. Sterling was the senior director of the New York chapter of the American Red Cross. She looked somber but confident in a high-collared black taffeta dress with matching jet earrings and necklace. In a corner of the room, under a portrait of the late Mr. Sterling, sat George Crosby.

George had attended many victory celebrations since the end of the war — marches, the laying of wreaths at cenotaphs, the unveiling of plaques, concerts in honor of the fallen. He had most recently been present at a ceremony at the hippodrome in honor of Marshall Foch, where the famous hero of the Lost Battalion, Lieutenant Colonel Charles Whittlesey, had sat on the stage among many wounded soldiers, some of them without arms or legs. George had observed that the war hero looked ill at ease with these men and had sat through the whole entertainment with an expression of profound despair.

But none of these memorial events had prepared him for the news of his sisters' suicides. Indeed, at first he refused to believe it, insisting they had boarded a different ship. After all, he had arranged their passage. Surely it was the *Providence,* not the *Provence,* on which they were traveling—an easy mistake to make. He had recently purchased a pair of fine Irish mares as a welcome-home present for them. They would certainly wish to see them. There was still hope, wasn't there? Ships' manifests were notoriously unreliable during times such as these. Adeline Wetherall had encouraged him in this view. "There was no sign," she kept repeating. "The girls had a brilliant future."

Mrs. Sterling called the group in her drawing room to attention. The reporters opened their notebooks. She cleared her throat and addressed her rapt audience.

"My only statement about the tragedy is this," she said in loud, clear tones. "Some of our young girls are not up to the stress to which they are exposed. That is what the Crosby twins, in their tragic deaths, are telling us. Therefore, I urge you, Mothers of America, to call your daughters home at once. They are no longer needed, now that the war is over. The relaxation from strain is clearly a serious problem and demands the immediate withdrawal of every one of our girls in the war zone." She paused to let her message sink in. "Again, I say, Mothers of America, call your daughters home from France. Now. Thank you."

With an imperious wave of her arm, she sent the reporters away. George Crosby got up and silently shook her hand. With head bowed, he followed the journalists out of the room, evading their questions. He would not go home quite yet, he thought. A drink at the club perhaps. He was not entirely ready for Lavinia. At least his son was a true Crosby. There was no mistaking the family likeness. We must look forward, not back, he told himself firmly.

As he walked down Fifth Avenue, George remembered he had been invited to a party that evening at the French Consulate to celebrate the French soldiers who had died at the front. That sad-looking

Lieutenant Colonel Whittlesey was the guest of honor and was expected to make a stirring speech. George decided that he would not attend.

Mrs. Sterling's statement was given generous coverage in the New York newspapers. Several mothers were quoted as saying they agreed with her sentiments and that they would do as she proposed. "It is a well-documented fact," observed Dr. Hermann Bach of the New York Psychoanalytic Society, in an interview on the subject, "that for patients suffering from depression, the risk is greatest not when the person is sickest but shortly after a course of treatment has been declared a success."

A response from Evangeline Booth, leader of the American Salvation Army, was also published: "I deplore the proposal suggested by the Red Cross to withdraw our girls from the war zone. I see no argument to justify discouraging young women prepared to make the ultimate sacrifice. The idea is preposterous."

Nothing more was written about the matter.